Raves
NASCAR

"Britton writes the kind of book that romance fans will read and reread on gloomy days."
—*Publishers Weekly*

"A fun NASCAR racing contemporary romance… which from start to finish line takes readers on quite a ride around the track."
—Harriet Klausner, *Amazon.com*

"[ON THE EDGE's] Adam is a great character, a near-perfect romance hero."
—*The Romance Reader*

IN THE GROOVE

"NASCAR fan or not, let IN THE GROOVE drive you to distraction."
—*Romantic Times BOOKreviews*

"IN THE GROOVE will keep you turning page after page until you have raced through the novel."
—Dawn Myers, *Writers Unlimited*

"IN THE GROOVE is a fun, light-hearted love story with racing as the backdrop and a feel-good ending."
—*Racing Milestones*

"What a great story! ... Ms. Britton makes the world of NASCAR come alive."
—*SingleTitle.com*

"IN THE GROOVE is a blast! It's funny, sexy and romantic."
—*Joyfullyreviewed.com*

Other Pamela Britton titles in the NASCAR Library Collection

On the Edge
In the Groove

And also by Pamela Britton

Cowboy M.D.
Cowboy Trouble
Scandal
Tempted
Seduced
Cowboy Lessons
Enchanted by Your Kisses
My Fallen Angel

Watch for Pam's next NASCAR Library Collection title

Total Control

coming from HQN in September 2007!

#8

PAMELA BRITTON

to the **limit**

HQN™

ISBN-13: 978-0-373-77187-5
ISBN-10: 0-373-77187-8

TO THE LIMIT

This edition published by arrangement with Harlequin Books S.A.

www.HQNBooks.com

Printed in U.S.A.

ACKNOWLEDGMENTS

This book was written during a very difficult time in my life. And so I'd like to thank all the wonderful souls who work at Cancer Care Center in Redding, California, and the equally wonderful people who work for St. Elizabeth's Hospice in Red Bluff, California. Angels on earth, one and all. Thank you for helping my dad die with dignity.

My wonderful assistant, Rae Monet, for taking care of business when my life spiraled out of control. What would I do without you? You're a godsend and I'm so thankful for your help.

My editor, Abby Zidle, and all the staff at Harlequin Books for being patient when the book was late. Thank you so very, *very* much for understanding.

Lastly, a big thank-you to my husband, Michael, for holding my hand through the good times and the bad. You keep me sane in an insane world, babe, and I couldn't do this without you!

to the **limit**

DEDICATION

For Daddy

March 12, 1938 – June 20, 2006

I miss you.

CHAPTER ONE

THE HELICOPTER JUST about landed on her head.

One minute Kristen McKenna was jogging along a sunny beachside path, waves crashing in the distance on her left, the next—*blam.*

"What the—?"

She stopped cold. Actually, what she did was cover her face with her arms, the sand kicked up by the helicopter's rotors pelting her face like a new age treatment at a health spa. Not that she'd ever been to a spa—no time for that.

Whump-whump-whump.

"Hey," she cried, wishing immediately that she hadn't opened her mouth. Her teeth suffered next. She moved her elbows to her side and tried to spit the grit out, wincing against the gnatlike stings. At least her glasses shielded her eyes, although at this rate she wouldn't be able to see out of them thanks to the sandblasting.

Gradually, the thing passed, enough so she could drop her arms. She watched in shock as the aircraft, one she thought at first might be military, sank to the ground like excrement from a bird. A Bell Jet-Ranger, she noted—3200 pounds heavy, 1487 pounds of load capacity. Maximum cruise speed of 213 kilometers.

What the hell was it doing?

Crashing? she thought. Some of her hair had come out of her ponytail, the mouse-blond strands flicking her sweaty forehead where they stuck for a moment before being ripped away.

Whump-whump-whump.

No. Not crashing, she realized, pushing her glasses up her nose. Its loss of altitude was too controlled for a crash. Plus, by now it was hovering fifty feet away, still off the ground but turned in her direction, the pilot in his insectoid glasses waving.

Definitely *not* a crash.

But then it backed up, its tail end spinning around so that she could see the side.

Knight Enterprises.

She straightened and absently rubbed her aching leg—it always hurt while she was jogging. Knight Enterprises.

Her employer. Actually, she worked for one of their small subsidiaries—a research-and-development facility that tried to figure out ways for Mr. Knight to make more money off his string of aircraft, usually by increasing fuel efficiency via aerodynamics.

Whump-whump-whump.

The helicopter dropped lower, the fronds of nearby palm trees cowering away. A half second later the pilot set down and cut the engines. That helped considerably. Slowly, the blades began to lose velocity and the turbine engine's whine became more pronounced. She watched the pilot turn and say something to a passenger. A second later the side door popped open and a man with burly shoulders and forearms the size of Thanksgiving turkey breasts dropped out, his black glasses reflecting the green lawn as he squatted beneath the blades. He had gray hair, oddly enough, that didn't move an inch.

"Are you okay?" Kristen called to the black-clad figure. "Do you need me to call nine-one-one?" she asked, patting the sides of her baggy blue jogging suit, the pants bulging on the left side.

Cell phone. Good.

"Kristen McKenna?" he called out, straightening now that he was away from the rotor. He had an earring, she noticed, and an earpiece, too, a spoon-shaped mic hanging by his left cheek.

Kristen's arms dropped.

"Are you Kristen McKenna?" he asked again, and when he drew a little nearer, she could see he was tall. And wide. Military looking, in a retired Navy SEAL sort of way. Short-sleeved black T-shirt and matching black pants. Scary looking, actually.

"Y-yes," she said. "That's me."

He pulled something from his pocket. A picture of her, she realized. *Of her?*

"Good," he said, after comparing her with the photo. "Come with me."

"Come with— *What?*" she asked, stepping back. "Who are you?"

"Rob Sneed. Head of security for Mathew Knight."

Mathew—

She blinked.

Mathew *Knight?*

The Mathew Knight? Her boss? The single richest man in the universe? She'd only ever seen him on the covers of magazines. Or on TV. Or in the newspaper—front page.

"Mathew Knight is looking for *me?*"

"Affirmative," he said, glancing at the picture again, and then his watch. Rolex Aviator. She'd coveted that watch since flight school.

"Well—" She blinked a few times, trying hard to focus her brain. "What about?"

"I'm afraid I'm not privy to that kind of information."

"Oh."

That made sense.

Wait a second. *None* of this made sense.

"Mathew Knight wants to see me?" she asked again, the import of the words suddenly hitting her. Before he'd passed away, her dad had often said that for a genius, she could be awfully dense.

The big man in front of her nodded.

"And he sent his helicopter for me?"

"You weren't in the office."

"No," she said. "I'm not."

"We were told to find you."

And so they'd sent a helicopter after her?

Kristen glanced down, noticing leaves and bits of debris stuck to the front of her jogging suit. "Look," she said, brushing at the stuff, tiny cumulus clouds of dust rising around her. "I appreciate the fact that Mr. Knight sent his helicopter for me, but I'm not so certain I should actually go with you." She glanced up, shooting him a nervous smile. "No offense. It's just that I have no idea if you are who you really say you are. I mean, obviously I'm pretty certain you're not some twisted sicko with a private helicopter, but still. I'd appreciate it if you'd tell Mr. Knight I'd be much more comfortable with a meeting at my office. *His* office, I mean."

He crossed his arms in front of him. "Negative."

"Negative?" she echoed.

"No time to meet you at the office."

"But he has time to send his helicopter after me?"

She straightened suddenly. "Although, I do have to wonder how you found me."

"Our intel revealed you like to jog on your lunch hour."

"Intel?"

"Affirmative."

"I'm outta here."

A hand on her shoulder stopped her cold.

"Hey," she said.

"Ms. McKenna," he said, his grip tightening. "I think it would be best if you met with Mr. Knight right now."

"And I'm telling *you,* I don't think so."

"You don't really have a choice," he said, pulling her toward him.

All right. That did it. She kicked him.

"Ouch," she instantly cried, drawing back and hopping around on her bad leg—never an easy thing to do. That had *hurt.* "What's your shin made of? Titanium?"

The human monolith didn't move. No. He stood there. Unflinching. Like one of those British soldiers outside of Buckingham palace.

"My, my, my," a masculine voice drawled. "When they told me you were a handful, they weren't kidding, were they?"

Kristen turned.

The man with the slicked-back black hair and the

dark suit was instantly recognizable: Mathew Knight. In the flesh.

"Oh...my...gosh."

MATHEW SAW HER MOUTH DROP open after she said the words, eyes wide beneath her thick-framed black glasses, foot still held in her hands.

He doubted she realized it, but her face was covered with a fine sheen of grit.

"Why didn't you tell me he was in the helicopter?" she asked, glancing at Rob, leg slowly dropping.

"You didn't ask," his security manager said in his deep, deep voice.

Mathew smirked. Rob loved to play security specialist to the hilt.

"You have something on your face," he said, wiping at his own cheeks in a way meant to suggest that she might want to wipe at *hers.*

She must not have heard him, or understood the silent gesture. "Look, Mr. Knight," she said. "While I'm sure the whole helicopter and special-agent thing might work well with some people, I'm afraid I'm still not comfortable with flying off with you. If you want to talk to me, I'd rather do it back at the office."

"Negative," Rob started to say, stepping forward.

But Mathew slid in front of him, holding out a hand. "I really don't have time to meet with you at the office. Not anymore."

Ms. McKenna looked at Rob again. "Does he sit and stay, too?"

"You have something on your face," he said again, ignoring her question.

She lifted her own hand then, one swipe revealing the full extent of the damage. "Holy—" She began to wipe at her cheeks furiously, using the edge of her jogging shirt. As the oversize jacket lifted he caught a glimpse of something, just a hint of flesh that was surprisingly tan and lithe, not the least bit lumpy, as her jogging suit had suggested.

"Rob," he said as she continued to wipe. "We can just do the meeting here." But her cleanup job hadn't helped much. She looked like a child who'd been playing with a box of chocolate.

Mathew gave up then, reaching into his suit jacket and pulling out a handkerchief. "You missed a spot," he said, handing her the handkerchief. Their fingers brushed.

He saw her chest cavity expand, and then still. She had an unusual face. Tiny chin. Thick lips. And—behind thick brown glasses—the world's largest eyes, he realized, suddenly meeting her gaze.

His hand dropped.

"Uh, thanks," she said, her chest starting to move again. She used the cloth, handing it back to him when she was done—albeit with a sheepish grin.

"You want to walk down to the beach?" he asked.

She smoothed her hair off her face, her focus suddenly locked upon the ground. "I'm supposed to be in a meeting in a half hour."

"Rob can let them know you'll be late."

"It's a class of sixth-graders. They want to see the wind tunnel. I'd hate to keep them waiting."

"We'll keep it short," he said.

She nodded and stepped up next to him, her stride a little uneven. Must be the injured leg he'd heard about. Severely broken right after high school. Permanently misshapen, and a disability she'd overcome. He'd been filled in by Rob, who did background checks as a matter of routine.

Wonderful.

That's how she'd been described. Wonderful. Brilliant. Unique, and in possession of a sense of humor that kept her team in stitches most of the time. His head of R&D had spent a half hour extolling her virtues, then another half hour telling him why he couldn't afford to lose her.

"Well?" she asked, Mathew catching a bit of a wince when her left leg took the weight of her body.

"You okay?" he asked.

"Fine," she said. "Just a little sore from jogging."

That leg was probably more than a little sore, from what he knew of the injuries she'd sustained, but he let it slide.

They walked for a bit in silence, Mathew taking

note of the scenery. He'd always liked Florida—great Palm Beach Polo Club. And even now, in mid-May, the breeze that flung itself off the ocean cooled things off, the sea a clear gray-green. If it weren't for the hurricanes he'd have bought himself a place out here years ago.

"Do you always send helicopters after your employees?" she said, interrupting his musings.

"No."

"Then it's safe to say that I'm the first employee in history who's been run down by one of your Rangers?"

"You are."

"Lucky me."

Close to shore he could see dolphins break the surface of the water. He stopped for a moment, intrigued.

"What do you need to talk to me about?"

The porpoises were forgotten the moment she reminded him of his task. "I need your help."

Her whole face seemed to lift in surprise. "*You* need *my* help?"

"I do," he said.

"With what?" she asked.

Fascinating, her eyes. Big and blue. They looked almost electrified from within, they were such a luminescent blue.

"Long story," he said.

"Then you'd better find a way to make it short."

Indeed, he probably should. "I recently embarked upon a business venture that could use your help."

"How so?" Blond eyebrows arched above the frame of her glasses.

"You have the special background needed for this project."

"What background?"

"Racing."

"What?"

"Your employee profile said you used to race open wheels."

She let out something that sounded suspiciously like a snort. "About a million years ago."

"And that racing is what got you interested in pursuing a degree in aeronautics."

"Before I realized women weren't really wanted in open wheel garages."

"From what I understand, NASCAR's much different."

"NASCAR?"

He wondered how much to tell her, realized he'd better tell her as much as possible, and so said, "Ms. McKenna, I've bought myself a race team." He smiled down at her, sliding his hands in his suit's pockets and jingling some change. "A NASCAR race team."

"Why'd you do that?"

Her honesty was refreshing and amusing. His bank had hemmed and hawed around that same question before one of them had finally gotten the courage to ask him outright—an hour later.

"It seemed like a sound investment. The sport's growing by leaps and bounds. I expect a healthy return on my investment. Plus, I like things that go fast."

"So you bought yourself a team."

He shrugged. "Some people buy themselves baseball teams. I chose NASCAR."

"Because when you have more money than God, why buy a second home or a new car when you can own a whole race team?"

"Exactly," he said.

"So what do you need *me* for?" she asked.

The breeze kicked up, strands of her hair whipping around her face. "You're my ace in the hole."

"I beg your pardon?" she asked, looking up at him from above the rim of her glasses like the Catholic nuns used to look at him when he was a boy.

"You're one of the best in your field, according to your employee profile. Plus, you have the background. Your psych profile tells me that you like to win and it just so happens you already work for me. Perfect."

"Perfect for *what?*"

"Engineering consultant for Knight Enterprises Motorsports."

"I beg your pardon?"

"You're eminently qualified for the job," he said.

She shook her head, slowly at first and then faster and faster, setting wispy strands of hair loose so that she probably resembled Medusa. "Do you have any idea how surreal it is for you to be standing here?" she asked. "In front of me, offering me a job designing race cars?"

"Didn't you spend your first three years in college learning to do exactly that?"

"Yeah, but that was before I realized how hard it was for a woman to break into the racing industry."

"And so you switched to airframes."

"Better job market."

"But wouldn't you like a shot at doing what you originally wanted?"

Unreal. Just unreal, she thought, staring up at him. She felt like an actress in a James Bond movie, but that might be because of his resemblance to a young Pierce Brosnan—and his helicopter entrance didn't hurt. But there was no denying that with his slicked-back hair, tanned face and born-with-money attitude, he seemed out of this world.

"And, actually, you wouldn't be the first person to cross over from aerospace to NASCAR. A number of teams have started to look outside of racing for their engineers."

"I can't believe this is happening," she mumbled, looking away from him.

The clouds started to part, shadows seeming to float and undulate across the ocean's surface like a living, moving thing. When she'd graduated college that's all she'd wanted to do—design cars. She'd spent her summers racing midgets with her dad back in Oklahoma. She'd been good—really good.

Until the accident.

She closed her eyes, willing away the bad memories.

"Look," he said, green eyes holding her gaze. "I have a plane leaving for North Carolina tomorrow morning. Why don't you sleep on it?" he asked, handing her a card.

A card. Of course. Probably with gold lettering. Yup:

Mathew Knight

CEO

Knight Enterprises

The Mathew Knight. Her *boss.* And he was offering her a job. Well, a new job. Designing *race cars.*

"Call the number on the bottom. My secretary will arrange things should you decide to take the job."

"Why?" she asked. "Why me? I haven't worked on car bodies in years."

"I don't want someone who's already in the industry. I want someone with a fresh mind. Someone who will think outside the box."

"Yeah, but surely there are other people better qualified than me?"

"Perhaps. But you happen to have the added benefit of already working for me."

"But I don't know anything about stock car racing."

"Even better. You won't be throwing around the same old, same old."

She began to shake her head. "This is crazy."

"Maybe," he said. "Maybe not. But I didn't get to where I am today by thinking like everyone else."

No. He probably hadn't.

"Just promise me you'll mull it over."

She nodded.

And with that, he turned away. Very 007ish, she thought as he strode back to his helicopter, hand in the pocket of his black suit pants, his security specialist crouching by the helicopter door.

Knight. *Mathew Knight.*

"Wait," she called out.

He half turned, cocked his head in her direction.

"How much does it pay?"

His hands jingled the change in his pockets again. "Two hundred."

"Dollars?" she asked, which was probably the stupidest question in the world she'd ever asked because *of course* she knew what he meant.

"Thousand," he called, his voice having risen because his helicopter's turbine engine had begun to spin, the rotors beginning lazy loops in the air. "For six months' worth of work," he added. "That is, if you make it through the sixty-day probationary period. But if it doesn't work out, you can have your old job back."

"Unbelievable," she muttered.

"Think about it," he called again, turning away and disappearing inside the helicopter like the secret agent he resembled.

"Um, sure," she mumbled to nobody but herself.

CHAPTER TWO

"THINK SHE'LL SHOW?" Rob asked the next morning.

"She'll show," Mathew said, not even glancing up from the papers he studied, the Knight2000's square windows doing little to keep the noise of the busy airport from penetrating the fuselage.

"I don't know," Rob said, his Bronx accent making him sound like a boxer rather than an ex-Army Ranger. "She seems feisty."

"You only say that because she tried to take you down."

"The operative word being 'tried.'"

"I'd have been disappointed if she'd succeeded," Mathew murmured. "I don't pay you an exorbitant salary to be felled by diminutive females."

"She's hardly diminutive."

"I hope not," he said, flipping to the next page.

"And I have a feeling she might surprise you."

"She'll show," Mathew repeated.

They sat in a makeshift office in the back of his jet, oak furniture that would have looked at home in his Madison Avenue headquarters reflecting the soft morning light, a nearby jet braking on the runway. Mathew looked up.

"Here she is now," he said, catching a glimpse of a plain-faced woman walking across the tarmac, her stride just the tiniest bit uneven. She pulled a suitcase behind her, one of the private terminal's staff escorting her to the bottom of his jet's stairs.

Rob looked left and out the window. "Well, I'll be damned."

"Given your penchant for card games and strippers," he said, flipping another page, "you probably are."

Rob spun back to face him. "You want me to greet her?"

"Not necessary."

"*You* going to greet her?"

"In a minute," he said, studying the words in front of him. "As soon as I'm done reviewing this."

"You want me to go out there?"

"If you want."

"Actually, I think I'll stay here," Rob said, leaning back in his chair. "I have a feeling this ought to be interesting."

Mathew ignored him. A few moments later he heard voices outside his office. There were six seats in the main cabin, any one of which Ms. McKenna could choose. She'd be perfectly fine out there while he finished up.

"*Really* interesting," Rob added.

Mathew looked up, shooting Rob a look meant to remind him that he had work to do.

"I'll shut up," Rob said, leaning back in his chair and placing his hands across his stomach. He grinned, but not a har-de-har-har, this'll-be-funny type of grin. No. It was more of a smirk.

Mathew's response was to shrug out of his black jacket and roll up the sleeves of his white dress shirt. He kept Rob around because he was good at his job, and with his high-profile life, it was necessary to have someone on staff to keep the riffraff at bay. He'd never expected the two of them to become friends, but he supposed in the strange way of two people constantly thrust together, they were.

"We're ready for takeoff," his pilot reported over the intercom a few minutes later. Mathew heard first one and then the other engine start up, their loud whine filling the cabin.

"Whenever you're ready," Mathew said, still studying the documents. There were dossiers on each of his new employees. Job titles like "chassis specialist" and "body hangar" were typed across the top of each page.

"Oh, good," said a falsely bright voice. Mathew glanced up in time to spy Kristen standing by his door.

"Hello, Ms. McKenna," Rob said, clearly amused.

"Hello, Mr. Sneed. Sorry to bug you, Mr. Knight. I just wanted to make sure I was on the right plane." She shot him a smile. "It'd be terribly embarrassing if I ended up catching a ride to South America with a Colombian drug lord or something."

With a parting smile, she stepped back and closed the door.

Rob sat in his chair, his chest vibrating with silent laughter while, outside the tiny window, the tarmac began to glide by.

"Something tells me the next few weeks will be interesting," Mathew said.

"You're just realizing that now?" Rob asked. "I knew it the moment she tried to kick me."

For some reason Mathew stood up, grabbing his jacket off the back of the seat. They were, indeed, getting ready to leave. His pilot had switched on the fasten-seat-belts sign, a silent way of telling the jet's occupants that they'd been cleared for takeoff.

"I think you like her," Rob said as Mathew opened the door.

"She's an employee."

"She interests you."

"Nonsense. I just met her. I've hardly had time to form any type of opinion about her."

Only after he stood above her, clutching the back of the seat in front of her to keep his balance, he admitted he really did find her interesting. She used to race cars. Given her small stature and womanly curves, that seemed strange.

Womanly curves?

Well, yes. Today, in her black suit, curves became noticeable. Indeed, she looked markedly different than she had on the jogging path. There was just a hint of lip gloss coating her mouth. A touch of mascara had been brushed onto the lashes behind her thick brown glasses. Light from the tiny window next to her—the shade drawn halfway down—coated her skin with a pale sheen that showed off skin as smooth as wet paint.

"I'll take the peanuts, please," she said. "And a Coke."

"Actually, all we have are granola bars," he found himself answering.

"Not even a snack box?" she asked, feigning disappointment.

"I'm afraid not."

The plane stopped moving. Mathew glanced outside. They'd paused at the end of the runway.

"Have a seat," she said, patting the smooth leather chair next to her as if he were a toddler asking to sit next to his favorite aunt.

He did as asked. He didn't know why. He really did have work to do. But something about her grin made him sit down.

"I'm glad you decided to take the job," he said, settling back in his seat and loosening his tie.

"Yeah, well, we'll see if I make it past the probationary period."

"I have a feeling you will."

"Do you?" she asked, lifting a hand and slipping off her glasses.

Remarkable eyes.

He'd noticed them yesterday, had wondered if they could possibly be as blue as he remembered. They were. The color of a Brazilian sky, pewter and blue and green all mixed into one.

"I have no doubt you'll do well," he said, and that rather surprised him. He didn't like to form instant opinions about people.

"Good. Because I have to tell you, I turned down Bill Gates last night. He wanted me to build him a solar-powered coffeemaker, but I told him I had a prior engagement building your race cars."

"A solar-powered coffeemaker?"

"Apparently, he's preparing himself for a global disaster." She smiled even more brightly. "He doesn't want to be without the creature comforts."

She *was* odd.

"Actually, it's a pretty good idea if you think about it. I mean, if the world were ending, wouldn't you want to watch it with a good cup of coffee?"

"I suppose I would."

"Anyway," she said, expelling a sigh that was coated with disappointment, "I chose to build your race cars. I mean, I don't know anything about building solar-powered coffeemakers, but I *do* know a tiny smidgen about race cars and so I figured why not? Why not chuck it all and try something different?"

"Why not, indeed?."

"So thank you," she said. "I'm pretty excited. In fact, I worked up some drawings last night."

"Did you?"

She nodded, leaning forward to reach beneath her seat. She pulled out a small duffel bag that had the outline of a square inside. A drawing pad, he realized.

She let the bag drop back to the floor, flipping open the cover a second later. "What do you think?" she asked.

Lightning McQueen from Pixar's *Cars* stared back at him.

She'd caught the personality of the car exactly, one eye wide with excitement, the other winking—all drawn in the long, swiping strokes of an artist used to drawing car bodies.

To his utter shock, Mathew found himself on the verge of laughing. He didn't, of course.

"Now then, NASCAR might have something to say about the aerodynamics, but you gotta admit, it's a unique idea."

"Actually," he said. "I think it's already been done."

"Nah," she said.

"I hate to break it to you, but Pixar did it a year or two ago"

"Really?" she asked, both eyebrows arching.

"I'm afraid so."

She sighed. "Well, then I guess it's back to the drawing board."

"Guess so."

"Too bad, too. I was really looking forward to calculating the airflow around his eyes."

The chuckle seemed to be plucked right out of him. "I see."

"Here we go," she said as the jet began to shoot forward.

"Here we go," he echoed, wondering just what exactly he'd got himself into.

And thinking it just might be fun.

HIS EYES TWINKLED WHEN he was amused.

She hadn't expected that.

In all the years she'd worked for Knight Enterprises, she had never imagined Mathew Knight would find her amusing. Well, okay, she'd never imagined sitting next to him on a private jet, either. But here she was. And that wasn't to say she hadn't thought about him a time or two. There wasn't a red-blooded female employed by the man who hadn't speculated about what it'd be like to shake his hand. But none of them had ever actually *done* that.

The sound of the jet's engine suddenly rose in volume. Kristen looked toward the window, feeling immediately better.

"Here we go," she said, clutching the armrest. This was her favorite—when twelve-thousand pounds of thrust was suddenly unleashed. It was as close as one could come to racing cars without twelve cylinders.

"You love it, don't you?"

She nodded without looking at him.

"You look like a downhill skier about to try her hand at a mountain."

"I can't help it. I'm always amazed every time I take off in a jet. Here we are, in an inanimate object, but in a few moments we'll be airborne thanks to the physics of flying."

She took a deep breath, then forced herself to face him again. "Did you know the Wright Brothers flipped a coin to see who would test-pilot the *Flyer* first? Wilbur won, but the plane stalled and so Orville Wright got his turn next and the rest, as they say, is history."

His brow wrinkled, dark brows lifting up over his south-of-the-equator green eyes. "Actually, I didn't know that."

She nodded, looking away once more, but only

because her stomach suddenly dropped, that sometimes dizzying, sometimes uncomfortable, feeling she got when a plane suddenly lifted off the ground, turning her breathless.

"Waa-hoo," she muttered under her breath.

"Waa-hoo," he repeated in a monotone.

"Don't *you* love it?" she asked, taking another deep breath before facing him.

His hands rested on his lap, and Kristen realized that he had really big arms. She'd never seen anybody whose forearms were muscular, but his were. And tanned. A slight dusting of hair turned golden-brown from the sun spread away from his rolled-up sleeves. Must work out.

"I guess I never really thought about it," he said.

"Really?" she asked, tipping her head in question. "But you own an airline."

He lifted an eyebrow, his look clearly asking, *And your point is?*

"I just sort of thought anyone who owned an airline must love to fly."

"Actually, I can't stand it."

"What?" she asked, thinking he was kidding her.

He didn't look as if he was kidding.

"You're seriously afraid of flying?"

"I am."

"But you look so calm," she said. But now that she dared to look at him a tiny bit closer, she noticed that lines bracketed around his mouth and his jaw seemed a little tense.

"It's taken me years to master my fears."

"You've got to be kidding me."

"I wish I was."

"But you—" She didn't know what to say. Well, she did, but she didn't dare say it. He was her boss, and somehow she didn't think he'd like her calling him a coward. "If you don't like to fly, why'd you buy an airline?"

"It seemed like a good investment."

"And you're good at spotting those."

"Actually," he said, "I am."

She was struck by a sudden curiosity. Well okay, to be honest, she'd been thoroughly fascinated by the man for years. Who hadn't? But now that he didn't seem as intimidating—she still couldn't believe he was *afraid* of flying—she asked, "What's it like to be one of the world's richest men?"

The brackets around his mouth eased, only to reappear again when the plane banked to the left. "Funny thing about wealth," he said, glancing out the window—perhaps to see if they were crashing—his hands easing on the armrest he'd suddenly cluched when they'd begun the turn.

Damn, he really was afraid.

"When you're struggling to make that first thousand bucks, you fantasize about what it'd be like to make a hundred thousand. But then, when you've got a few hundred thousand, you wonder what it'd be like to make five hundred thousand, and then a million, and then a billion."

"Are you trying to tell me that you don't feel wealthy?"

"No. What I'm saying is that it's all relative."

She leaned close to him. "Here's a news flash."

He drew back a bit, the lines around his mouth easing again.

"You're not just wealthy, you're really, really, *really* wealthy."

"I know that," he said sharply, as if she insulted his intelligence by pointing that out.

"In fact, you're so wealthy I bet your toilets flush on their own."

"I beg your pardon?"

"You know. They probably have those sensor things. When your butt lifts off the seat, they flush."

The tension had completely eased from his face by now and Kristen thought that it was a nice improvement. He looked worn out. Oh, he was still handsome with his five-o'clock shadow and his intensely green eyes, but he looked tired and in sore need of a little fun.

"I saw it on MTV's *Cribs,*" she added. "This baseball player had self-flushing toilets. I found myself thinking, what a great way to know if you've made it or not. Self-flushing toilets."

"I *don't* have self-flushing toilets."

"No?" she asked, disappointed. "Well, that's good. A little manual labor never hurt a person."

"I'd hardly consider flushing a toilet manual labor."

"You might think so if you were used to them flushing on their own."

He gave her one of those looks people give when they're not sure if they should take a person seriously or run in the other direction. "You know, you really do say the damnedest things."

She didn't take the words as an insult. Quite the contrary. "Who told you?" she asked with a small smile.

One side of his mouth lifted, which was about all the smile she ever got out of him, she realized.

"Mr. Knight," his security guy interrupted. Rob Sneed, she remembered.

They both looked up.

"You have a phone call."

"No self-flushing toilets, but you have a private phone on your jet," she said with a laugh.

Rob looked at her strangely. So did her boss.

"It's all relative," he reminded her.

CHAPTER THREE

THEY LANDED LESS than an hour later. Kristen slipped into a limo that was every bit as plush as the jet she'd just left behind, right down to the mahogany armrests and slick leather seats.

And then Mathew Knight took a seat next to her and she forgot all about plush interiors and concentrated on trying to ignore him. But how did you ignore one of the most eligible bachelors in the whole entire world? Sure, he was a bit of a cold fish, but he was a handsome cold fish.

To be perfectly honest, he terrified her. Not only did he rarely laugh at her jokes, but now that they'd arrived in North Carolina, she suddenly felt woefully inadequate. Surely he had someone else in his employ who was better qualified?

But one thing she'd learned about working for Mathew Knight—he liked to do things differently. The airline he'd purchased and then completely reorganized, Fly For Less, was a prime example. He'd grown the company on one basic principle: give the consumer what he wanted at rock-bottom prices. He'd done whatever he could to make that happen—slashed prices, serviced less populated routes and, later, commissioned the design of a new airframe with a sleeker design that gave better fuel mileage. The rest, as they say, was history. Fly For Less was now one of the nation's most popular airlines. *Everybody* knew Mathew Knight. He was the Bill Gates of the skies.

"You look worried," he said, interrupting her musing.

"A little," she admitted.

"Afraid you might have bitten off more than you can chew?"

That was unexpectedly perceptive of him. Was she that obvious? "A whole elephant's foot," she muttered, the car moving smoothly forward.

"It won't be that bad."

"I bet that's what they say to virgins before they push them into volcanoes."

Kristen glanced out the window. North Carolina was green. Really, really green—rolling hills covered by lush foliage and tall trees that framed two-lane roads. Southern-style brick homes dotted the landscape, the occasional palatial estate thrown in. It was pretty, she admitted, feeling instantly at home. The homes gave way to commercial buildings and then to a mall of some sort. She caught a glimpse of the street name. Speedway Boulevard. They must be near the track.

She ducked down, peering out the front windshield. "Is that—"

She didn't finish her sentence, because there was no need to. It was, indeed, a racetrack.

"That would be the speedway," Mathew said, shifting on his seat, his rear end brushing hers. She scooted away.

"It's, ah…it's huge." The speedway, not his rear end.

"It is," he agreed.

The steel structure seemed to sprout up before her eyes, like a giant metal flower that bloomed larger and larger the closer they drew. Outbuildings stood all around it, the track circled by roadways. They stopped at a traffic light and Kristen realized they were going straight inside, not turning.

"Wait a second. Is the shop at the speedway?"

"We'll be touring the shop later. At present we're meeting the Cup team. They're testing right now, and so I thought it'd be an excellent opportunity for us to introduce ourselves."

"Uh…okay."

They turned right. Soon she had to crank her head back to see the metal beams that crisscrossed the back side of the grandstand and held up the seats like a king-sized erector set. A flag with the racetrack's name fluttered lazily in a breeze, its shadow gliding across the surface of black asphalt.

And she'd thought IRL tracks were big. *Ha.*

They entered a tunnel, then shot out the other side and into bright sunshine. She looked out the window and toward the infield. It was so huge it took a moment to simply absorb the enormity of it all. Around the perimeter, grandstands rose up as tall as ten-story buildings, every square inch filled with multicolored seats. And above that, suites. It felt like being inside a giant gray bowl, she thought, one with huge, angry bees buzzing around the rim. Race cars. Their loud engines penetrated the interior of the limo. She closed her eyes for a moment because until that exact instant, until that very moment, she hadn't realized how much she'd missed that sound.

"Are you ill?"

Her eyes sprang open. Her boss stared at her with a look of concern.

"No. I'm…ah…I'm meditating," she said.

He lifted an eyebrow—very Mr. Spock.

"You should try it sometimes," she said. "It's great for calming nerves."

"I'll keep that in mind," he said, looking away.

He must think she was nuts.

So much for trying to impress him.

The limo came to a stop right next to what she

presumed was the garage, at least judging by the multitude of race car transporters that stood opposite the single-story, gray building. People buzzed about, darting to and from the big rigs. Those rigs had huge sponsor logos on the sides. She recognized more than a few household names.

"Wow," she said.

"Let's go," Mr. Knight said, not even waiting for Rob to open the door.

Kristen scooted out, and the moment she did, the moment she stood, it all came back to her. The smell. The sound. The very *feel* of a racetrack.

It brought tears to her eyes.

She'd missed it. She'd given racetracks a wide berth after the accident. She hadn't even followed the Silver Crown series. And now here she was at a NASCAR track.

"Are you okay?"

Kristen hadn't realized she'd stopped or that she'd closed her eyes again. She looked up. Her boss had the same look on his face as he had when he caught her "meditating" earlier: a kind of concern mixed with what looked to be fascination. Or maybe revulsion.

"It's nothing," she said, straightening her suit jacket, which had the annoying habit of straining over her breasts.

"Are you crying?"

"Just dirt in my eye."

He didn't say anything. She didn't, either, just lifted her chin.

"I see," he said.

Before she could respond further, his secret service agent—or whatever he was—stepped into place, which meant she was left following in their wake like a dog at its master's heels. They crossed through a spiked rail fence, the big rigs even larger upon closer inspection.

Vrr-*rrrrr.*

She heard the sound even from all the way outside the garage. Air ratchet.

Vrr-*rrrrr.*

Klug-klug-klug-klug.

Tires being pulled on and off. Ah, yes, she knew the sounds well.

Nobody glanced up as they passed, men still rushing between the haulers and the garage. Some of the stalls were empty. A few had cars in them, card tables with computer monitors and printers and other electronic devices set up near the front. Groups of people stared at the data streaming across the screen.

"Here we are," she heard Mr. Knight say before looking left and right and crossing the road between the parked transporters and the garage.

Todd Peters, read the sign hanging above the garage. Number eighty-two. Curious, she scanned the car, surprised to see the name of a video-game software company on the back, side and front of the hood. Arcadia. One of the largest manufacturers of interactive entertainment in the world, its black-and-blue color scheme matching the packages their games came in.

"Floyd?" Her boss called.

A man with thinning hair and a belly that protruded above his dark blue work pants turned to greet them. He stood near a group of men, all of them except for one wearing headphones.

Todd Peters. The driver. She could tell by his fire suit. She resisted the urge to study him. If he was like other drivers, he was probably used to being stared at. And since she refused to cater to anyone's ego, she focused instead on the man called Floyd. For a split second she saw something flit through the man's eyes. Annoyance, maybe, but it seemed to be directed at her boss.

"Mr. Knight," he said, the smile on his face doing little to match the look in his eyes. "Good to see you again."

Floyd's silver headset hung half on and half off one side of his head; Kristen knew he did that so he could still hear things. Her boss came forward and shook the man's hand, others in the crowd turning to look at them, including Todd Peters, his dark hair and dark eyes raking her black suit up and down before immediately dismissing her. Story of her life. Actually, she was pretty certain that unless she'd been a tall Swedish blonde, he'd have done that anyway.

"This is Todd Peters," Floyd said, turning to the man in the dark blue fire suit. "Your driver."

"I know," Mathew said, coming forward to shake his hand. "I recognize you from your picture."

They'd never met?

"And this is Dan, your crew chief, and Victor, our chief engineer."

"Rob Sneed," Mathew said, "my security specialist, and Kristen McKenna, one of my aerospace engineers."

"You don't look like an engineer," Todd said, dark eyes raking her again.

She gave him a gamine smile back. "I left my pocket protector and slide rule at the office."

His bushy black eyebrows swooped upward.

"But you got the suit right," he offered.

"I know," she said with a wrinkle of her nose. "Don't suppose there's a clothing store around here that might sell me some jeans?"

"There's a mall right down the street," Todd said.

"Great. Can I borrow your ride?" She pointed to his race car.

"Don't think so," Todd said with—could it be?—a smile?

She caught her boss's gaze. He looked puzzled

by her banter, as if he couldn't figure out why she bothered.

"Okay. Well," Floyd said, all but clapping his hands. "Thanks for stopping by, Mr. Knight. Nice to meet you, Ms. McKenna, Rob. See you at the shop."

Something was wrong. Floyd's dismissal was a little too abrupt. A little too heavy-handed.

"Good to meet you, too," she said, studying him closely. "I'm looking forward to getting to know everyone."

Floyd reluctantly shook her hand. "I'm sure they're all dying to meet you, too," he said, before turning back to the computer monitors.

"How are we doing so far?" Mr. Knight asked, causing Floyd to turn back.

He looked irritated by the interruption. "He's nineteenth quickest."

Didn't Floyd get it? Didn't he understand this was Mathew Knight he spoke to? Owner of the newly formed Knight Enterprises Motorsports?

"Is that good or bad?" her boss asked.

Todd crossed his arms, seeming to adopt a defensive stance.

Floyd seemed to smirk. "There's only twenty teams testing today."

"That good, huh?"

They all turned and stared.

She met the onslaught of their glares bravely,

only to transfer her gaze to Todd. "I've heard flapping your arms can help."

Todd lifted a brow.

"Used to work for me, at least," she said.

That made the driver perk up. "You used to race?" he asked, uncrossing his arms.

"Midgets. But I stank," she lied. The truth was, she'd been better than good...*before.*

"Then I switched to designing cars."

"What team did you work for?" Victor asked, suddenly looking interested, too.

"Haven't worked for a team. Been working with airframes mostly."

Silence. And then she caught a softly muttered, "That ought to come in handy," from Floyd.

"Actually, it probably *will,*" she said. "Equations such as Bernoulli's p over ρ plus V squared, plus gz over two will work on both large and small bodies. Of course, if I get the two *ps* confused, I'll be SOL PDQ."

That last alphabet soup was meant as a joke, but they all looked at her as if she'd just used her hair to pull her head off her shoulders. Todd crossed his arms again, but there was a glint of amusement in *his* eyes at least.

And she'd thought academics were stuffy.

"Well. Make yourself at home," Floyd said. "Since you're new to the sport, I'm sure you'll want to see how things are done."

And there it was again, that hint of something in the team manager's voice. Malice? Yeah, that was it.

"I'm sure there'll be a learning curve," Mr. Knight said. "But I've never had any trouble picking up on things before."

"I'm sure you won't," Floyd said. "But I'm also certain you'll find that owning a NASCAR team is nothing like owning an airline."

Silence. A tension-filled silence. The kind that usually followed a serious medical diagnosis.

"I'm certain it isn't," her boss said with a cold smile on his face. "So we'll be sure to stay out of your way. For today." He met the eyes of each and every team member.

The only person who appeared unaffected was Todd, the driver. "Nice to meet you," he said to Mr. Knight, holding out his hand.

"Looking forward to having you drive my car," Mr. Knight said. "And to learning the ropes."

And that was that. With tight smiles all around, he turned away, Kristen and Rob following in his wake. She almost didn't say anything. After all, it wasn't her place. But she'd never been any good at holding her tongue and to be honest, she didn't see any reason to start now—boss or no boss.

"Do you mind telling me what was going on back there?"

"What do you mean?" he asked.

She glanced over her shoulder. The entire team had turned their attention back to the computer monitors. And though it might be warm beneath the late-spring sun, the atmosphere inside the garage had the distinctly chilly feel of a meat locker.

"Methinks your new race team isn't impressed by the conquering hero."

Todd glanced back then, meeting her eyes. To her surprise, he smiled.

She blinked a few times to cover her shock, then asked, "Why don't they like you?"

He shrugged.

She shook her head, crossing her arms in front of her and feeling the suit tug across her back. She'd started to sweat. Kristen could feel the loose hairs that had escaped her bun sticking to her face.

"Don't give me that," she said. "Those men in there looked like they might be thinking of dragging you behind one of your own race cars. What'd you do? Bump off the previous owner? Win the team in a game of chance? Corporate takeover through the purchase of stock?"

"Nothing that dramatic," he said, his voice rising to be heard over the sound of a car that had just taken off.

"Well, in case you hadn't noticed, whatever nondramatic move you used, it didn't go over particularly well."

"And your point is?"

He stood there, looking out of place in his black suit with his swept-back hair. Like a peacock in a pen of roosters, out of his element and yet...not. His type of commanding attitude was home anywhere.

"Obviously, if there's a problem I need to know about it."

"You're here to do a job, nothing more."

Well, now, that stung a bit. "Actually, that's not true."

"Excuse me?" he said, drawling the words in such a way that she was positive he hadn't been contradicted in a while.

"If you're the enemy then I'm an enemy."

He appeared to consider her words, at least he half turned toward the garage as if trying to gauge for himself whether he had trouble on his hands. But then he swung back to her. "Someone else was poised to buy the team before I came along."

"Who? The Dalai Lama?"

He didn't even crack a smile. His funny bone must be the size of a decimal point, Kristen thought. "No. A former crew chief turned team manager."

"Whom everybody loved," she said, instantly

grasping the problem. "No wonder they looked at you like you were NASCAR's version of Attila the Hun."

"They don't have to like me," he said. "I own the team and that's that. You, however, appear to have an admirer."

The words shocked her because, quite frankly, she never would have expected him to crack a joke. "Oh, yeah. Floyd whatever-his-last-name is. I can tell working with him is going to be loads of fun."

"I was talking about Todd Peters."

Shock held her speechless for a second, and then she felt laughter build in her chest. "Oh, pul-leeze," she said. "Todd Peters has about as much interest in me as a dog does nail polish."

"I disagree."

"Then you've been working too hard. Todd Peters is a race car driver. A celebrity. One who's used to buxom blondes on his arm. Not—" she waved to herself "—someone like *me*."

It was his turn to stare her down, something that made Kristen acutely aware of the fact that he, too, was a celebrity. Although as far as she could tell he didn't appear to date a whole lot. She'd never seen a picture of him with a woman on his arm. Well, okay, maybe once, a long time ago.

"You know," he said, his eyes suddenly intent on hers. "Sometimes a woman's mind is more attractive than any amount of blond hair."

She snorted. "Yeah, right."

"I'm serious."

"I know. And I'm serious, too," she said, glancing toward the garage again and deciding a change of subject was in order.

"So what's the game plan today?" she asked, heading for the hauler. "I don't suppose we're going to stick around all day?"

"Actually," he said, falling into step beside her, Rob five steps behind, "I thought we'd stay for a bit."

"Fine. But before we do, I'd like to change."

"Why?"

"I think we'll fit in better in more casual clothes."

His green eyes swept over her with the thoroughness of an X-ray machine. "Good point."

"I'll just go get my bag out of the limo," she said, changing direction and heading for the parking area.

"No need. I'll have the driver bring it to you."

She stopped. They stood across from the garage, near a stack of tires, their rubbery smell causing her nose to twitch. "Will he bring me a burger and fries, too?"

"Are you hungry?"

Funny bone the size of a decimal point, she reminded herself. "No. I was just joking," she said. "The suitcase is all I want."

"I see."

"Don't suppose you're going to change, too, are you?"

"Should I?"

"Do you even own a pair of jeans?"

"Actually, no."

"Why am I not surprised?" he heard her mutter.

"I'll send the limo driver out for a pair after he delivers your suitcase."

"Wow. Delivery boy. Personal lackey. What doesn't your limo driver do?"

"Perform sexual favors."

He said the words so deadpan she found herself thinking… But, nah, it couldn't be. He couldn't have just made a joke, could he?

"I'm not going to ask how you know that," she said, lifting her hands and pretending to be scandalized.

But once again Mathew Knight proved how utterly serious he was. "It's part of the contract."

She must have looked stupefied because Rob stepped in and said, "It's part of the agreement we sign with the limo service. Apparently a few of their clients have used their limo drivers to arrange, shall we say, escorts, and so we have to sign something that says we won't do that."

"You're kidding."

"No, I'm not," Mr. Knight said.

"What *is* this world coming to?" she said in mock dismay, slapping a palm across her cheek. "Oh, well, I suppose you can let your fingers do the walking if it comes to that." She took a step backward. "In the meantime, I'm going to go powder my nose. Just have Guido put my suitcase over there." She turned away, strangely, unaccountably, overcome with mirth.

Contracts. Escorts. Who would have thunk?

Apparently, Mathew Knight.

She had a feeling he thought of everything.

CHAPTER FOUR

"SHE'S HILARIOUS."

Mathew turned toward Rob. "She is different."

"I like her."

"Really?" Mathew said, flipping open his cell phone and pressing the direct connect button for the limo driver whose name he didn't know. He couldn't recall Rob "liking" anybody quite so instantly.

"Hello," Mathew said after the beep.

"Yes, sir."

"I need you to go out and purchase a pair of jeans for me."

"Jeans, sir?"

"Yes. The denim type."

"They only come in denim," Rob said, clearly amused.

Mathew waved at him to be quiet.

"What size, Mr. Knight?" the limo driver asked.

The question caught Mathew by surprise. "I'm not certain," he admitted after pressing the call button, having to yell a bit when a nearby car started up, the sudden burst of sound causing him to wince.

"I'll need a size, sir."

Yes, he supposed he would. "What size do you think I am?" Mathew asked Rob.

"You telling me you don't know what size jeans you wear?"

"I don't need to know my size," Mathew said. "When I want jeans, I go to Ralph and he brings them out to me."

"Ralph?"

"Lauren."

"Turn around," Rob said, motioning with his index finger. "Lift your jacket."

Mathew did.

"Bend over."

"Rob," Mathew said, turning toward his security specialist in disgust.

"Tell him to try a thirty-one waist, thirty-four leg," Rob said, lips twitching.

"Thirty-one," Mathew said into the phone, "with a thirty-four leg."

The direct connect beeped, Mathew not even giving the man time to comment before slipping the phone back in his pocket. "Come with me."

"Where are we going?"

"To the garage. We'll wait for Kristen there."

"I think she had a point about your new employees not wanting us around."

"And as I said to Ms. McKenna earlier, what they want is immaterial."

Rob fell into step beside him, looking left and right—a habit of his—but all there was to see was a member of the safety crew, the reflective stripes on his fireproof jacket glistening beneath the sun.

"Just out of curiosity," Rob asked, once the guy had passed. "Whatever possessed you to buy a NASCAR team?"

Mathew shrugged. "I believe that in the long run, it'll be a good investment. If NASCAR ever decides to franchise team ownership, the entire operation might well end up worth billions."

"Yeah, but you've bought companies before and never had any interest in running them."

Mathew considered for a moment. Truth be told he'd said as much to himself once or twice. Generally, he did keep his distance from the less expensive investments, such as a race team. But he supposed if he were honest with himself, he'd bought the team because something about the sport excited him. He'd flown down to a race, experienced it firsthand, and had determined then and there that he wanted a team of his own. Never would he forget how it had felt to hear over forty cars start up and then take off down the homestretch.

"It seemed like a good investment," he said again. He'd learn what he needed to know along the way. Ms. McKenna would take care of that. It was one of the reasons he'd hired her.

"I see," Rob said, sounding disappointed by his response. So be it. Mathew didn't need Rob to know that lately things had gotten a bit stale. As he'd explained to Kristen, wealth was all relative. Making money didn't cause the same thrill as it had once upon a time. Buying a race team seemed as good a way as any of injecting a little excitement into his life.

"HE'LL BE GONE WITHIN a year," Floyd said.

Todd glanced in the direction of the new team owner, but Mathew Knight and his goon had disappeared. Probably off to watch the cars out on the track, which was where *he* should be—if they could ever figure out what the hell was wrong with his damn car.

"Men like him," Floyd was saying, "they like to live in the moment. Just as soon as the glamour of owning a race team wears off, he'll be gone."

"I don't know, Floyd," Todd said. "From what I've read, he's not the type to quit."

"He'll quit," Dan, his crew chief, said. "He'll get tired of dealing with all the crap, especially when he realizes most teams are lucky to get more than one win a year."

"Hey," Todd said. "We'll win more than that this year."

"Mr. Fancy-Pants there is probably expecting you to be in the winner's circle every month," Floyd said. "Like you're a damn race horse or something."

Todd crossed his arms, thinking they were wrong. He had a feeling Mathew Knight knew *exactly* what he was getting into. He wasn't the type of man who did anything without looking at all the angles. One of the youngest billionaires in the U.S., if rumors were to be believed.

"You ready to get out there?" Dan asked.

"Sure. But maybe we should wait for the new boss to get back."

"Why? He won't know what he's looking at, anyway," Dan said.

"Maybe," Todd said, thinking that Dan really had a stick up his butt where the new owner was concerned, so much so that he couldn't resist riling him a little. "That engineer friend of his might."

"The woman? She's just a science geek," Floyd said.

"Knows something about racing," Todd said.

"Yeah," Dan said. "Probably from watching ESPN."

"I don't think so," Todd said. "But even if she doesn't know anything about race cars, sure sounds like she knows something about aerodynamics."

"Are you sweet on her or something?" Dan asked.

"Sweet on her?" Todd said, shaking his head and thinking the joke had gone far enough. "I just met the woman. Besides, you know me better than that."

"I do. That's why I'm surprised to hear you sing her praises. You only ever do that if you're hoping to get some woman's number."

It was true. Todd loved women. Most of his friends did, too. Okay, maybe not Lance Cooper, but that was only because the sap had got himself snagged by some good-looking kindergarten teacher. But academics weren't his type. He preferred women with a little more pizzazz. Women who turned heads. The taller, the better.

Kristen McKenna looked like his third-grade teacher. Definitely *not* his style.

"Believe me," Todd said. "I have no interest in dating someone like her."

"That's what I thought," Dan said, turning and grabbing Todd's helmet, its dark-blue-and-black finish reflecting a square patch of light off the top of the car. "Let's get going. Our new boss can catch up later."

Still, Todd hesitated for a moment. He didn't exactly want to piss off Mathew Knight, especially since the man owned his car. Then again, the man wouldn't be stupid enough to try to fire him. No way.

Todd slipped inside the car, the space between

the window and the door frame seeming to get smaller the older he got. Too many slices of pizza last night, he thought, slipping his HANS device over his shoulder, then plugging himself into the radio. The tape over the earpieces had lost its stickiness, but he'd fix that later, he thought, slipping his helmet on and then his leather driving gloves.

"You there?" he heard Dan say.

"I'm here," Todd answered.

"Crank her over."

Todd flicked on the switch, the starter chug-chug-chugging for a second before the boom of all eight pistons roared through the garage. He put it in neutral. A couple of his crew guys came forward and helped to push the car backward. Todd put it into gear once they cleared the garage. The vehicle lurched forward.

And off he went, Mathew Knight and the geeky engineer forgotten as he pointed the eighty-two car toward the track. He had to squint against the sudden brightness of the sun. Chrome surfaces on the haulers reflected light, and crew members and pedestrians darted out of his way. He made a left past the gas pumps and then turned right onto pit road and then the track.

"Okay," Dan said. "So we've got some new shocks. We changed the sway bars. Put on some fresh tires and cleaned the window for you."

“Did you fill her up, too?”

“Sorry. Forgot to do that, buddy.”

“You’re slackin’ on me, Dan.”

“I know, I know,” his crew chief said.

He liked Dan, the two of them one of those rare driver/crew-chief combos that’d been together longer than most marriages. Course, that might all change now that they had a new boss man in town.

“Who’s out here with me?”

“You’ve got the fifty-three, the seventy-six, the sixty-three and the eighty-six.”

Fifty-three. Lance Cooper. The man had a hot car this time out. If he could keep up with him, he’d be doing all right.

The problem was: he couldn’t keep up with anybody.

“It’s total crap,” Todd said after the first few laps. “I’m so loose the back end feels like it’s coming out from under me.”

“Just give her a minute, driver. See if she comes back to you.”

But Todd doubted it would. He shook his head, disgusted. Just what he needed. To fall on his face in front of his new boss.

“Comin’ up behind you,” a voice said. Gary. His spotter.

Todd looked up. A red star filled his rearview mirror.

Lance.

Todd almost waved him around, but something made him clench the wheel. Probably the competitive edge that had plagued him ever since he was five years old and he'd gotten upset when his big brother had beaten him down the bunny slopes. It had been his first experience with speed and he'd never forgotten the rush he'd felt.

He felt that same sensation now.

Lance ducked down low. Todd blocked the groove, knowing he'd piss Lance off. But that was okay. He liked jerking Lance's chain. The guy was a Goody Two-shoes, but he was one of the nicer drivers on the circuit. He could take a joke and it really was a joke, to think he could hold him off.

Lance backed off. Todd knew he was just biding his time. They were approaching turn three, which meant he was about to get looser than a stripped-out lug nut. Lance knew it, too.

"High," Gary said.

Yeah. He could see that, Cooper having ducked to the outside, and the moment Lance's front end took the air off his spoiler, his car's back end broke loose.

"Whoa," he said to himself.

Lance shot by.

"Thanks a lot, buddy," he said as the white-and-orange car swooped down in front of him.

"Clear," Gary said.

Todd's heart still pounded. That would really make his day—putting his car into the wall. Shit.

"What happened?"

"She gets loose in dirty air."

"Damn," Dan said.

"Coming up behind you," Gary said.

"Son of a—" As bad as he was right now, he didn't dare risk trying to hold people up. He ducked down low.

"Outside high."

This was bad. This was really bad because it wasn't just one car coming up behind him, it was a pack. Three of them, to be exact, and one of them had no place to go but right up his ass, which meant when he was clear to pass, he'd dart right and—

He saw the driver do exactly that, Gary saying, "Outside high," right as the guy brought his nose around the right side of Todd's car.

His back end hopped right, then left.

"Oh, crap."

CHAPTER FIVE

"WHAT'S GOING ON?" Kristen asked as she came up behind him. On a monitor embedded in a toolbox, Mathew watched as a car spun. "Hey," she cried. "That's Todd."

"Is it?" Mathew muttered crossly, watching as the car did lazy circles on the track. Nobody had said a damn word since he'd arrived on pit road, although their faces were looking more and more grim as time went on.

"It is," Kristen moaned as the car slowly came to a stop—thankfully without touching the wall.

Other cars swerved around Todd, the multicolored and plain gray bodies of the race cars whoosh-whoosh-whooshing as they whizzed by them in real time a few seconds later.

"What happened?" Kristen asked.

"I have no idea," Mathew muttered, vexed.

Kristen turned to Victor, tapping the man on the shoulder and waiting for him to lift the right side of his head phone before yelling, "Is he okay?"

"No, he's not okay. He just about had it in the wall a second ago," Victor said just before the earphone slapped back into place.

"That's good," Mathew heard Kristen say. "We need scanners." She turned back to him.

"Scanners?" Mathew asked, suddenly peeved. He should know this. Then again, that's what Kristen was here for.

"Come on," she said, and turned away.

She had a nice butt. The jeans she wore accented it perfectly.

Mathew immediately looked away, embarrassed. How completely unprofessional to be staring at her rear end. She had ample breasts for her frame, too, her white button-down emphasizing those as well.

Mathew!

"Here we go," she said when they made it to the hauler. Dan, the crew chief, was still atop it. Without so much as a by-your-leave, she opened the sliding-glass door and Mathew was surprised to feel a blast of air-conditioned air seep out from between the tinted-glass doors. Inside he caught his first glimpse of what his millions of dollars had bought him.

A hauler, he learned, was like a mobile command center. Dark gray carpet ran down a long, central aisle. On a counter to his left sat a coffeepot, and a box of sweet-smelling doughnuts next to it. Their aroma made his stomach grumble. They passed cabinets that were labeled with stickers: "hand cleaner" and "shop rags" and "blue fan" (whatever that was). Kristen stopped before one labeled "radios."

"Should you open that?"

"It's yours, isn't it?" she asked, shooting him a small, almost mischievous smile.

"Yes, it is," he agreed.

"Here," she said, reaching inside and pulling out what looked to be a transistor radio.

He glanced inside the cabinet. A row of headphones hung suspended from a bar. In a drawer, numerous scanners sat at attention. A few of them had names on top of them. Kristen didn't take those, he noticed. She handed him an unlabeled headset and took one for herself.

"Don't press the button on the side," she said, showing him how to plug the thing into his device and then slip it on.

It felt like wearing a giant vise grip. "I don't hear anything," he said.

"There's no need to yell," she said back, her voice trembling with laughter. At least he thought that's what she said. It was hard to tell. She sounded as if she was talking to him underwater. "We need to find out what frequency they're using."

"How do you know all this?" he asked.

Mouse-blond eyebrows swept upward. "Are you

kidding? Every race fan knows how to operate a scanner."

But as far as he knew, she didn't follow racing anymore. Did she?

"Come on," she said, grabbing one more scanner and headset and then squeezing by him. He supposed they were for Rob, who'd stayed outside.

"He won't use it."

"Huh?" she asked, turning back to him.

"He won't take the headset. Won't be able to listen for trouble."

"You're yelling again."

Was he? His cheeks reddened. "You might as well put them back."

"You're probably right," she said, returning them to their cabinet.

And then she squeezed by him again, only this time their bodies touched.

Mathew jerked.

She didn't seem to notice a thing. "C'mon," she said.

He didn't immediately move. Instead he stood there, analyzing what he'd just felt. Probably static discharge from the atmosphere, he deduced. That happened a lot after a flight. Something to do with ions in the atmosphere.

"What frequency?" she asked Victor when back on pit road. She pointed to her scanner.

Victor looked from her to the scanner, then back at her again. His expression seemed to say, *Where'd you get those?* She ignored the silent question, just continued to stare at Victor with lifted eyebrows and lips that were pressed tight together.

He liked Kristen, Mathew thought.

He had no idea where the thought came from, but he realized in an instant that it was true. Not only was she good at what she did, but she managed to comport herself with a confidence that was admirable for a woman in a man's world.

Victor unclipped his scanner and then turned the face toward Kristen. "Thank you," she said, turning away so she could program his next.

Mathew heard voices.

"...gonna slide into the wall if I'm not careful."

"You want to bring it in?"

"Think I'm gonna have to. She's only getting looser with tire wear."

"All right then. Bring her on in."

Victor shot up from his position on the wall, heading back toward the garage without looking in their direction.

"That's it?" Mathew yelled, lifting up one side of the headphones, something that was difficult to do since they didn't bend all that easily. "We went through all that just to hear him say he's coming back in?"

She was laughing at him again. "It wasn't for nothing," she said, sliding her headphones off her head and loosening a few strands of hair. She swiped them away impatiently. "We learned he was loose. That's why he came in."

"And what, exactly, is loose?"

"I was just about to explain that," she said, her eyes bright with—was it excitement?

Yes. Very definitely excitement.

"Loose is when the back end of the car slides around on the track. It's not a whole lot of fun because your car feels like a fish's tail." She demonstrated with her hand. "They'll need to do something called tightening the car up to get the rear end some traction."

"And how do they do that?"

"They'll make some adjustments to the car. In fact, they may even use aerodynamics. Sometimes just changing the angle of a rear spoiler can help tighten a car up."

He nodded.

She smiled. And off they went.

Yes. He'd *definitely* done the right thing.

Todd was just pulling into his garage stall when they made it back, a group of people hovering yet again near the front of his car.

"What are they going to do?" Mathew asked.

"I don't know," she said. "Let's find out."

She walked right into the stall, past Dan who was lowering the net for Todd, and up to Floyd and Victor who were consulting their computer monitors again.

"Well, how's it look?" she asked.

"Excuse me?" Victor said, his headphones resting on his shoulders now. Mathew did the same thing with his own headset. So did Kristen, he noticed.

"What adjustments are you going to make?" she asked, only she ignored Victor. The question was aimed at Dan, the crew chief.

"We're thinking of changing shocks. Maybe go to a different track bar, too."

Kristen nodded as if this made perfect sense. "Are you going to futz with the aero?"

"Not right now," Dan said, his face growing tense as he stared past her.

Todd walked toward them, his hands busy unzipping his fire suit, face sweaty despite the fact that he'd only been in the car for a short time. "That was bullshit," Todd said.

Mathew caught Kristen's gaze, but she didn't seem fazed by Todd's outburst.

"I know, I know," Dan said. "But we'll get it right."

"You better hope so because I'm not going back out until you make some changes." He swiped a hand through his sweaty hair. "The *right* changes."

"I'm telling you," Kristen said into the silence that followed. "Flapping your arms works like a charm."

Silence. Even the team members working on the car behind them paused in their tasks.

Todd met Kristen's gaze. She smiled. Todd's whole face seemed to relax. "I'll keep that in mind," he muttered.

Some of the tension seemed to fade.

"Can I take a look at it?" Kristen asked Todd, pointing to his car. "Just in case, you know, I come up with a better idea than flapping your arms."

"Help yourself," Todd said, looking past her and to the computer screen.

Kristen motioned for Mathew to follow. She walked toward the back of the car, squatted down near the back corner, tipped left, then right, then left again.

"What are you looking for?" Mathew asked in a low voice.

"Damned if I know," she whispered back.

Her response almost startled a chuckle out of him.

"But I don't think I'm going to hurt anything given the way the car's driving now."

"I think you're right."

She straightened. "Actually," she said, "I am trying to get a feel for the car's aerodynamics. For instance, the metal strips on the roof are there so a vacuum doesn't form over the top of the car when it's out on the track."

She pointed to a metal ridge that stretched from the front windshield to the back window.

"And I'm wondering if we're allowed to play with those, or if NASCAR regulates their placement. I'll need a copy of the rule book," she said.

Mathew nodded.

"And I'm wondering if the window clips can be played with. See how they stick out there across the front windshield? If we could recess them, we'd have a smoother airstream, one that might create more down force across the back end. You'd be amazed at how a tiny little thing like window clips can influence aerodynamics."

She stepped around the side of the car. Mathew stayed where he was.

"She's good," Rob said.

Mathew had forgotten about his security specialist's presence. "I think you're right," Mathew said.

And she was.

He watched her finger the ridges around the cockpit, peer into a duct of some sort located near a rear side window. She squatted down near the back end of the car again, her expression intense as she stared across what would be the trunk on a street car. And as he watched her he realized that she'd been joking earlier. She really did know what she was looking at, or rather, she knew what she was looking for: ways to improve something. She headed toward the front of the car. He moved to follow.

And almost fell.

"Careful," she said without looking back.

He looked down, trying to figure out what his foot had made contact with. A piece of lead?

"Are you okay?" she asked when she saw what it was.

No. He wasn't okay. His ankle was killing him, and it took everything in his power not to limp. "Fine," he clipped out.

"That's a dangerous place to leave a scale," she said.

Is that what it was?

"I'll ask someone to move it."

"No, don't," he said, glancing toward Rob. His security specialist had turned away, ostensibly to keep an eye out for trouble, Mathew thought, although it might well be so Mathew didn't see him laughing.

"Those things are heavy," she commiserated.

"I need NASCAR lessons."

"I think you're right."

"I don't know a thing about what's going on and I'm very frustrated."

"Frustrated?" she asked. Terrific. Now she was laughing at him, too.

"This isn't a laughing matter."

"I know, I know," she said. "I just never figured you'd be the type of man to let car racing 'frustrate' him."

"What type of man do you think I am?"

She stared up at him for long seconds. "You want the truth? Or do you want me to sugarcoat it?"

"The truth," he said, staring into her big blue eyes, nearly as blue as the garage floor was painted.

"You're a genius," she said. "You don't do a thing without a lot of thought, whether it's starting an airline or buying yourself a race team. I read about how you got started. First in real estate, and when you made a mint at that, airplanes. You started your airline because you thought it was a good investment and your genius IQ helped you make it into a household name. And now you've bought a race team. But if you're looking for someone to teach you something about NASCAR, you're barking up the wrong tree. I don't know much more about the sport than you do."

"But you know race cars."

"Open-wheel cars. It's different from NASCAR."

"Not so different."

"Yes, it is."

"I bet you know what a blue fan is."

"A what?"

"A blue fan," he said with a wide smile.

"No, actually, I don't."

"But you'd probably realize what it was when you saw it, which is more than I would do."

"Look, Mr. Knight, I doubt I'd be very good at teaching a subject I don't know."

"That's where you and I differ, Ms. McKenna."

"Kristen," she corrected. "Unless you find that too informal?"

"No, Kristen will do. And as I was saying, you know far more about racing than I. I just need some help learning the basics. Thus, if you're willing to work with me for a few days, I'll make it worth your while."

"You're already paying me too much."

"There's no such thing as too much money."

"Easy for you to say," she muttered.

"It'd only be for a few days."

She glanced into the garage. "A few days, huh?"

"We can meet at my new home in North Carolina. In the evenings. I'll pay you time and a half."

"Your home?"

"I bought a house."

"Why am I not surprised?"

"I'll even give you a few days to study."

She let out a snort. "Gee, thanks."

"And for your first task, find out what a blue fan is."

"*You* go find out."

His spine went rigid in surprise. He wasn't used to people contradicting him. "Very well," he said. "If you insist."

"No, no," she said when he turned away. "I'll go find out." She shook her head at him as if she couldn't believe he'd actually considered listening to her, then set off. Only after she left did he realize she hadn't technically agreed to teach him.

"You sure this is a good idea?" Rob asked.

Mathew glanced back at his security specialist, surprised to see him standing nearby. "What do you mean?"

"You've never taken direction well."

"And how do you know that?"

"Dr. Samson."

Mathew straightened. "He asked me to do the impossible."

"Yeah, slow down."

"I've taken his advice. I've relinquished control of my company. I'm no longer the majority shareholder."

"And it just about killed you to do so," Rob said.

"The point is that I did it."

"Yeah, but I wonder if you shouldn't do the same thing with this new venture of yours. Let others run the show. That seems to be what they want."

"Immaterial. I've chosen to 'relax' by buying a NASCAR team. Ms. Mckenna is going to teach me the ropes."

"And why are you in such a hurry to learn the ropes?"

"I'm going to run the team, eventually."

"You're kidding."

"You know me better than that," Mathew said.

"Unfortunately, I do."

They both looked up as Kristen approached again. "Victor says it's used to cool off the brakes."

Just then the group of men erupted into laughter. There were several covert looks in their direction, too. Mathew tried his best not to let his irritation show.

"NASCAR lessons, huh?"

"Yes," he said.

"All right," she replied, with another glance in the men's direction. "I'll do it."

"Excellent," he said, although part of him wondered if she'd only agreed to educate him out of pity. "Next can you find out why they need generators behind the cars when they're on pit road?"

"Sure," she said. "Although I'm pretty certain they're there to warm the engine oil."

"Find out for certain."

"You're going to run her into the ground," Rob said.

"Something tells me it would take quite a lot to do that," Mathew said.

Nice butt.

He shook his head.

"Still, you better hope she sticks around," Rob said.

Indeed, he hoped she would. But there was a part of him that wondered if he wanted her by his side because of her mind, or her nice butt.

"She'll stick around," he muttered.

He would make certain of it.

CHAPTER SIX

IT WAS THE WEEK from hell.

Not because of anything anyone said or did. People didn't exactly welcome her with open arms, but nobody was overtly hostile. Even Ralph Helfrick, the head of engineering, treated her fairly, if a bit condescendingly. That she could deal with. What she couldn't deal with, what made her fall into bed each night exhausted, was trying to cram as much NASCAR knowledge into her head as humanly possible. She'd gotten a call from Mr. Knight's secretary on Monday, the woman telling her their boss would be available for his first lesson the following Friday. She'd been studying ever since.

Fortunately, the condo Knight Enterprises provided for her was a welcome refuge. Not that she used the bed all that much. Just as she had in college, she stayed up late studying, often waking in the morning with her head in the middle of her book, ink stains on her forehead.

She saw Mr. Knight around the shop from time to time, but not as often as she'd thought she would, and all they ever did was nod to each other. She'd heard through the grapevine that he was making his presence known by trying to learn as much as he could about the sport, too. She'd also heard that, in addition to her, he'd brought in two other Knight Enterprises employees—one of his COOs, a woman named Gloria who now ran the team's human resources department, much to the chagrin of the current HR manager. And Rob who headed up—you guessed it—security.

So that was it. Mr. Knight, Rob and Gloria.

And her.

The one responsible for teaching her boss about NASCAR. Talk about the blind leading the blind.

She drove out to his new house at the appointed time a week later. Maddie, the receptionist, had given her directions, so armed with *NASCAR for Dummies* and pages and pages of notes, she turned off the main road and into Mr. Knight's driveway. As she drove down the blacktop, she found herself pulling to a stop in surprise.

Did she have the right address?

She pushed her glasses up her nose. It was a farmhouse, the yellow paint taking on the color of the pink sky above. Two stories tall, it had white shutters that flanked the old-fashioned, lead-paned windows. A cute little porch hugged one corner, a white railing that had obviously seen better days encircling it. The other corner was rounded like a turret. More than one chimney intersected the steep pitched roofline. About the only thing that was as she expected was the view. Behind the house Lake Norman caught the sun's last few rays, the water seeming to sparkle like diamonds.

She had the right house, because in the gravel drive sat a silver Porsche, a New York license plate proclaiming it to be MRKNIGHT. There was another car parked next to it. A state-of-the-art Roush Mustang—a Stage Three—that had Kristen salivating. Must be Rob's car.

The sound of her own door slamming startled frogs into silence, but only for a split second—the impromptu choir erupted into song well before she'd reached the five or so steps that led up to the lead-paned door. She stopped at the bottom of the steps, taking a deep breath.

The front door opened.

"Well, well, well, if it isn't the little pencil pusher," Todd Peters said, slowly descending the steps, his jeans and beige button-down shirt making him look even more tanned.

"Well, well, well," she said back. "If it isn't the conquering hero."

He smiled, Kristen thinking he either needed to

shave, or was going for that haven't-used-a-razor-in-a-week look.

It really was a pity he had such a huge ego because that smile was pretty nice.

"What are you doing here?" he asked, stopping when his feet hit the driveway.

"NASCAR lessons."

"Excuse me?"

"I'm here to teach the boss a little something about racing."

Todd let out a breath that could only be called a snort. "Good luck."

"What about you?" she asked. "What are you doing here?"

"I was summoned."

"I see," she said, hiding her amusement, because it was obvious Todd didn't like being "summoned." "What'd he want to talk to you about?"

"My contract."

That got Kristen's attention. "Is he releasing you?"

"Hell no," Todd said. "The man's not stupid. He wanted to tell me we're dropping our current sponsor."

"We are?"

He nodded. "Seems Mr. Knight there wants to sponsor his own cars. Starting next year, Fly For Less will be on the hoods."

"Really?" she asked, although she supposed it wasn't all that surprising. If the team lost money,

Mr. Knight could write off both expenses. "What'd Arcadia have to say about that?"

"Nothin'. Apparently Mr. Knight's going to start up a second race team. That's what he really wanted to pow-wow about."

"And how do you feel about that?"

"Crap, you sound like my shrink."

"You have a shrink?" Kristen asked.

He crossed his arms. "None of your business."

She gave him a big old grin and said, "That explains a lot."

"*You're* the one that's not normal."

"Definitely not," she said.

"And I'm stoked about the second team. We've been at a disadvantage for years. I can't wait."

She nodded. "Good. Sounds like you and Mr. Knight will work well together."

He nodded, too, leaning down close to her and saying, "*We* could be good together," in a low, seductive whisper.

She drew back. But a split second after he said the words, she knew he was just trying to be funny. "Ha," she said. "You had me going there for a second."

"I did?"

"You did. But I know you're not serious," she said, taking the steps two at a time.

"Wait. What makes you think I'm not serious?"

She waved the silly question away.

"Kristen, wait," he said, causing her to turn back reluctantly. "Maybe I *am* serious."

"Todd, please stick to driving cars because your acting skills are no good."

She turned away before he could interrupt her again.

"I think I was just insulted," she heard him say.

The front door opened.

"Cute house," she said to Rob after he stepped aside. He must have been waiting for her.

"If you say so," the bodyguard said, glancing past her. She followed his gaze. Todd still stood there.

"See ya," she said again, going inside and closing the door behind her. "Is the boss man in?"

"He is," Rob said, his ever-present black shirt stretched across his wide chest. "What'd you say to Todd that had him looking so peeved?"

"Did he look peeved?" she asked, glancing around. The inside of the house looked as worn as the outside. "I didn't notice. And I said nothing, really. Where's Mr. Knight?"

"He's in there," Rob said, pointing to a quaint little dining room that her boss had apparently converted into an office. Antique furniture hugged the walls, its dark-oak surfaces polished clean. Mathew had his business papers spread atop them, his seat creaking as he leaned forward.

Have a seat, he mouthed to her.

Her boss was on his cell phone. Or a cordless. Whatever. She couldn't tell since it was held up against his head, his black hair mussed and rumpled, as if he were frustrated with the way things were going on the other end of the phone.

So she sat. And pulled her leather briefcase into her lap, the smell of cowhide filling the air. Inside were cars. She took them out, placing the miniature vehicles atop the table.

"Are those Hot Wheels?" he asked after he'd hung up.

"Tough day?"

Somewhere along the way she had lost her fear of him. How that had happened, she didn't know precisely. Maybe on their tour of the shop when she'd realized he really was as clueless as she. Ignorance had a way of leveling the playing field. Still, she wanted to make it past the sixty-day probationary period, which meant she needed to work hard to impress him. But as she scooted her chair forward—causing a nearby china hutch to rattle, the dishes inside clinking and clattering—she realized she didn't feel the least bit intimidated.

"You could say that," he said, swiping his hand through his hair. He looked down at the cars again. "What are those for?"

"Guess," she demanded with an encouraging smile.

She'd worn her work clothes, which meant she

sat across from him in jeans and a dark blue polo shirt with *Knight Enterprises Motorsports* stitched across the left breast. He, however, wore his standard-issue white dress shirt, sleeves rolled up yet again, and dark gray dress slacks. Those eyebrows of his were also in their standard, upraised position. "I suspect you're going to use them to teach me a little something about race cars."

"Very good," she said. She'd had a college professor who'd used tiny airplanes to demonstrate airflow. The lessons he'd taught had always stuck with her and so she hoped it worked just as well with her boss. "Here." She reached inside the briefcase again and pulled out a belt.

"I hesitate to ask what that's for."

"Worried I'll use it on you?" she asked, after reaching across the briefcase and creating a circle out of the leather strap.

He drew back as if she'd poked him. "No."

"Or are you the type that enjoys that kind of thing?"

"I beg your pardon?"

Decimal-point sense of humor, remember.

"It's the racetrack," she said. "You'll have to use your imagination for the infield, though. She reached inside one more time, only this time she lifted out three tiny dolls. "I went to McDonald's today and they were giving these away in the Happy Meals. Thought they were perfect. They're race fans."

When she caught his eye, he stared at her as if she'd left her brain beneath the golden arches. She smiled—her standard response to such looks, and she'd gotten a lot of them in her lifetime.

"Okay, so here we go," she said, suddenly nervous, but not because of him. No, she just hoped she could explain things so that he'd understand. "Let's start with the basics. Race car performance."

He leaned back, the wood chair creaking so loudly she worried it might break. But then she got a mental image of him sailing over backward and she smiled. Wouldn't that be something?

"The other day Todd said his car was loose," she said, her lips flexing in suppressed amusement. "And I was explaining to you that that meant his back end was fishtailing around." She demonstrated with one of the colorful cars.

He nodded. "I remember that."

"Well, good, 'cause the opposite of 'loose' is being 'tight.'"

He nodded again. "I heard the term used while watching a broadcast this past weekend."

"Then you might have also heard them use the term 'push.' When a car has a 'push' it's the same as being 'tight' and tight is when the car won't turn." She put the car on the inside of the race track and demonstrated what she meant by having the front of the car head straight for the wall instead of turning the corner. She even made a crashing sound.

"Charming," Mathew said.

"Shh," she admonished. "Pay attention." When she glanced up at him she realized it'd been a long time since someone had shushed him. He'd gone all stiff. "Now, you don't have to be tight going *into* the turn. You can be tight through the middle, too. That would be right here." She placed the car in the middle of the turn, then had it crash into what would effectively be turn two's wall, complete with sound effects again.

"Now," she said, swiping a stray bit of hair away from her face. She'd taken to wearing her hair in a ponytail around the shop, but it had come loose after a ten-hour day. "There are a number of ways to fix a car that's tight and/or loose."

She reached into her briefcase again.

"If you pull out a kitchen sink, I'm leaving."

She looked up at him in surprise. "That was a joke, wasn't it? Way to go, Mr. Knight. There's hope for you yet. And, no, this isn't a kitchen sink. It's a spring rubber." She held up a doughnut-shaped piece of rubber. "This is called a 'full spring.' There are half rubbers, too. You put them in a car's spring so they don't flex as much. That stops the back end from hopping around, thereby helping to make a car less loose."

"I see."

"And for a tight car, you can make an adjustment on this." She turned the Hot Wheel car over. He leaned forward. So did she. "Look, isn't this cool? It's got the whole undercarriage. See that little line right there? That's a track bar. You can move those up or down. Up will loosen a car, down will tighten. You can change them out, too, or change out the shocks or sway bars. You know what a shock absorber is, don't you?"

"Of course." He was back to looking serious again. Too bad.

"You can play with tire pressure, too. Or with something called wedge." She pulled out pen and paper and illustrated how a wedge adjustment was made, which basically meant putting more weight on the rear axle by controlling tension in a wheel's spring.

On and on she went, pulling out her *NASCAR for Dummies* book next and going over some of the terms in the glossary. "Here, you can have this," she said, shoving the book with its bright yellow cover across the table. "You can also have this," she said, pulling out another research book. "You'll have a test on all this next week."

"You can't be serious."

No, but apparently he was—in spades. "Actually, I thought I'd let you absorb some of this over the next few days. I can come back before the race next weekend."

"Dinner's ready, Mr. Knight."

They both looked up. Kristen couldn't stop the smile that slid onto her face when she spied Rob standing there, an apron around his waist that read Bite Me on the front. "You cook, too?"

"Rob has many talents," Mathew said. "And later next week will be fine."

"Okay, great," Kristen said, removing the glasses that had caused the bridge of her nose to sweat. She rubbed at it. "I'll just be on my way then."

"You can join us for dinner if you like," Mathew said.

Dinner? With him?

"No, thank you," she said, replacing the glasses but removing her ponytail. The thing had started to fall out anyway and so she pulled the hair band free, raking her hairs with her fingers. "Do you want me to leave the Hot Wheels?"

She looked up to find her boss's eyes upon her. But it was the look on his face that took her aback. He seemed to be analyzing her. It made her self-conscious.

"No," he said. "That's all right. I'll make do without."

Sarcasm? Or maybe a joke? Hard to tell.

"Fine. I'll be on my way."

"I'll show you out," Rob said.

"No need. I'll do that," Mathew said, taking Kristen by surprise.

"That's okay, Mr. Knight. I can go with Rob."

"I insist."

She was afraid he'd say that. The way he was looking at her made her feel like a test part being monitored in a wind tunnel.

"So," she said, as he walked her out. The interior of the place was done in a light yellow, the paint worn and faded. Antique photos hung on the walls. It looked as if he had bought the place lock, stock and barrel, and it was in desperate need of a good overhaul. "I must say I like this house."

"I'm tearing it down."

CHAPTER SEVEN

"WHAT?"

Her mouth hung open, Mathew noticed. She did that a lot. Most unprofessional. And yet…on her it looked adorable.

Adorable?

"I bought the house for the view, nothing more."

"Yeah, but you don't have to tear the house down for a view. You've already got one."

"This house is too small."

She paused by the front door. "There are only two of you. How could it be too small?"

"Ms. McKenna—"

"Kristen."

"Very well, Kristen," he quickly corrected. "I have a lot of business interests. Most of those interests come with obligations…entertaining and meetings and whatnot. This house is too small."

"Can't you rent someplace for meetings?"

"Sometimes I have guests."

The frown on her face clearly made him wonder

if she thought his "guests" were of the feminine variety.

"But the house is historic," she protested.

"Immaterial."

"Immaterial," she repeated. "Doesn't all this antique furniture mean anything to you?"

"I'm donating it to a local charity."

"That's supposed to make me feel better?"

"No, actually. I just didn't want you to think it would go to waste."

She blinked, emotions flitting through her eyes and across her face. "Whatever," she said with a small shake of her head. "It's none of my business."

It wasn't, but he found himself surprisingly curious nonetheless. "Why do you care?"

He didn't encourage familiarity between himself and employees, yet he still found himself saying "Kristen" easily. Odd.

She pushed away from the wall. "Never mind," she said. "I don't want to get myself in trouble."

"You won't get in trouble. I value those who speak their minds."

Her eyes narrowed for a second, as if she searched his face for the truth of his words. "Because it has history," she said, motioning around her. "There's charisma to this house. Doesn't that mean something to you?"

"No," he said matter-of-factly.

She looked speechless, and he noticed once again that she looked different with her hair down and loose around her face. In fact, she might even be considered pretty.

But enough of those distracting thoughts. He watched her carefully, rather enjoying the way she wore her emotions on her sleeve. Frankly, he'd been enjoying himself for the past hour or so. She did and said some of the most unexpected things. But of course, creative people were always a bit different. Still, he hadn't expected to find her quite so...he searched for the right word. He found her delightful. She was mischievious, outspoken and highly intelligent. A very interesting mix.

"Mr. Knight—"

"Mathew," he reminded her. Funny, too. Not even Rob was allowed to call him Mathew.

"Mathew," she said. "Old houses are like—" She searched for her own word. "People. They're like people. They have stories to tell. Interesting things that only they know about."

"'They' being the house."

"Yes."

"You're starting to sound suspiciously like a psychic."

"Maybe I am," she said. "In fact, I bet I know something about this house you don't know."

"And what is that?"

She headed back to the the kitchen. Rob stood there, serving up pasta, looking quizzically at her when Kristen came storming into his domain. "I bet if I open this here—" she went to a door that he'd never noticed before "—I'll find—" she swung the thing wide. "Uh-huh," she cried, turning back to him, self-satisfaction clear in her eyes. "Look."

He peered into the darkened cabinet, but to be honest, he didn't see anything of particular interest. Just cans and boxes.

"What am I looking for?"

"These," she said, waving a hand.

"What?" he asked again, genuinely perplexed.

"Don't you see it?"

"See what?" he asked, starting to grow irritated.

"This," she said, pointing to the doorjamb.

Mathew leaned forward. Actually, he did see something then, something that looked to be black smudges beneath the white paint.

"What is that?" he asked.

"It's a growth chart."

"Growth? Whose growth?"

She looked flabbergasted. She even took her glasses off—as if she couldn't possibly believe she was seeing him right.

She looked pretty without the thick frames concealing her face.

"Didn't you have one when you were growing up?"

Images of the numerous homes he'd lived in flashed through his mind. The dark, the dingy, the inhospitable. "No," he said sharply.

She leaned toward him a bit, her eyes narrowing. "You grew up in foster care, didn't you?"

It was a well-known fact, so he didn't deny it. "For a short while. But then I settled down."

"And your foster parents never tracked your height?"

"There was no need," he said, knowing his words sounded terse but failing to see her viewpoint. "I was fairly tall by the time I was fourteen."

"You were bounced around from home to home until you were fourteen?"

"Ms. McKenna, I fail to see where this is going."

"You were calling me Kristen a moment ago. And I don't have a point," she said. "Well, not really," her forehead wrinkling as she frowned. It was a habit of hers, he'd noticed. "Actually, I guess I do."

"Well, thank God for that," he said.

She looked at him, askance, then said, "My point is that this house has a story. One that at first glance you wouldn't notice, but if you look a little deeper, it's there."

"And how do you know that?"

"My mom has a house just like this."

"Excellent. I suggest you go and visit her when you're in the mood for some history."

"I can't."

"Why not?"

She fidgeted with a thread on her sleeve for a second. He stared at her closely. "Never mind," she said, brushing the thread away. "Obviously, you don't understand."

"Where are you going?"

"Leaving."

He followed her down the hallway. She put her hand on the door, turning the knob with a bit more force than necessary.

"What's wrong?" he asked, stopping the door from opening.

He didn't need to become embroiled in his employee's affairs, he told himself. Except the pain he'd momentarily glimpsed stuck with him like spots from a camera flash.

"Nothing's the matter. I'm just ready to leave."

To his utter amazement, he found himself reaching out and touching her—just her shoulder, and it was a light touch.

She leaned away. "I'll see you in a few days," she said.

"Don't," he said, completely frustrated that she didn't do as he asked.

"Excuse me?"

"Don't go," he clarified, more softly this time.

"I have to."

His hand stopped the door again. "Is it because of what happened with your sister?"

She felt as if the breath had been sucked right out of her. *"What?"*

"Rob researched your background."

Don't let him see it. Don't let him know. It's none of his business—

"Goodbye, Mr. Knight," she said, ducking her head.

"Kristen," he said, once again resting a hand on her shoulder, his touch uncertain, as if he wasn't used to public displays of emotion.

And when she looked up, she saw it. Kindness. Sympathy. Understanding.

It was all there in his eyes.

"It's never a good idea to hide from your past."

"I'm not hiding," she said, each tiny pressure point where his fingers brushed her seeming to pulse. Her face heated.

What was he doing touching her?

"Have you been back home recently?"

Her sister's grave. Her father in stasis right beside her.

No, she hadn't been back. She refused to go back.

She swallowed hard. "I've been busy."

His hand dropped from her shoulder and clasped

her fingers. Did his thumb actually brush against them? She saw his eyes widen.

He released her hand as if it had suddenly turned into dry ice.

"Maybe you should slow down," he said gruffly.

"Maybe you should do the same," she found herself saying.

This time *he* looked up sharply.

"You work too hard. Every time I see you, you're in a meeting, or you have papers in front of you, or you're on the phone, or taking a phone call."

"I didn't get to be where I am today by resting on my laurels."

"No, but there comes a point in time when you should slow down and enjoy yourself."

"Maybe I'm doing that now," he said softly, his face relaxed as he looked off into the distance. "Maybe that's why I bought this race team."

"Then leave the running of your airline to your chief executives and hang around with me this week at the shop."

What? Had she just offered to spend *more* time with him?

"I don't want to be a bother."

"You won't be a bother," she said, pushing her glasses back up her nose and wondering if she'd lost her mind.

"I usually stay out of the trenches."

"But racing's a team sport. Everyone expects you to get your hands dirty. If you don't do that, people will start to talk."

"Perhaps I don't care for other people's opinions."

"Perhaps you should." She'd noticed a certain dissension within the ranks in recent days, especially when her boss happened to be nearby. The covert glances seemed to carry with them even more ill will than before. Given that every time she'd caught a glimpse of him he'd looked as friendly as a tiger with a toothache, that wasn't surprising. He really did need to warm up.

"I'll consider it."

"You're the boss." She tried to open the door again.

His hand shot out to stop her.

"You know," she said, "maybe you could lock the door on me. That might make keeping me inside easier."

His lips didn't so much as twitch. "Do you really think this is important?"

She swallowed because he looked as if he might actually be considering her suggestion. "I do."

He stepped back from the door. "Fine. I'll have my assistant give you a call."

"Terrific," she said.

He opened the door for her.

"I can leave now?" she asked.

"You may," he answered.

"Great, because for a minute there I thought I'd have to file a missing person's report on myself."

She waited, studying his face, hoping to find a spark of amusement *somewhere.* Nothing. Not even the tiniest hint of a smile in his green eyes.

"Have a good evening, Mr. Knight."

"You, too, Ms. McKenna."

So much for using first names.

CHAPTER EIGHT

HIS ASSISTANT CALLED her the next day, informing her that Mr. Mathew Knight would be pleased to join her starting on Wednesday if that fit her schedule. Kristen had been half tempted to tell the woman no, but she chickened out at the last moment.

So Wednesday it was.

She almost called in sick. Except she knew if she did, her boss would reschedule. He wasn't the sort of man to give up on an idea easily, and she'd practically goaded him into accepting.

She showed up to work on the appointed day, settling down behind her desk—if that was what one could call the long plastic counter that stretched from one end of a shoulder-high cubicle to the other. But at least she had a window, she thought, staring out at the tree-studded landscape outside. She'd had an office back in Florida and so the dark-gray walls of her cubicle would take some getting used to.

Mr. Knight probably had an office.

Well, of course *he has an office, you dodo. He's the boss.*

It'd been awfully nice of him to pick up her hand like that, to try to reassure her….

Knock it off, Kristen. He was only trying to be kind.

She'd pegged him as a royal stick-in-the-mud, except it turned out he had a human side, one that was rather nice….

"Trouble in paradise?"

Kristen jerked.

Todd Peters. What the heck was he doing here?

"Hey, Todd." Kristen found herself thinking it was no wonder he remained one of the sport's favorite drivers, especially with the female population. Yeah, he was stocky, but in a black T-shirt she could see that that "stock" was actually muscle. With his shoulder resting against the dark gray plastic that made up one of her "walls" and that shirt of his tight around his bulging forearms, she could easily understand the appeal.

"What's up?" she asked.

"I came by to see how you're doing."

Right. "How nice." What did he want?

"No, I did," he said, obviously taking note of her disbelief. When he moved Kristen caught a hint of his aftershave. Something like Irish Spring.

She leaned back at the same time she pushed her glasses up her nose. Only she wasn't wearing glasses. For some strange reason she'd found herself a local eye doctor the day after her evening with her boss, and asked for contacts. It was actually something she'd been meaning to do for years, but she'd been especially keen on the idea now because she was working around cars so much; the glasses had become something of a pain.

Or that's what she told herself.

But then why had she gone to a hairdresser, too, one who'd pulled her mouse-blond hair down from its customary bun, proclaimed her natural hair color "blah," and convinced Kristen that she'd look GREAT! with a few highlights.

"You look different," he said.

"I have my contacts in," she said, as if she'd always had them and just chosen not to wear them before now.

"It looks nice."

He wasn't handsome, she realized. Not the way Mr. Knight was. But there was something ruggedly appealing about the driver that had Kristen wanting to back up her chair. "Thanks," she said, glancing at her computer monitor. She had work to do.

"Did you draw those?" he asked.

"Um, yeah," she said, glancing at the cartoon sketches she'd done for their boss.

"That's great."

"Thanks," she said, trying to concentrate on data

that had been collected from the wind tunnel. The truth was, her job was boring. Nine times out of ten all she did was study numbers—like now. It didn't exactly make for a stimulating day, especially when hunky NASCAR drivers were nearby.

Hunky?

"You know, Todd," she said, forcing herself to concentrate. "Now that I think about it, I do have a question for you."

"Oh, yeah?" he asked, leaning toward her.

She had to resist the urge to lean back again, every Dangerous Male alert button clanging and clattering in her head.

What *was* it with the man?

He was not, absolutely not, the kind of guy she'd go for. Too cocky. Too aware of his own sex appeal. Too *too*...if that made sense.

"Um, yeah," she said, forcing herself to concentrate. She had less than fifty days to prove herself to Mr. Knight and so she needed to get on the ball.

But Todd made that nearly impossible to do, what with the way he scooted closer. He didn't stay out of the no-fly zone like most men would. No, Todd got so close she could actually feel waves of heat oozing off his compact body. "I have some questions about the handling problems you had while testing at—" she checked her notes "—Michigan last year."

"You want to ask me about handling problems?"

He'd put an emphasis on the word "handling," and just in case she missed the double entendre, he lifted one thick brow, his eyes sparking in flirtation.

Okay, definite trouble here. No question about it.

"Yeah," she said, trying to keep it professional. "I know Dan played with the rear spoiler that day, but does he ever mess with this area?" She closed some screens, then pointed to a picture that showed Todd's car in the wind tunnel, a slipstream of smoke wafting over the body. The area in question was just behind the rear window, near the top of the "trunk."

"Uh, no. I don't think so."

"Humph," she mused. "I wonder if that's because it's regulated by NASCAR."

"Well, it sort of is," he said, leaning away from her and crossing his arms. "I mean, NASCAR has templates that body styles have to adhere to, so if he was to deviate from the accepted shape, NASCAR would find out."

"I know," she said, turning back to her computer screen. "But there's more than one way to skin a cat, and we can do it while staying within the rules."

"Oh, yeah?" he asked, back to being flirtatious. "How?"

"I'm not ready to share that with you yet," she said, hoping that if she gave him the cold shoulder again he'd quit his little act. "It's just an idea."

He uncrossed his arms and leaned toward her, his breath wafting over her ear as he said, "You can share other things with me if you want."

"Yeah, right," she said, rolling her eyes.

"I could think of lots of things," he said. "Things that would involve—"

"Hello, Todd."

They both sprang apart, Mr. Knight looking ever the businessman in his dark suit and matching pants. His black hair was swept back smoothly against his head.

"Hey there, boss man," Todd said. "Come to see what's up with our sexy engineer?"

Black eyebrows lifted, Mathew looking between the two of them. "Actually, I have an appointment with her."

"Do you?" Todd asked. "Lucky man."

"You ready?" Kristen asked, feeling the need to say something before Todd got too out of hand.

"I am," Mathew answered.

"Where are you two going?" Todd asked, a hint of innuendo in his voice.

"Mr. Knight's going to accompany me on my rounds today."

"Really?" Todd asked.

She nodded, catching the "you can't be serious?" look on the driver's face.

"Right this way, Mr. Knight," she said, nailing

Todd with a glance that told him to behave. "I was just explaining to Mr. Peters that I might have an idea on how to improve his car's performance. I thought perhaps you might want to accompany me to the fabrication shop where I hope to coax one of the body men to instigate a new design I have in mind."

"Certainly," Mathew said.

Kristen gave Todd her most professional smile as she stood up. "Thanks for the info," she said.

"Anytime," Todd said with a sexy grin. "I'll give you my cell-phone number in case you have any other questions."

"No need," Kristen said.

"You certain?' he asked. "Maybe you might want to call me about something else?"

"Not likely," she said, knowing that Todd's flirtatious ways were merely a matter of habit. He wasn't serious.

"Follow me, Mr. Knight," she said, walking down the center of the office, her fellow employees' heads popping up as they passed by.

"Mr. Peters certainly seems friendly," Mathew said.

Was that a hint of condemnation she heard in his voice? "He's a driver," she said, as if that ought to explain matters.

"He seems interested in you."

She shot him a glance. "Not likely."

Why would she think that? Mathew wondered.

Didn't she realize she was pretty—in an unconventional way?

She led him through a door and into the administrative portion of the upstairs offices. More heads poked up. He ignored them, as he always did.

The multilevel complex had cost him over a million dollars. And as always, he marveled that beneath them was a race shop. The shop wasn't like he'd pictured. He'd pictured a garage similar to what one would find at the high-end dealerships he'd frequented over the years. But this was more like a business complex that just so happened to have a race shop on the bottom level. U-shaped with a wide, grand entrance in the middle, his NASCAR NEXTEL Cup team occupied the right "arm" and his Busch and truck teams the left.

"I thought we'd visit with Sam Scott. He's the body man."

"And the purpose of our visit is?"

"Just an idea I have," she said, smiling at him mysteriously. "I can introduce you to the other guys while we're down there, too."

"You know their names?"

"Of course," she said, turning right and leading him down the carpeted steps that led to the first floor. On the wall hung pictures of various race cars, all with the same number on the side.

"I've been making a pest of myself in recent days,

trying to learn all I can about how the cars are put together. It's different from airplanes, obviously."

"Did you get contacts?" he asked, suddenly realizing that something about her was different.

"Hi, Maddie," she said at the bottom of the stairs, her smile wide as she waved at the main-floor receptionist.

"Morning, Ms. McKenna, Mr. Knight," said the twenty-something receptionist, a look of apprehension on her pretty face, her phone beep-beeping with an incoming call.

"I did get contacts," Kristen said as they walked toward the back of the building, her limp slightly less pronounced today. "I've been beneath so many cars in recent days that my glasses were getting in the way."

"Your hair's different, too."

"Yeah, I know," she said, stopping in front of a door, a plastic sign with the words Race Shop next to it. "I got shanghaied by a local hairdresser." She punched the keypad, the numbers chirping every time she pressed a button. "I went in to get a trim and the next thing I knew, bam, I had pieces of foil all over my head. I looked like a walking cell-phone tower."

She pulled open the door, and any comment he might have made was cut off by the sound of an air ratchet.

"Ah, the smell of a race shop." She sighed, pausing

and inhaling. "Race fuel and rubber. My favorite." When she turned, Mathew realized his feet had stopped working.

What a smile.

"Okay," she said, heading for the center aisle. On either side of the tile floor, race cars sat in various stages of assembly, their dark blue bodies reflecting the dome-shaped lighting fixtures above them. "Obviously we've had a tour of the race shop, but that was a lot of information to take in. I wouldn't blame you if you don't remember what each department does. So let me just tell you that each of your cars is worked on by specialists. You have your tranny guy here—that's a transmission specialist." She pointed to a pair of feet hanging out from beneath a car. "Your rear-end specialist is there," she said, indicating the far corner of the shop. "And your electronics guys are there—"

They were attracting attention, Mathew noticed. Men were peering out from beneath the cars, or bending around to see. One guy stood in an empty engine compartment making him look as if he was wearing the car around his waist.

"The fabrication area is through here," she said, turning left and walking toward a door that had triangular warning signs posted on it. He knew from his tour that there was another shop on the other side, though at the time he hadn't known the difference between the two areas. But now he looked around. A guy squatted next to some box-shaped tubing, his welder's mask making him oblivious to the new arrivals.

The door slammed closed behind them as Kristen said, "Over there is Terry. He builds the frames for your race cars. Opposite him is the senior fabricator, Bill."

It seemed hard to believe that the pieces of metal would be shaped and welded into a car, but they would. In one corner of the shop, a dark-haired man worked with a metal press of some sort. He was cranking on a lever that spit a slightly bowed sheet out one end. He'd seen that particular device before—at his own airframe fabrication shop. The shape of the metal could be controlled by how many times it went through the press.

"Bill," Kristen called.

Bill stopped, the metal making a wha-wha-wha sound in protest. "Hey," he said by way of greeting, his expression turning wary when he saw who stood behind her, not that it'd been particularly warm to begin with.

"Have you met Mathew Knight?" she asked, motioning to him with a hand.

"No, ma'am, I haven't," he said, wiping a hand on black work pants before holding it out to him. "Nice to meet you, Mr. Knight."

"Nice to meet you as well," Mathew said, watching as Bill pulled his shoulders back, his dark blue, button-down work shirt nearly pulled from the waistline of his pants. He couldn't be much older than twenty-five. Surprising, really, that he was a "senior" anything.

"Bill," Kristen said. "I have a question about how you fabricate the rear deck lid of the cars."

"Yeah?" the man asked.

Kristen went over to the car he was currently putting together. The back end was complete, and it was clear what was being fabricated now were the sides. "My question concerns this area here," she said by way of an answer, pointing to the spot right below the rear window, or where the window would be if one had been put into place. "Does NASCAR examine this area closely?"

"What do you mean?"

"Do they take off the sheet metal? Or press down on the rear deck to check for integrity?"

"They work around the area, when they're measuring or using the templates," Bill said, "but they don't actually tap on the sheet metal or nothin' if that's what you're asking."

"Kristen, what are you thinking?" Mathew asked, intrigued.

She crossed her arms, her expression as serious as he'd ever seen it. The engineer in her suddenly emerged, and Mathew was reminded of the fact that she was considered one of his best.

"A few weeks ago," she said, "before you just about landed that helicopter of yours atop my head, I received a bulletin from AeroSkin. They have a new product they're testing, a poly-enhanced metal that expands and contracts under pressure. They were suggesting it for the ultrasonics, but I don't see why it wouldn't work for race cars. It looks just like sheet metal, or it would once it was painted. The piece they sent me was quite impressive. You could actually twist and flex it like it was a thick piece of aluminum foil."

"How would this give us an edge?" Mathew asked.

"Well, as you may or may not know, the tear-drop design is by far the most efficient way to move large objects through airspace. Obviously, this presents a problem for race teams because NASCAR mandates the shape of the car. But what if the car merely started in the correct shape? What if while out on the track we were able to gain an inch or two of lift in the back here?" She pointed the rear quarter panel. "I don't think it'd be obvious, certainly not in a way that other teams would notice."

"You think that'll give us an edge?" Bill asked, doubt written on his face.

"I do."

"How?" Mathew asked.

"Because the area behind the rear window is known for its flow detachment, which, as you might know, Bill, is an area of high vacuum. If we harness that energy by using a material that will lift when it's pulled upon by the vacuum, we'll likely decrease some of the drag, since our car will be a little closer to the optimum tear-shaped design. All we'd need to do is use the special metal here and here." She pointed to the trunk lid and the window frame. "And maybe even on top of the quarter panels. And the *really* great thing is, if this works, we could find out which combinations work best for whatever specific track."

"Maybe," Bill said.

"There's no way to know unless we try," Kristen said.

"Do it," Mathew ordered.

Bill didn't look terribly pleased by his decision. "Well, heck, Ms. McKenna, why not use your special metal on the top of the car, too?"

Mathew bit back a sarcastic retort. Either Kristen missed the condescension in the man's voice, or she chose to ignore it.

He glanced at Kristen. She ignored it.

"I thought of that," she said. Mathew was surprised that he could read her so easily. But it was easy to do, given that the fun-loving, usually smiling

Kristen was gone. In her place stood a woman who was calm, confident and firmly in control of her emotions.

Impressive.

"I've actually been working on this idea for several days," she added. "And my biggest concern with using the material on the roof panels is that it might not be as structurally sound as regular sheet metal, and I wouldn't want to risk a driver getting injured by putting something above his head that might tear or break apart and maybe slash into him."

Bill didn't move. Maybe he'd finally grasped that Kristen was good at what she did.

"And even if it turns out that we can't use the metal, I think we might be able to create a loose-enough skin through here—" she pointed to the back of the car again "—that it'll lift up some when under vacuum. Don't you think?"

"Maybe," Bill said grudgingly.

"Well, we can try. Maybe even on this car. What do you think? Or are you building this one for a specific race?"

"I was building it for one of the speedways," Bill said.

"Perfect. I think we should do it then, with your permission, of course," she said, looking Mathew in the eye.

"You have it," Mathew said.

"Terrific," Kristen said.

"Tell him what you need," said Mathew, glaring at Bill when the man crossed his arms and squared his shoulders. It appeared that Mathew needed to have a talk with his staff about gender bias.

"I'd like to have something to test for the wind tunnel by next week. Can you schedule that for me?" she asked Bill.

"I can make a call."

"Great," Kristen said. "I'll go order the material." She turned away. "Come on, Mr. Knight. We need to go back to my cubicle."

"Do as she asks," Mathew said on his way out, making sure Kristen was out of hearing distance, "and your job working for me will be a lot easier."

Bill looked ready to say something sarcastic again, but he must have remembered who he was talking to. Mathew had been called "intimidating" in the boardroom. That wasn't for nothing.

"Understood," Bill said.

"What was that about?" Kristen asked when he caught up to her.

"I just reminded Bill that time is of the essence," Mathew said.

"Really?" she asked, letting them out of the shop. "Because if you were talking to him about adjusting his attitude, don't bother. I'm used to men treating me like that."

"Not while you've been working for Fly For Less."

She stopped. They were tucked back in a corner of the main shop, people looking in their direction again. Kristen didn't seem to notice. "Are you kidding? When I first started working for you it was an uphill climb. I was young, just out of college, and none of your male engineers wanted to listen to a woman. I worked my butt off proving myself to everyone and now I've got to start all over again here, not that I mind. I'm always up for new challenges, but I don't suspect it'll be easy convincing men who have years of working for race teams that I'm someone they can trust."

"But you have a racing background, too."

"Yeah, but they don't know that."

"They will if I tell them."

"They'll either hear it through the grapevine or they'll figure it out on their own," she said, her chin lifting. "My work speaks for itself."

"But it might make it easier if I smooth the way—

"Don't," she said quickly. "That'll only create friction. Men don't react well when something's crammed down their throats, especially a female something."

He supposed she had a point. What's more, she seemed perfectly capable of handling the situation herself.

Good for her.

"Very well. I won't say a word, but if you encounter out-and-out hostility, I'll expect you to let me know."

Her face softened then, the light back in her eyes. "Are you kidding? That's not going to happen when I'm showing the big cheese around."

He found himself smiling at his new title.

"Well then," he said. "I suppose you'd better take the big cheese back to your office. I'm curious how much this new material might cost me."

"Aw, don't worry, boss. It's only twenty thousand a foot."

"I beg your pardon?"

The sound of her laughter echoed through the shop. Heads turned again. Mathew stared, wondering at the strange way she made him feel.

"Just kidding," she said.

"I should hope so."

"It's only fifteen thousand."

She was trying to keep a straight face, he could tell. "Well then, perhaps we should order more," he said. "It being such a bargain and all."

The smile she gave him was as bright as spotlights at a movie premiere. "Come on," she said, motioning him to follow. "Let's go spend your money."

CHAPTER NINE

TO KRISTEN'S ABSOLUTE SURPRISE, she found herself enjoying her boss's company. By the end of the day she was even calling him Mathew easily, something that she'd have never thought possible earlier that morning. Her boss was a brilliant man, not surprising given his success. He was also a quick study, and personable when he put his mind to it. She would bet half the females in his employ went home thinking about him at night. She certainly did.

She was actually looking forward to the next day, until his assistant called and informed her that Mr. Knight wouldn't be joining her. He'd been called out of town.

But that was okay. His absence gave her time to focus on the changes she wanted to make to car body sixty-one—that was the identification number they used. It took most of the week, due in large part to the fact that their computer modeling system was so outmoded. It took her days to enter the data specs for her rear deck lid—and that was just one portion of the car. Heaven forbid she had to build a whole vehicle. But the data she'd gleaned from her hours of work looked promising, enough so that Ralph Helfrick—chief engineer—promised to let her use some of the much-coveted wind tunnel time to test it.

Mathew wouldn't be there. Whatever business he was conducting, it kept him away.

So the day they were due to test came all too quickly. Kristen woke up hours before she was due at the office. She used the time to go jogging in the hope that it would help clear her mind. It didn't. She was a nervous wreck by the time she showed up at Jet Systems, the wind tunnel place. Kristen smoothed her hair back from her face and tucked some loose strands into her ponytail. Her hands shook.

Well, of course they did. She was anxious. Who wouldn't be?

The building was three stories tall and looked more like an airplane hangar than a test facility. Tiny square windows dotted the front facade. A single door sat near the middle. The only thing that marked it as a state-of-the-art testing facility was a small white sign with black lettering that read Jet Systems in the upper left-hand corner of the buff-colored building.

The parking lot looked empty.

When she recognized Dan's white Explorer, Kristen wondered if everyone had come over in one vehicle. Probably. Big surprise that she wasn't invited to ride along.

"It's a colossal waste of our time."

Kristen paused with her hand on the front door. The building only had a few windows, but obviously her co-workers hadn't been looking out them because it was Floyd who spoke next. She recognized his voice.

"I know," the general manager said. "But we have to humor her. Boss's orders."

Stay calm.

"How long do you think she'll stick around?"

Dan. That's who'd spoken the first time.

"Just until her design's a proven flop," Floyd said. "Then she'll be out of our hair."

She had to step back from the door, had to take a few deep breaths.

A colossal waste of time? Ooh.

Her heart pounded. Little did they know.

She composed herself and pasted a wide smile on her face as she breezed inside the office. "Hey, guys," she said brightly.

Dan and Floyd immediately stopped talking. But what surprised her, what hurt—even though it shouldn't—was that Ralph was there, too. She'd thought he'd warmed up to her.

"We ready to go?" she asked.

"Just waiting on you," Floyd said.

Was she late? She glanced at her watch. No. She swiped a loose strand of hair away from her face, a nervous habit. She was so mad she could barely contain herself.

They were shown into the observation room a moment later, a space dominated by a large projection screen that hung on the wall to their left. On either side of the monitor sat flat-screen TVs—six in each unit. A few were turned on and showed the image of car body sixty-one already strapped down inside the wind tunnel.

"Welcome, everybody," a man said, his white shirt with Jet Systems stitched in black lettering on his pocket, his name—John—stitched above that. "Just take a seat."

Chairs screeched against the white linoleum floor as they were pulled away from the desk, if one wanted to call it that. It looked more like something you'd find at a bar with its half-moon shape, the thing made out of gray Formica. Kristen took a seat, but she ended up all by her lonesome at one end, her fellow engineers at the other.

"Most of you have been here before," John said, his gray hair looking white beneath fluorescent lights, and his long, skinny frame making him appear more like an ex-ballplayer than an engineer. "But for those of you who haven't—" he glanced in her direction "—I'm John and I'm the general manager here. The first thing we're going to do is go over a few safety measures."

It was all pretty basic. Kristen had been to wind tunnels before, but she gave the guy her undivided attention anyway. Or she tried to. It was hard to concentrate with anger beating in her chest. She picked up a pencil, began to turn it over and over again in her hands.

"When you're ready to get started, just let Chad there know." He pointed, near the door they'd just come through, to a heavyset man with a nearly bald head. "He'll fire up the fans—"

The door opened.

Kristen almost dropped her pencil.

"Am I late?" Mathew asked.

The other engineers all straightened. Dan said, "Uh, no, actually. You're not. We were just about to get started."

"Excellent," Mathew said, his eyes sweeping over the room. His gaze found hers. He moved in her direction.

Kristen turned away, her heart pounding even more but for another reason altogether.

"Good morning, Mr. Knight," she said when he sat down next to her.

"I thought I was going to miss it," he said as he took a seat.

"You're just in time," she whispered back.

He looked different this morning, she thought, peeking at him. More casual. Dark blue polo shirt. Tan slacks. Slightly mussed hair. He looked good.

And she was happy to see him.

"All right then," John said. "You ready to do the first test?"

"Light 'em up," Dan said.

The projection screen flickered. A giant spreadsheet suddenly appeared, the fields empty.

"What am I looking at?"

"Data fields," Kristen said, her voice low. "When the fans are brought up to maximum speed, air will begin to flow over the car's body. We'll collect data from thousands of sensors beneath the car and in the tunnel. With that data we'll be able to gauge air pressure, velocity over certain parts of the car, and, most importantly, create a two-D model."

"I assume you'll use the model to gauge whether your new material is doing what you want?"

"We will. This particular car was already tested once this week. The numbers generated from that test will be compared to those we get today."

Mathew nodded.

He heard a sound, a low hum that quickly grew louder. He glanced at Kristen. "The fans," she said.

She looked pale. And tired. And, he thought as her hand fiddled with a pencil, nervous.

"Relax," he found himself saying. "If this doesn't work you can go back to your old job."

She shot him a glance, her hair flicking behind her. "Thanks," she said. "That's reassuring."

He said the words in jest. But, of course, it hadn't come out sounding that way. That was one of the reasons he never joked around with employees; it always came out wrong.

"I meant that you have nothing to worry about either way."

"I know," she said, her shoulders relaxing a bit. "I'm just stressed."

"I'm not surprised," he said, thinking she smelled nice. Like flowers and cinnamon rolls all rolled into one.

Cinnamon rolls?

He must be tired, not surprising since he'd had to catch an early-morning flight from New York in order to get to North Carolina in time for the test session. He was exhausted from a busy week, on edge, and a bit irritated to have found Kristen sitting alone at one end of the table while the rest of his engineers sat on the other.

"Here we go," she said as the first string of data started to pop up on screen.

"What are we looking for?" he asked.

"The column marked 'Cd two.' 'Cd' stands for drag coefficient. We want lower numbers in that column than the one marked 'Cd one' which is from our test earlier this week."

The numbers started to fill in, slowly at first and then faster and faster. It was like watching a Keno game in Las Vegas.

Kristen straightened.

Mathew jerked upright, too, because the numbers weren't just a little lower, they were *a lot* lower.

He glanced at Floyd. The head of engineering looked thunderstruck. Dan, sitting next to him, looked pleasantly surprised.

"How quickly will we have the modeling?" Kristen asked.

A man he hadn't noticed before, but who obviously worked for Jet Systems judging by his shirt, said, "Just a couple of minutes. Takes a bit for the computers to crunch all the numbers."

Kristen nodded. Her grip on the pencil tightened. She stared at the television screen as if she could see actual streamers of air as they flowed around the car.

And then the spreadsheet disappeared. A line drawing appeared in its place.

"Split the screen," Kristen said. "Show us the two-D model from earlier this week."

The Jet Systems engineer did as asked. A second image appeared by the first one's side.

Even Mathew could see the difference.

"I'll be damned," Floyd muttered.

"It's working," Kristen said.

Indeed it was. Even Mathew could see the noticeable lift in the back section of the car. It wasn't much, but on a super speedway, where tenths of a second could count, it just might be enough to give them an edge.

"Congratulations," Mathew said.

Her eyes appeared lit from within. They even changed colors, seeming to turn sky-blue instead of royal blue. Mathew found himself unable to look away. He'd missed her this past week. Missed her offbeat sense of humor and her bright smiled.

He'd missed *her.* He rarely had occasion to socialize with women. He'd enjoyed every minute spent with Kristen.

She leaned forward and every nerve in Mathew's body seemed to freeze.

"I so want to rub Floyd's nose in it," she said in a low voice.

"I don't blame you," he said gruffly.

"I'll fall over dead if he congratulates me."

"I wouldn't hold my breath," he said.

She turned beautiful when she was happy.

"Would you like to go to lunch to celebrate?" The words slipped out before he could stop them and he immediately regretted it.

She looked speechless, as well she should. What the hell was he thinking? He couldn't take her out to lunch. Not only would that look odd to his other employees, but it was against his principles to get personally involved with his employees.

"I don't think that'd be a good idea."

No. Of course not.

"I mean, I'm flattered, but I—"

"I just thought you might like to go out and celebrate," he said, trying to hide his chagrin. "There's nothing more to it than that."

"I...well, thank you."

"But I perfectly understand your reticence. What's more, I agree. It might very well ostracize you even more if I begin to show you favoritism."

"Yes. I mean, no. That wasn't what I was going to say, but that's a very good point."

"So tell me what happens next," he said, changing the subject. He must be sleep deprived to have said something like that.

"We'll run the test at different speeds, see how the rear deck lid performs under different loads. It'll be a long day."

"So!" a voice boomed from the back of the room. "What'd I miss?'

Everyone turned, including Kristen. Mathew followed her gaze although he recognized the voice.

"Todd," Dan said. "What the heck you doing here?"

"I was in the neighborhood," the driver said with

a wide smile. "Wanted to see if our new engineer was as smart as she is good-looking...whoa!" he said, his attention having caught on the screen. "Look at *that.* Obviously your new material worked."

"It did," Kristen said. Mathew watched as color spread into her cheeks. Did she like the driver?

"What sort of gains will we see?"

Kristen looked at Ralph, almost as if she expected him to answer, and when he didn't she said, "We should see anywhere from a half-second to a full-second gain in your lap times."

"Outstanding," Todd said, walking up to Kristen, bending and putting an arm around her. "Not only are you brilliant, but you smell good, too."

Like cinnamon rolls, Mathew thought.

"I think this is cause for celebration."

"She's too busy," Mathew said.

All eyes turned to him.

"You working her too hard?" Todd asked.

"Actually," Kristen started to say, "he's right. I—"

"Kristen works whatever hours she chooses, but I happen to know those are long hours. She doesn't have time to go out with you."

"Not even for dinner?"

"No," Mathew said firmly.

Silence.

Kristen stared between the two of them. Her mouth went flat. "Mr. Knight is right," she said. "I don't have time for victory celebrations. But I'm perfectly capable of working out my own schedule." She looked at Mathew. "And answering my own questions."

Everyone in the room held still. Mathew knew he sounded like a fool, and that made him feel an even bigger ass. What the hell was wrong with him?

He liked Kristen.

He was attracted to her wit and to her intelligence and to her unique personality, all the things Todd Peters wouldn't give a damn about.

But it was none of his business, he realized. She was free to do what she wanted and he should *not* be forming an attachment to her.

"I beg your pardon," he said to Kristen. "You're right. I shouldn't have answered for you. I'm tired," he offered by way of explanation. "Long night."

"We're all tired," Kristen said, glancing around the room. "Now, if you'll both excuse me, I have work to do."

And that was that, Mathew thought. Dismissed by his own employee, not that he blamed her.

"*You* want to go to lunch?" Todd asked, leaning toward him.

"I have work to do, too," he said.

CHAPTER TEN

"WHAT WAS THAT ABOUT?" Kristen asked Mathew when they were on break a couple hours later.

"What was what about?"

But she was certain he knew *exactly* what she meant.

"I'm perfectly capable of scheduling my own lunches. Or dinners," she said, crossing her arms and leaning against a wall.

A microwave binged, the smell of blueberry muffin filling the air.

"I was merely trying to intervene in the event you were uncomfortable with…" He seemed to have to search for a word. "Rejecting his offer of a date."

"He wasn't offering a date."

His brow lifted in scorn. "No?"

"No," she said firmly, pushing herself away from the wall and pouring herself a cup of coffee. Her stomach growled.

"You might want to watch yourself with Todd," he said.

"Todd's a flirt. That's all."

"Don't be naive."

The other engineers were shooting them covert glances. Kristen leaned forward and lowered her voice. "The only one being naive is you. Todd Peters would flirt with a two-legged newt. It's a sickness with him. He probably can't control himself."

"And the fact that you're a talented, beautiful, brilliant engineer has nothing to do with it?"

Was that how he saw her? She flushed, her eyes darting away for a second. "Well, I—"

What was she supposed to say?

"I doubt he even knows the color of my eyes," she mumbled.

"Don't sell yourself short."

Mathew's eyes were green, with blue flecks around the pupil. The left one had a tiny dot near the rim of the iris.

"I need to get back," she said.

"Kristen," he said, capturing her arm before she could turn away. "Don't think your disability makes you any less desirable to men."

How did he…? She lifted her chin. "I don't think that."

He didn't say anything.

"I don't," she repeated.

"I hope not," he said, releasing her arm.

Kristen watched him walk away, her shoulders

suddenly slumping. When she looked around she noticed the other guys were all staring at her. She shook her head, her lips pressed together.

"What?" she asked them.

"Nothing," Dan answered, but there was quiet laughter after he turned away.

Brother.

THE REST OF THE TEST ONLY confirmed their earlier findings. The new material worked like a charm, so much so that they decided to test it on the track. The Michigan speedway was perfect for that task. She just wished everyone else felt as enthusiastic. The tension in the engineering department was palpable. She knew that was due, in part, to her successful test. Nobody liked to be shown up, especially if the person doing the showing up was a woman in an all-male environment. But there were undercurrents, too. After Mathew's outburst, and then their whispered conversation at the wind tunnel, half her co-workers suspected they were having an affair.

Damn it.

She worked hard to come up with new ideas and make her own way in a mostly man's world. The last thing she'd needed was for everything to be completely undermined by gossip, but that's exactly what had happened.

She focused on work, the only thing she *could*

do. Her boss had disappeared again, but that was probably a good thing. It kept some of the gossips at bay. Todd, however, kept poking his nose into her business. He did it all under the guise of wanting to be kept "in the loop," but his attention caused more eyebrows to rise.

So when Kristen stepped out of the company van with various other team members not long after, she was heartily grateful to be away from the office. Of course she was nervous about testing her new design in an actual race, but her anxiety was tempered by anticipation.

"Scared?" a crew member named Rick asked, climbing out right behind her.

Rick was part of the B team. Kristen had learned that race teams had A, B and sometimes C teams that flew in and out during a race weekend. The A team were the guys who went over the wall, and they were only flown in on race day. The B team were the grunts, but Kristen noticed Rick didn't seem bothered by that. He was one of the few men on the team who didn't seem to mind having her around, probably because he was just happy to have a job working in racing. His eyes were as bright as the Trinitron big screen in the infield.

"Not scared," she said. "Apprehensive."

It was an overcast day, but Kristen still had to squint against the glare to look up.

"Well, I guess we'll know in a few hours," Rick said, the duffel bag he carried bouncing against his back. "Practice starts soon."

Yes, it did, and she knew she'd be sweating every minute of it. Not only was this her first official race, but it was her first time in a NASCAR garage and she had to admit that she felt a healthy degree of apprehension at being at a track.

It brought back memories.

Memories she'd rather not think about.

"When's Mr. Knight coming in?" Rick asked, wiping at a spot of something on his blue crew uniform, the name Arcadia plastered across the front. They wouldn't switch to the red-and-gold Fly For Less colors until the end of the season, or until Arcadia signed off on a new driver for the second team Mathew was assembling.

"I don't know," she said. And she didn't care. She was still peeved at Mathew's high-handed behavior.

And still wondering if maybe he was right. Maybe she *did* shy away from men because of her disability. She certainly had reason to do so, but that was another memory she'd rather forget.

"Show your ID when you get to the gate," Rick said as they exited the crew member parking area off to the side of the garage.

"Right," she said, digging it out from the neckline of her dark blue Arcadia polo shirt. She wore tan slacks, which, given the heat, would make for an uncomfortable day. Rick's work pants looked worse—they were black denim.

She flashed the credential, which looked like no more than a credit card, at a sunburned security guard. She'd been handed the ID last week, her smiling face staring back at her. The picture was taken pre-contact lenses and she marveled at how different she looked now without glasses. She'd even begun wearing a tiny bit of mascara on her upper lashes.

"Go on," the white-shirted security guy said, waving her through, his shiny gold badge refracting sunlight.

"Where do we go?" she asked Rick, looking around.

The garage reminded her of a local tire shop, one that had roll-up doors and glossy concrete floors. Only it was way bigger than a tire shop. She counted twenty-five stalls just on one side, and there were another twenty-five on the back side of the garage, and a whole other garage parallel to the first.

"Well," Rick said. "The haulers are parked according to where they are in the points standing. They use the points from the previous week. Todd's in fifteenth place."

"Fifteenth? Isn't that bad?"

"Not really," Rick said, the corners of his eyes

creasing as he glanced around. "We'd like to be in the top ten, of course, but we had some bad luck early in the season."

"You think there's time to catch up?"

"We're only halfway through the season," Rick said, guiding her past the first ten stalls. There were car numbers above the stalls, she saw, and the names of the drivers right next to them. "And we've moved up five spots in the past few weeks. There's time."

"Especially if my new design works."

"A win would certainly help," he said, his voice lowering. "But be careful what you say around here."

Kristen looked around. The race car transporters were parked opposite the stalls, just as they'd been at the test session at Charlotte. And once again, crew members dashed back and forth between the garage and their big rigs like worker bees around a hive. Some of them carried car parts. Others looked to be deeply troubled by the state of the world's economy, at least judging by the expressions on their faces. Either that or their jobs seriously stressed them out, probably the latter if her own job was anything to go by.

"I take it some teams like to steal ideas."

"You bet," he said, stopping at the back of the number eighty-two hauler, Arcadia scrawled in white vinyl letters on the tinted sliding-glass door.

"Hardly sportsmanlike."

"Nope, but it's the way the game is played." He leaned closer to her. "The thing is, nobody will be able to figure out what you've done. That new skin looks like regular sheet metal."

"It *is* sheet metal. Just a new kind. I hope it works," she said.

Rick straightened. "I'm going to go stow my bag. You should have a look around. See what the other teams are up to. There's an aisle that runs down the middle of the garage. If you walk down it, you can look into garage stalls."

"Won't I be a little obvious?" she asked, motioning toward her team shirt.

"Nah. You're new so nobody knows who you are. The other teams will think you're a fan. Just tuck your ID beneath your shirt and nobody will be the wiser."

"You mean you guys keep track of faces from week to week?"

"Sure. Especially a pretty girl like you. You're bound to stick out." He clamped his mouth closed, almost as if he was embarrassed by his own words. Maybe he was, she thought, because she was pretty certain that was a blush she saw staining the base of his neck.

"Thanks, Rick," she said. "Thanks for everything. You've been a big help."

"No problem," he said, but he didn't meet her gaze.

But Kristen was hard-pressed to know what to do with herself, despite Rick's advice. She felt like an ice-skater at a football game. And as she looked around, she realized how much she had to learn. Sure, she knew a lot more than she had a few weeks ago, but it still wasn't enough. At least poking around gave her something to do until practice time. She peered beneath open hoods, bumming a notepad off someone so she could jot down ideas or questions. She was so engrossed in what she was doing, she didn't even notice the person coming up to her.

"Well, hey there, little lady. You gonna help me out today?"

There was only one person on earth who would dare to call her "little lady."

"Hey, Todd," she said, turning toward him and closing the cover of her notepad. He'd caught her at the end of the garage, and Kristen noticed that they were attracting quite a bit of attention. Men and women whom she assumed were fans—judging by their colorful T-shirts and the cameras around their necks—stared in their direction.

"What you writing there?" he asked.

"Just a few notes."

"Let me see."

There was a waist-high metal fence that separated the observation aisle from the actual garage stalls. Todd pulled the thing toward him, inviting her in.

"Mr. Peters, can I get your autograph?" a man called.

"Can I get a picture?" a woman said.

"Will you sign this?" someone else called.

Kristen was startled. A moment ago she'd been standing by herself, but all at once race fans were pressing against her. She slid into the garage right as Todd said, "Not right now, guys," he said. "My engineer here has something important to discuss with me."

"You're an engineer?" a middle-aged woman asked, the brim of her visor proclaiming her to be the fan of another driver.

"Yes, ma'am," Kristen said.

"Really?" the woman said. "Can I get a picture with you?" she asked, holding up her digital camera.

"Ah, in a second," Kristen said, completely befuddled. Why would someone want a picture with *her?*

"Because you work for a race team," Todd said when she voiced the question out loud, guiding her toward his own pit stall. "Fans are like that. Here," he said, holding out his hand. "Let me see what you've got there. Hey, Adam," he said, waving to another driver who looked to be in a serious discussion with his crew chief and a pretty redhead.

"Hey, Todd," Adam said, smiling.

"Does everybody know everybody?" she asked. She'd asked much the same question of Rick, of course, but she was still curious to hear his response. Back when she'd been driving, she had pretty much kept to herself. Then again, as a woman, she'd been an outsider.

Story of her life.

"Pretty much," Todd said. "When you're with the same people week in and week out, new faces tend to stand out. The race fans are easy to spot. The women wear skimpy clothing, the men wear T-shirts with their favorite driver on it. They always have cameras. Usually they're wearing a hat of some sort. They stand out like sore thumbs. What's this?" he asked, showing her the page he'd flipped to.

She looked at the page in question, the disk-shaped design she'd drawn recognizable only to her. She'd done that on purpose in case she lost her notepad. Rick had her paranoid.

"That's something I'm working on."

"Yeah, but what is it?"

She glanced around. They'd reached his pit stall, and a few of the crew members that she'd flown to the race with nodded in her direction. At least they were acknowledging her presence. "I could tell you what that is," she said, "but then I'd have to kill you."

Todd had a look on his face that was a cross between amusement and pique. "You're kidding, right?"

"Actually, I'm not," she said. "I don't tell anybody my ideas until they're a done deal."

He squared his shoulders. "Yeah, but I'm the driver."

"Doesn't matter," she said. "To me you're just the monkey that pilots the car."

He leaned back, his nostrils flaring. Uh-oh. She'd made him mad. She almost told him she was kidding, but something made her stop. Instead she peered up at him with a challenging look on her face.

"You know, I could have you fired for saying that."

"Mr. Knight won't fire me."

And then he started to look amused.

"Time to suit up," Dan said, coming up behind them.

Todd didn't turn, just lifted his hand, staying the crew chief with a wave.

"Jeez, is it that time already?" Kristen asked, pretending to glance at her watch. "Guess you've got to go."

"You know, Kristen," Todd said, leaning toward her. "Something about you really gets under my skin."

His breath wafted across her neck in a way that she was certain had been done on purpose. Mathew's words came slamming back to her.

"Really?" she asked. "That's too bad."

"Actually, I think it would be good," he said softly, leaning even closer. "Very, very good."

He's not serious, she reminded herself. He is *not* serious.

"I'll have to take your word for that," she said, stepping back. "In the meantime, drive carefully out there."

She turned.

"Kristen," he said.

She told herself not to look back. "Yeah?" she asked, doing exactly that.

"See you after."

"Yeah, after," she echoed, holding his gaze.

He was the one to break eye contact, Dan having come up to him with a clipboard in hand. Kristen turned away, too, not really sure where she was headed but needing to get away. She couldn't stand Todd and yet she was starting to think he really was interested in her.

But why?

She couldn't figure it out. Todd Peters, famous race car driver, didn't date engineers. Drivers dated actresses or models or television personalities.

He must be bored, she told herself. Or maybe he was between girlfriends and she was just someone he could flirt with to fill the time. That must be it.

But what if there was more to it than that?

She thought about all the times he'd come by to visit her and blushed.

Good Lord. What if there was?

HE LIKED MESSING WITH HER, Todd thought as he drove onto pit road less than fifteen minutes later. He had no idea why, but something about the female engineer amused him to no end.

"You got a pack of cars coming up on your rear," Gary, his spotter, said.

"I see them," Todd said, glancing in his mirrors. He wasn't up to speed yet and so he stayed down low, waiting until the other cars passed. They did in a blur of color, Todd spotting the fifty-three car and the seventy-six in that pack. If he could keep up with them, that'd be a good test of his car's performance.

He smiled beneath his helmet, the foam inserts pressing against his cheeks. He couldn't get the look on Kristen's face out of his head, the one she'd given him when he'd intimated how good it'd be between them.

"How's she feel, driver?" his crew chief asked.

"Good so far," he said, his head tipping to the right as he rounded turn two. It was partly cloudy—rain was predicted for later in the day—and so that might affect his lap times. Shade meant lower track temperatures, and a cooler track meant faster laps.

"So far the fast cars are running twenty-eights."

"Roger that," Todd said. "Twenty-eights."

He was almost up to speed. Todd glanced out his rearview. He couldn't see the deck lid, but he assumed the new material was holding up. If not, the drivers behind him would have a nasty surprise in the form of sheet metal coming at them. Very likely NASCAR would have a few questions, too.

It struck him then.

It was quieter. Usually the wind rushing by sounded like the inside of a tornado. Not today.

"Coming up on them," Gary said.

Todd could see the backs of the other cars, the logos of their team sponsors like tiny billboards. He pointed his car right for them.

"Fast time's now a twenty-seven," Dan said.

Todd took note of the time. He wouldn't be given his own until he completed his current lap. He eyed the pack of cars in front of him, pretty certain he was gaining on them.

When he exited turn three he knew he was right. "She's handling good," Todd said. "But maybe we could make the car turn a little better." He threw his car into turn four. "When I'm on the gas out of the corner, she wants to lurch to the right."

"Roger that," Dan said.

But he was still gaining on the field in front of him, so much so that he was really curious about what his lap time would be. When he crossed beneath the start finish line, he found himself holding his breath.

"You just ran a twenty-six."

Hot damn! That was almost a full second faster.

"Check your engine temperature."

Todd smiled to himself. "It's fine," he said, knowing that Dan didn't really care about his motor temp. Well, he *did,* but not at that moment. The words were a code to take it easy. They didn't want to show their hand just yet.

Todd eased off.

Still, his next lap was only a fraction slower.

"Still running cool?" Todd asked.

"She's fine," Todd said. "I'm doing all I can to keep her cool." Which meant he was *trying* to slow down. Holy crap. What had Kristen done?

"Twenty-seven-oh-eight," Dan said.

He caught the pack, Todd picking off his competitor's car in such an easy fashion that he found himself grinning all over again.

"How long do I need to stay out?"

"We're trying to figure fuel mileage so it'll be a few more laps," Dan said.

"Roger that."

The new part would alter how much gas they used. Faster cars usually meant more fuel consumption. Then again, maybe not. If his car was moving through the air more efficiently, they might actually be *saving* fuel.

"I think she's tightening up in turn three," he

said, which really meant that he had a rocket ship on his hands.

"Roger that. We'll work on it when you come in."

Todd almost laughed. They wouldn't be *touching* this car. No way.

His optimism only improved the longer he ran. He could practically pick off cars one-handed.

"Okay, you can come on in," Dan said a few laps later.

Todd immediately ducked down low, riding the apron until he hit pit road.

He had a car he could win with.

And he had Kristen to thank.

When he turned into the garage, NASCAR whistles blowing to warn pedestrians that he was coming, he felt more chipper than he had in ages. It was hotter than snot inside the car, but Todd hardly noticed. He couldn't wait to tell Dan about his ride.

He found his garage stall, one of his crew members standing outside to direct him in, more whistles blowing. It took a second for his eyes to adjust when he entered the building, Todd hitting the brake a split second later.

But not because he was about to run into the toolbox.

No. He mashed the pedal because once he could see clearly, he spied Kristen talking to Mathew Knight.

Todd flipped his visor up.

And it wasn't until that moment, that *exact* moment, that Todd realized how bad he had it.

He hadn't been flirting with her because he wanted to rile her up.

He *liked* her. He was hot for Kristen.

She gave him shit. And she blushed whenever he got too close. He found that cute. But most of all, he liked that she knew how to make a car go fast. She talked his language. Blondes with big jugs were only good for one thing, and it wasn't talking. Kristen knew her way around a race car. It had him wondering if there were other things she might know her way around, too.

And what he'd have to do to find out.

CHAPTER ELEVEN

"CONGRATULATIONS," DAN SAID, coming up to her and shaking her hand, much to Kristen's surprise. It was his first public display of acceptance.

"Thanks, Dan," Kristen said, meeting Mathew's gaze. He'd shown up just before Todd had pulled into the garage, Kristen so surprised she'd been momentarily tongue-tied.

"How'd it feel?" the crew chief asked Todd when he removed the window net. Todd's helmet came out first, Dan taking it and then placing it up on the roof. Gloves were tossed out after that. Kristen watched as Todd disconnected himself from his HANS Device and tugged off the tape that held his earpieces in place.

Their eyes met.

Kristen tensed. She knew Todd had said on the radio that he liked the car, but she was dying to know if he *like-liked* it.

Nothing.

His lips didn't so much as twitch. He stared at

her unblinkingly, intensely, as if he were trying to see through her skull and directly into her head.

"Well?" she mouthed.

He looked away, shifted a bit and then wiggled out of the car, his rear end resting on the door frame for a second as if he were trying to catch his breath before he swung his legs out.

Maybe he was trying to keep his feelings to himself so the other crews and drivers up and down the garage wouldn't become suspicious. Yeah. That must be it.

She saw Dan duck down next to his ear. Todd whispered something back. Dan broke into a smile, but only for a split second, then Dan turned to Kristen and winked. That should have made Kristen's spirits soar—more proof that Dan was coming around. But what Todd did next made Kristen grit her teeth. He turned away and headed back to the hauler.

Without a single backward glance.

"I guess that means we're good?" her boss said, still managing to look suavely debonair despite the more casual polo shirt and dark slacks.

"I guess it does," she said.

"He said it's a rocket ship," Dan finally clarified, stopping in front of them. He glanced around before he whispered his next words. "He said there's no doubt he'll nab the pole."

"Congratulations," Dan said again.

"Yeah, thanks," Kristen said.

"Excellent work," Matthew added, nodding his head.

Kristen met his gaze. She wanted to bask in his approval, but she couldn't get Todd's cold-shoulder treatment out of her mind.

"Will you excuse me for a second?" she asked. "I'll be right back." Because, damn it, she wanted to know what Todd's problem was.

"Of course," she heard Mathew say.

But she was already gone, Kristen following in Todd's wake. Race fans had spotted him, again, notepads and racing apparel pulled from pockets and fanny packs and backpacks and then held out for autographing. He ignored them all.

"Todd, wait up," she called. But he was too far ahead of her to hear. There was maybe only forty feet between the garage and the hauler, but he'd crossed that distance in a flash.

"Damn it," she said, pausing for a minute in the middle of the road. It had turned overcast, a breeze having kicked up. An official blew his safety whistle at her, reminding Kristen that there were still a few more minutes of practice left. She darted toward the hauler, a car roaring up behind her and slipping into the garage. She could feel the heat and smell its exhaust.

"Is Todd in the back?" she asked one of the crew guys standing in the hauler's aisle, a Ford-blue spring in his hand.

"Yeah, he's in the lounge, but I don't know if I'd follow. It takes him a minute to calm down after driving."

"Tough titties," she mumbled, squeezing by the guy and heading toward the closed door at the end of the long walkway.

She turned right at the end of the cabinets, pausing at the top of three small steps that hugged the right side of the rig. There was another entrance in and out of the hauler at the base of those steps—a single door that led outside. For a moment Kristen thought about using that door to escape, but only for a moment. Steeling herself to be firm—

Arms wrapped around her and pulled her to him.

"What the—"

Todd kissed her.

Kristen stiffened.

His mouth pressed down harder. She tried to wiggle away, her gasp of surprise bringing the taste of him right into her mouth.

And then she went slack.

He tasted…good.

No. No way. No way. You are not liking his caveman-type tactics.

But she was.

His lips were hot, his body musky beneath his fire suit. And she *liked* it. She could feel the heat radiating off him. And for a second she lost herself to the pure, unadulterated, deliciousness of being kissed by Todd Peters—race car driver.

Oh, yeah, Mathew was right. Todd liked her.

His tongue touched her own.

She drew back. "Todd, stop," she said, torn between horror and amusement.

Amusement?

Hysterical laughter, she told herself, because she could not believe she'd just let Todd Peters, racing's bad boy, kiss her.

"I don't want to stop," he said, brown eyes turned black as tar. He tried to pull her toward him again.

"No," she said firmly. Her chin felt raw from where his razor stubble had rubbed against her. She touched the spot absently. "Crap, Todd. What the heck's gotten into you?"

She expected a flip answer, maybe even a cocky, c'mon-baby-tell-me-you-like-it. Instead he appeared to consider her words and muttered, "I wish I knew." He looked irritated and uptight and—Lord help her—turned-on.

"Well, whatever it is, you need to stop." But she was ashamed to recall just how little she *had* wanted him to stop.

"Why?" he asked, his dark eyes holding her own

in a way that made it impossible to look away. Behind him a TV flickered, the thing recessed in a cabinet above a corner desk. But the brightness of the flat-screen monitor wasn't half as bright as the glint in Todd's eyes.

"Because, Todd, I—"

"Kristen, are you in there?"

They both stiffened, Kristen looking toward the door.

It was Mathew.

Oh, great.

"Come on in," Kristen called, because she knew if she didn't answer right away, it'd look suspicious.

When he opened the door his eyes darted between the two of them. Could he tell what Todd had done? Was her chin still raw? Her lips still red?

Mathew's eyes narrowed.

He could.

"Am I interrupting something?" he asked, arms crossed in front of him.

Todd chose that moment to shrug out of his fire suit, a dark blue T-shirt beneath. "Nope," he said. But to Kristen's surprise, he didn't stop at his waist. He tugged the fire-retardant fabric down, exposing jockey shorts beneath. "I was just showing Kristen how much I appreciate the improvements she made to my car."

"Mr. Knight, I—"

"Showing?" her boss asked, stepping into the room.

"In my own unique way," Todd said, flashing his cocky grin.

"Excuse me," Kristen said, just wanting to escape. But she had to brush by Mathew in order to do so. Her boss caught her gaze. Kristen stumbled midstep. He reached out to steady her, but she drew back. "I need to write down some notes," she offered by way of explanation.

Yeah, note to self: don't let Todd kiss you again. And if you do, don't let Mr. Knight catch you.

"WHAT'S GOING ON BETWEEN you two?" Mr. Knight asked right after Kristen closed the door.

Todd ignored him for a second, opening a cabinet door behind him. Inside were his clean fire suits—three of them—and spare clothing for the team. He pulled a pair of his own khakis off the hanger.

"She's something else, isn't she?" Todd asked, turning back to Mr. Knight to gauge his reaction. He stepped into one of the legs, tugging the pants up.

"She's a valued employee who I'd hate to lose because of an office romance," he said, eyes glinting with fury.

Aha. So that's the way the wind blew?

Todd let out a little laugh. "Spoken like a true tight-ass."

"I beg your pardon?"

He pulled off his shirt next, exchanging it for a new team polo shirt. He left it hanging out of his pants. "I said you're a tight-ass. Anyone can see that. Maybe you should loosen up a bit more. Might help you score."

His new boss seemed to straighten, and Todd knew if he were any man but Knight Enterprises' star driver, he'd have been fired on the spot. Damn, that amused him.

"I'm *not* a tight-ass," Mathew said. "And I don't need help to 'score.'"

"Hey, don't get so defensive. As it happens, I don't blame you for liking Kristen."

"Excuse me?"

"C'mon, boss man. You going to tell me you haven't noticed the hot body beneath those loose shirts she favors?"

"I don't know what you're talking about."

"She's smokin'. Like one of those librarian chicks, all prim and proper on the outside, but probably a real wild woman in bed."

"You're out of line," Mathew said, fists clenching. It occurred to Todd then that they were roughly the same age. He didn't know why he'd thought the guy was older.

"I'm just pointing out the obvious," Todd said. "But if you're not interested, great. I'm going to ask her out, and *this* time I won't take no for an answer."

"I wouldn't advise that."

"Why not?"

"Dating a fellow employee is against company policy."

"I don't work for you."

"You most certainly do."

"I'm a private contractor. A driver for hire. You can't control me."

"I can too."

"Why don't we be honest here? You don't want me dating her because you want her for yourself."

"*Excuse* me?"

"You want her for yourself," Todd said again, enjoying the way the great Mathew Knight seemed incapable of speech for a moment.

"I do *not* want her for myself."

"Denial. I love it. But that's okay. A little friendly competition is good for the soul."

"You're fired." The words were clipped, his boss's jaw muscles so taut Todd wondered if his teeth ached. "I don't care what your contract says—pack your stuff and leave."

"Not going to happen," Todd said.

"It very well *will* happen. My attorneys will see to it."

Todd shook his head. “Give up, boss man. I’m driving your car and dating the girl and that’s that.”

“No, you are not.”

“We’ll see,” Todd said, scooting by him. Mathew Knight would learn soon enough that his contract was ironclad. He had every right to date whoever the hell he wanted, and that included Kristen McKenna.

CHAPTER TWELVE

HE'D FIRED HIS star driver.

Mathew turned a full circle in the small room, more frustrated and angry and conflicted than he'd ever been in his entire life.

Maybe buying a race team hadn't been such a great idea.

"So that wraps up today's practice, where Todd Peters appears to be the fastest driver on the track."

Mathew turned toward the TV.

"Yeah, but only *some* of the time," a second announcer said, a smooth-haired man smiling into the camera. "We'll be back later today for qualifying, when we'll see if Todd Peters really is the fastest car out here."

The first announcer said, "If we don't get rained out."

"That is *definitely* a concern," the second guy said. "But we'll be sure to keep you posted."

The two announcers smiled, their bleached teeth glowing under the lights. Closing credits started to roll. Mathew sank down on the leather couch that jutted out from the wall opposite of the door.

What did it matter if Todd Peters dated Kristen?

It didn't, Mathew reassured himself. Not really. But to be fair, he should have a talk with Kristen about the situation. It wasn't right to threaten Todd and not do the same to Kristen.

Threaten her.

Is that what he was going to do? As opposed to firing her like he had Todd? Would he unleash his fury on Kristen, too? Because that's what he was. Furious.

She'd been kissing Todd.

And he didn't like it. Not one damn bit. And it had nothing to do with company policy.

Mathew sank down on the couch, completely in shock.

He liked Kristen.

"Have you seen Todd?" someone came in and asked.

"I believe he went that way," Mathew said, pointing toward the exit. "Excuse me," he said, leaving the room.

She'd been kissing Todd.

"Have you seen Ms. McKenna?" he asked the first crew member he ran across.

"Saw her go that way about five minutes ago," the man said. "Looked like she was headed toward the bathroom."

The sun had disappeared, leaving a gray day in its wake. Practice appeared to be over, which made it easier for Mathew to make his way across the garage and toward the restrooms. But she wasn't there, either.

He gave up then, flicked open his Nextel phone, and alerted her with a chirp. "Ms. McKenna, I would like to speak to you, please," he said, then immediate regretted the words. He sounded too terse. Too much like a—he shook his head—too much like a tight-ass.

"Certainly, Mr. Knight," she said, sounding equally cool. "Where would you like to meet?"

He scouted the garage, as if she might suddenly appear out from behind a stack of tires or one of the giant toolboxes that stood at the entrance to the garage stalls. All he saw were crewmen from other teams, their multicolored uniforms blending in with race fans and other team personnel.

"Back at the hauler, if you don't mind."

"Not at all," she said.

He turned on his heel, wondering if he was making a huge mistake. Perhaps he should leave it alone—

"What's up?" Kristen asked right then.

Where had she been? Right behind him?

"Let's go inside," Mathew said.

But when he had her to himself, he didn't know what to say. Not at first. And then, "I fired Todd

Peters," came out in a rush, which wasn't what he'd wanted to say at all.

"You *what?*"

"I fired him," he repeated.

"You're kidding."

"He was kissing you."

"So you *fired* him?" she asked, not even bothering to deny it.

"Of course."

"You can't do that."

"I assure you, I can…and did."

"But…" Her mouth hung open a second. "He's one of the best drivers on the circuit."

"Immaterial."

"Do you know how hard it'll be to replace a driver like Todd Peters?"

"Of course, but—"

"Good drivers don't grow on trees."

"I realize—"

"You need to un-fire him."

This conversation wasn't going at all the way he'd planned. "Excuse me?"

"Tell him you made a mistake. That you thought—I don't know—that maybe I wanted him fired for what he did."

"Don't you?" He held his breath, waiting for her answer.

"Of *course* not."

"Do you *like* Todd Peters?"

"What kind of a question is that?"

"I'm merely curious," he said, pretending to be unfazed.

"Why?"

But of course he couldn't answer that. He couldn't tell her he was curious because he wanted to know if she might be amenable to an evening out with him.

"He seems to be quite the ladies' man."

She didn't say anything for a long moment. Mathew realized an instant later that she was studying him, analyzing his face and arriving at some sort of conclusion.

"*You're* interested in me."

It was like she'd hit him. Like she'd taken a battering ram and shoved it right at his gut. "I beg your pardon?"

"You like me."

How the hell had she figured that?

"*Of course* I'm interested in you," he said, having learned in the boardroom not to deny an accusation if it was true. The trick was to turn it around. "You're a wonderful engineer. I want to keep you happy."

"That's not what I meant and you know it," she said. "You're interested in me as a *woman*."

"I am not."

"You are, too," she said. And then she turned

away, only to turn right back around. "I don't believe this. What? Am I emitting some sort of man-attracting pheromone today? First Todd and now you."

"Ms. McKenna. I am *not* interested in you."

But his neck was turning red. A sure sign that he was flummoxed. What's more, she saw it too. Her eyes narrowed, and Mathew was suddenly reminded of her genius IQ. No fool, she.

"Look, Mr. Knight," she said. "I'm flattered. Really. And if you weren't who you are..." She motioned with her hands as if he might not understand that he was her boss. "If you weren't who you are, I'd be delighted to date you."

"Ms. McKenna, really—"

"No, no," she said. "Don't deny it. I can see it's true. But firing Todd is a huge mistake. Don't do it because of me."

"I'm not doing it because of you."

"No? Then why *did* you do it?"

Because I was so jealous of the man I couldn't see straight.

"Todd Peters is trouble. We can field a stronger race team without him."

"No, we can't. Hire him back. Immediately. And if you won't do it, I will."

Was *she* bossing *him* around?

"Understood?"

She was.

"I'll think about it," was as much as he would promise.

Her brow furrowed. "And as far as you and I are concerned, I don't have time for a man. *Any* man," she stressed. "I'm flattered that you like me, but my career is more important than anything else, and if you and I were to—" she stumbled over the word "—date, it'd make a mess of my life. I've had enough messy days, thank you very much."

With that she turned around, leaving him standing there at the back of the hauler like a chastened little boy.

"Women," one of his crew members said, having obviously overheard the last part of their conversation. "Can't live with them, can't shoot 'em."

Actually, Mathew felt like shooting *himself.*

CHAPTER THIRTEEN

QUALIFYING ENDED UP BEING rained out, so she was able to avoid Mathew the rest of the day. She avoided Todd, too. She avoided *all* the men in her life, finding a nice quiet corner of the racetrack to do her fuel mileage calculations.

But she couldn't concentrate.

Mathew Knight. Who would have thought?

Of course, there was an outside chance that she'd been wrong. He'd certainly denied it loud enough. But, no. She'd looked him in the eye and seen something there that had made her knees weak.

Jealousy.

He *liked* her.

The heavens suddenly opened up again, sheets of rain pouring down in a way that completely contradicted the late summer. Kristen decided to finish her work from her hotel room, the rain allowing her to slink away from the track like a wet cat heading for shelter.

But one afternoon's grace didn't mean she'd be

able to avoid Mathew and Todd for the rest of the weekend. She had one more early-morning practice to get through, NASCAR allowing the teams to practice before qualifying. What would she say to Mathew when she saw him next? What would she say to Todd?

She knew the answer to one question the moment she entered the garage the next morning because who was standing at the back of their Arcadia big rig but Mathew Knight, his arms crossed in front of him and looking extremely ownerlike in his dark blue polo shirt and Ray-Bans.

"Good morning," she said politely, her heart beating like a rubber mallet against the side of a race car.

"Ms. McKenna," he said coolly, politely.

Yesterday's rain had completely vanished, leaving in its wake a muggy, uncomfortable day. Of course, that could just be the company she kept.

"Okay, well…um. Have a nice day."

"Kristen, wait," someone called out when she moved away.

Kristen froze. It was Jennifer, Todd's PR rep. She'd bumped into the woman at the shop, the tall, willowy brunette always making her feel like a mutt compared to Jennifer's purebred lines. But beautiful women always made her feel that way, especially when her leg ached like it did today.

"Todd's been looking for you."

Kristen darted a glance at Mathew who cocked a brow at her. Guess that answered the question as to whether or not Todd was still employed. Boy, would she like to have been a fly on the wall for *that* conversation.

"Oh, yeah? What does he want?"

"Probably to show you his bed," she heard someone mutter.

Kristen turned on Mathew, but her boss pretended interest in a group of fans who tramped by.

Jennifer stared between them, obviously wondering if she'd heard correctly. "Anyway, Todd wanted me to track you down because he was talking to a journalist yesterday, Rick Stevenson, and he told him all about you. Rick is a bigwig in the world of motorsports and he was impressed with your credentials, so now he wants to talk to you, too."

"You're kidding."

"Nope," she said, a smile lighting her face. "But the thing is, the guy's on a tight deadline, so I need you to come with me now."

"Oh, ah...sure."

"I'll have her back soon," Jennifer said to Mathew.

"That I doubt," Mathew said.

Kristen shot him another look, but her boss didn't bat an eye. She shook her head, fed up with the whole situation. It wasn't *her* fault Todd had kissed her. And it certainly wasn't her fault that Mathew Knight liked her.

Or did he? He didn't act like it this morning. She just about had freezer burn after the cold look he'd given her.

"He sure is cute, isn't he?" Jennifer asked as they walked away from the back of the hauler, oblivious to the undercurrent swirling around her.

"Uh, yeah. I suppose."

"Is he seeing anybody?" Jennifer asked.

"I don't know," Kristen said, stepping around the back end of a toolbox.

"I haven't heard anything about a girlfriend."

He wanted *her* for a girlfriend. Or maybe not. Damn it, she didn't know what to think.

They stepped into the flow of foot traffic that crossed the garage. Crew members darted in front of them, white-clad NASCAR officials standing by.

"He works really hard," Jennifer said. "I heard he's been jetting between New York and North Carolina ever since he bought the team."

"Yeah, I heard that, too."

"His bodyguard, Rob, told me he bought the team as a way to relax. Doctor's orders."

"Really?"

"Yeah, but he's a workaholic. Rob said he's going to drop dead from a heart attack by the time he's forty if he doesn't slow down."

"Where are we going?" Kristen asked in an attempt to change the subject. She didn't want to talk about her boss, and they weren't headed toward the garage. The were moving toward the parking area which was out past the garage, golf carts and motor vehicles whizzing to and fro.

"Helicopter pad."

"Heli— What?"

"The reporter's not at the track," Jennifer admitted.

"He's not?"

"Nope. Todd's conducting his morning interviews from home. He's at his cabin on Lake Geneva."

"Huh?"

"Todd has a house on the lake," Jennifer added. "That's where we're going."

CHAPTER FOURTEEN

TODD HEARD THE helicopter coming in long before he actually saw it. He leaned back in his wrought-iron patio chair and studied his feet. He needed new sandals, he thought. The frayed leather straps were starting to sag.

But as he rested his foot on the gray marble, he couldn't help but feel a pleased smile come to his face.

Outwitted.

And the bitchin' thing was, Mathew Knight had no idea he'd been outfoxed. Ha!

Above the oak trees that framed his pool, he could see the white dot of his helicopter. Kristen McKenna. Right on time. It'd only taken her—he glanced at his watch—ten minutes to get here. Not bad. He wondered if he should greet her, but then immediately decided against it. The fancy Greek columns and sparkling blue water never failed to impress.

That fact was confirmed when Jen arrived with Kristen in tow. The little engineer with the hot lips looked a bit shell-shocked by the vast expanse of his back patio, most of which was covered in dark gray marble and wrought-iron furniture, off-white patio umbrellas pointing toward the sky. Out beyond the twinkling blue pool the lake stretched far and wide. It wasn't a huge piece of property—his lakefront property in North Carolina was much bigger—but it was right on the water's edge. A tray of early-morning goodies sat on the glass table in front of him. He wasn't going to eat any of the stuff, not when he had to practice in a couple hours. But he thought Kristen would be pleasantly surprised. They could fly back to the track together with Mathew Knight none the wiser.

"Here we go," Jen said with a wide, professional smile.

He glanced over at Kristen, caught the "holy shit" look in her eyes and found himself wanting to smile. "Hey," he said. "Thanks for coming."

"Jeez, Todd, what'd you do? Buy the house from an Arab prince?"

He chuckled. "Take a seat."

Jen said, "I'll just be inside if you need me."

"Orange juice?" Todd asked, pushing a glass toward her right as Kristen pulled a chair out, the metal legs scraping against the marble slab.

"Uh, no thanks. I never drink orange juice on an empty stomach."

"Have some food then."

"I'm too nervous to eat. Where's the reporter?"

"There isn't a reporter."

Her eyes shot to his like a loose car down a high bank. "Excuse me?"

"That was just the excuse I used to get you out here this morning."

"You did not."

"I did," he said, hooking his fingers together and resting them on his stomach. "Or rather, I tricked our boss into *letting* you come here. I figured that uptight Goody Two-shoes wouldn't allow you to leave the track if I made the mistake of asking, not when he's got the hots for you himself."

She didn't say anything for long seconds, and Todd wondered if she'd known their boss liked her.

"You mean you made up that story about a reporter wanting to talk to me?" she asked.

"Yup," Todd said. "Although Jen doesn't know."

Kristen shot up.

"Hey."

"I'm going back to the track," she said, her ponytail flicking around as if it belonged to an angry horse.

"Kristen, wait," he said, having to work to shove his chair back. Damn, these things were heavy. "Don't go," he said.

"You can't leave," he said when she stepped around him.

"Yes, I can."

"But I thought we'd pick up where we left off yesterday."

"You thought wrong."

He dropped his hand and, before she could step around him again, said, "You mean you didn't enjoy our kiss?" She was short, which he suddenly found himself liking. Yesterday, she'd fit the shape of his body perfectly.

"I want to go back to work, Todd," she said, ignoring his question. "I want to go back to work very badly, because when Mr. Knight finds out that there wasn't really an interview, he's going to be furious, and the longer I stay here, the worse it looks for me."

"But he won't know there wasn't an interview unless you tell him."

"Trust me, I'm going to tell him."

"What? Why?"

She didn't answer. What she did was dart around him again, stomping toward his helicopter pad as if a pack of angry race fans were at her heels.

"Wait," he said again, rushing to catch up to her. "You never answered my question. Did you like our kiss yesterday or not?"

"I can't believe you're asking me that."

She looked really cute as she stormed along the faux stone path that snaked its way beneath tall trees, sunlight flicking across her smooth skin. She wore jeans and a black jacket, one of those KEM

Motorsports work shirts beneath. It was your standard-issue polo shirt. Nothing special. Yet it hugged curves in a way he hadn't noticed before. It also made her blue eyes look violet when she glanced his way, which wasn't often because, quite frankly, she was pissed.

P.I.S.S.E.D.

His pilot was still in the cockpit, no doubt doing a postflight check. Todd got an idea then. "Hey, Brian," he said, the man opening his door when he saw Todd.

Kristen headed to the other side, pulling on the handle and sliding inside without so much as a goodbye. She even pulled headphones on.

"What's up, boss?"

"Slip on out," he said in a low voice, glancing across the blue leather seat at Kristen who, judging by the way she ignored him, hadn't heard his request.

"What? Why?" Brian asked back in an equally low voice.

"I'm going to fly her back."

Brian glanced at Kristen, whose face was as blank as a new piece of paper. "What about your meeting?" Brian asked.

"Canceled," he lied.

She snorted.

Aha. So she could hear with her headphones on.

Todd glanced over at her and smiled. She looked so perturbed, so absolutely peeved, that it amused the hell out of him.

She *had* to have liked their kiss. She just didn't want to admit it.

"C'mon," he said, motioning with his head that Brian should get out.

"What are you doing?" Kristen asked when Brian pulled off his sunglasses at the same time he started to slide off the seat.

"I'm flying you back," Todd said with a wide smile.

"You are not," Kristen immediately countered.

"Actually, he's a licensed pilot," Brian said.

"I don't care if he's authorized to fly Santa's sleigh, he's not piloting this bird back to the track."

"With all due respect, Ms. McKenna," Brian said. "He can do whatever he wants. He owns this Eurocopter."

"Fine," Kristen said, so furious she nearly broke a nail undoing the seat belt she'd just pulled across her lap. What the hell was it with men? Why didn't they understand that she'd worked hard to get to where she was? The last thing she needed was for some man to come along and muck it all up, which Todd would if their boss caught wind of what he'd done.

"Kristen," Todd said, intercepting her near the front, sunlight arcing off the helicopter's curved window and beaming them with heat like some sort of space-age weapon. "If you take a taxi home you won't be back for over an hour."

"So?"

"You might not make it back in time for practice," he said. "Race traffic."

"To heck with practice."

"You don't mean that."

No, she didn't. Damn it. If she missed practice, she'd be in even more trouble.

"C'mon. Let me take you back."

"Fine."

He smiled his Todd's-so-cute smile, but she wasn't buying it. Not one bit.

The helicopter rotors began to whine—louder and louder, and then louder still. She stared out the front, firmly ignoring Todd.

"Here we go," he said, pulling back on the cyclic.

She ignored him. Todd kept staring at her, but he must have finally given up because he slipped his own headphones on. She sat next to him and fumed as they began to lift off then skate over the tops of oak trees, their lush foliage turning as gray as battleships the higher they climbed. The Eurocopter's shadow chased the ground beneath them, getting larger when it crossed over the tops of hills or buildings.

"You look as riled as a hen whose eggs were just

stolen," he said when he was finished talking to local air-traffic control.

Ignore him, Kristen.

"And if you've never seen an angry hen, you're missing out."

If I don't say anything, maybe he'll give up.

"The feathers on the tops of their heads get all puffed up."

Sooner or later he'll realize I'm well and truly pissed.

"And their eyes get all red. Seriously. They get almost demonic looking."

The voice went quiet. Beneath the helicopter she could see a river, the water twisting lazily to the left and right. She wondered what the river's name was.

"It's the Sikonie River."

She glanced over at him, gave him a look that said, *Drop dead, butt-head.* But with each passing minute she could feel her resolve weakening. To be honest, there was a part of her that was—all right, admit it—*flattered* that he'd go to such lengths to pursue her.

Todd Peters. Pursuing her.

"Aw, come on, Kristen. Loosen up. What's wrong with wanting to spend some time with you?"

Sunlight blinded her on the right side so that she had to squint to see him properly. "That's my point, Todd. I didn't *want* to spend time with you. You knew that and yet you went over my head and arranged all this."

"No, I didn't know that, not after our kiss yesterday."

"About that kiss."

"It was good, wasn't it?"

"You shouldn't have done that, either."

"That's not the way it seemed what with the way you kissed me back."

"I did *not* kiss you back."

"You didn't pull away, either."

No, she hadn't. But that was because he'd surprised her. "You didn't give me *time* to pull away."

"Most women would go gaga if I showed them any interest," he said.

"I'm not most women."

"And that's why I like you."

"But *I* don't like the way *you* do whatever you damn well please, to hell with the consequences."

"I go after what I want."

"Yeah, but not the way a *normal* person would."

"I disagree."

"The way you do it pisses people off."

"No, it doesn't."

"Look at the guys at the shop."

"They love me."

"Oh, really?" she asked, glancing over at him. She hated being so brutal, she really did, but she needed to make him understand. She might be secretly flattered by his attention, but there were reasons for keeping that attraction at bay.

"Yeah, really," he said.

"You know what they call you?" she asked. "His Holiness."

"So?"

"I don't think you should be flattered."

"I'm not flattered, but I'm sure not *everyone* calls me that."

"Yes, Todd, they all do. *Everyone*."

He looked out the front, his face revealing a myriad of expressions. Amusement. A hint of anger. Disbelief. "My teammates don't have to like me," he said at last.

"Why not?" she asked, leaning back in her seat and crossing her arms. "Why shouldn't they like you, Todd? Or haven't you figured out yet that you catch more flies with honey?"

"Racing's not about honey, Kristen, it's about money. And the sooner *you* realize *that,* the better off *you'll* be."

"But all the money in the world won't buy you teamwork. That has to come from the heart, your teammates' hearts."

"My teammates aren't worth crap to me when they're all interchangeable."

"They're not interchangeable."

"Bull. They move around from team to team like fleas on a dog. Why should I get close to them?"

"That's a bad attitude to have." And it was even more evidence of why, ultimately, she should steer clear of him. He just wasn't her type.

"It's the truth."

"No, it's not. You have teammates that would do anything to help you go faster. People like Dan and Victor keep you ahead of the competition on race day. And people like Bill and Andy back at the shop work long hours to get your cars built. They're all trying to keep you out front and a little appreciation for their efforts might go a long way toward making them like you."

"I appreciate them."

"Do you?"

"Sure I do."

"Have you ever told them that?"

"That's not my job."

"You shouldn't consider praising people a job."

He said something to air-traffic control, and pitched the bird sideways. Kristen clutched the sides of her leather seat, but she didn't panic. She'd spent too many hours up in the air not to know that the maneuver wasn't an accident.

"Nice view," she said when he then dropped altitude so fast it was like riding the back of a bowling ball tossed from a rooftop.

"Thought you might like to get a closer view of the river," he said, leveling off.

"Oh, I do. It's great. Thanks. And you're not going to get off the hook that easily. You need to stop being such an ass."

"If I'm such an ass, how come this is the first time I'm hearing about it?"

"Oh, come on," she said. "You mean to tell me you've never read a newspaper? Never heard yourself called racing's bad boy?"

"A lot of drivers are called that."

"Yeah, but you're the *king* of all bad boys."

"Not as far as I know."

"All right. Fine. So you don't read about yourself in the press. But have you ever noticed how the shop goes quiet when you walk in?"

"That's just because I'm famous."

She snorted, then said, "Keep telling yourself that, Todd."

He glanced over at her. She lifted a brow. He looked away.

Something must have clicked with him because he didn't say anything more, not for a long while at least, and then he said, "I am who I am, Kristen. Just because I supposedly treat my crew like crap doesn't mean I'd treat you like that."

Didn't it, though?

It was her turn to look away. "That's what you say."

"That's what I know."

But she refused to believe it. She *couldn't* believe it, because if she was wrong…

If she was wrong, she'd end up starting to like him, heck, maybe even she'd go on a date with him, and that just wasn't a good idea.

Not when she'd sworn off ever getting close to another man.

CHAPTER FIFTEEN

"WHAT DO YOU MEAN there's no interview with Rick Stevenson?" Mathew asked Maddie.

"That's what I'm trying to tell you, Mr. Knight," his recently promoted receptionist said on the other end of the line. "When I asked Mr. Stevenson to please send us a copy of the article, he sent me a one-word reply—'Huh?'"

Mathew caught Rob's eye, as his security specialist lifted an eyebrow in question.

"Excuse me, boss," one of the crew guys said, trying to squeeze between them with something that bore a great resemblance to a giant metal ice-cream cone.

"When I responded to his 'huh' he told me he'd never heard of Kristen McKenna, but if Todd Peters wanted to call in to his radio show, he'd be happy to talk."

What's going on? Rob mouthed. Mathew waved his hand, signaling that he'd tell him later.

"What do you want me to do, Mr. Knight?" Maddie asked.

"Nothing," Mathew said. "I'll handle it from this end."

He flipped his phone shut with a snap.

"What's up?" Rob asked, arms crossed, his big body blocking the left side of the hauler. He wore his customary black shirt, his blue eyes scanning the garage even though Mathew had told him he didn't need his services in the garage.

"Kristen doesn't have an interview with Rick Stevenson."

That made Rob straighten in surprise. "No?"

Mathew filled him in on the details, and as he did, he felt his cheek begin to twitch, a sure sign of anger.

"What's she doing with Todd?" Rob asked when he was done.

"I have no idea," he said,

But he knew, and he didn't like it, not one little bit.

"You gonna can her?"

"No," Mathew answered instantly. His stomach turned. "I don't know. Perhaps."

He *should* fire her. He should fire Todd, too. Again.

"They seeing each other?"

His stomach flexed once more. "I don't know. I suppose so."

"Wow. I'd have thought Kristen would have better taste."

He would have thought so, too, but obviously that whole conversation the other day about "dating" and "making a mess of her life" wasn't true. Obviously she'd been meaning to go off with Todd the whole time.

"Well, if you're going to fire her, here's your chance."

Mathew followed Rob's focus, stiffening in shock. Kristen.

"She looks pissed," Rob observed.

And she did.

"Has anyone seen the keys to the rental car?" she asked as she walked up to the back of the tractor-trailer, clearly agitated judging by the way she looked around, her hands clenching and unclenching.

"No. Why?" Rob asked, crossing his arms in front of him.

"Because I need to use the car to run over Todd."

Rob grunted then said, "What'd he do? Spoil your big date?"

"What big date?" she said, staring between the two of them.

"You didn't really have an interview with Rick Stevenson," Mathew replied in a monotone.

Her eyes went wide. "You know about that?"

"Maddie," Rob said. "She called Mr. Knight here to tell him Rick Stevenson had no idea who you were."

And then her eyes narrowed. "And you thought

I knew that before going off with Jennifer," she said to Mathew.

"Do you blame him?" Rob answered.

"Given our conversation yesterday, I am surprised." She met his gaze head-on. "I would have thought you'd have known better," Kristen said.

"So you didn't know the interview was a sham?" Rob asked.

"No," she said firmly, glancing at Rob. "Todd cooked the whole thing up on his own. The jerk actually thought I'd be grateful to spend some time with him."

"You truly didn't know?" Mathew asked, and the relief he felt couldn't be denied.

Her eyes swung to his. "No," she said firmly, "I didn't."

And there was one thing that proved her words to be true more than anything else: she'd been gone less than an hour. If she and Todd had truly been seeing each other, she'd have been away much longer than that—or so logic dictated.

He would have kept her away all day.

"I'm going to fire him," Mathew said sharply.

"No, you're not," Kristen said. "Not again."

Mathew glanced at Todd. Rob's eyes opened wide. "You fired Todd?"

"Yesterday. But I had Gloria rehire him."

"Smart move," Kristen said.

"Yes, but today he's crossed the line," Mathew said.

"He has," she said. "But it doesn't make any more sense to fire him today than yesterday."

"Fine, then I'll have a talk with him."

"If you do that, he might walk. Don't take the chance."

"He deserves my censure," Mathew said. "And yours."

"He does," Kristen said. "But I think he finally realized it today."

She'd left her hair down again, the ends of it looking as soft as kitten fur. Mathew wondered what it'd feel like against his face, then immediately chastised himself for impropriety.

Impropriety?

Yes, impropriety, but he didn't care. He just didn't care. He wanted Kristen McKenna. No more denying it. Frankly, he'd never have gotten anywhere in life if he hadn't recognized and then pursued the things he desired.

Mathew caught Rob's eye, then signaled he wanted to be alone. Rob hiked up an eyebrow in question, but Mathew quietly shook his head.

But his security specialist wasn't stupid. His gaze moved between Kristen and him, understanding dawning. Good lord, the man was intuitive. Of course, that was why he kept him around.

"I'm going to scope out the rest of the garage," Rob said, sauntering off.

"And I've got work to do," Kristen said, her head held high as she prepared to turn away.

"Kristen, wait," Mathew said.

She turned back to him, her blue eyes wide and filled with wounded pride.

"I'd like to talk to you."

"About what?"

"Our conversation yesterday."

Her expression turned suddenly wary. "There's nothing further to say," she said.

"Yes, there is, and I'd like to talk to you about it now."

He thought she might hold her ground. Kristen was that way. A fighter, he realized. He liked that about her.

"Please," he added, a rare word for him to use, if she'd but known.

"Fine," she said.

"Come on," he said, leading her toward the lounge.

"Mr. Boss Man," Dan said when they moved inside, his gaze sliding past him, a smile coming to his face. "Hey, Kristen."

"Hey there, Dan," Kristen said back.

"We'll be in a meeting in the back," Mathew said gruffly. He waited until the door was closed before turning to face her, but once he did, he suddenly lost

his power of speech. There was a look of apprehension on her face, mixed with concern. He fidgeted with the change in his pocket and then suddenly blurted, "Go out with me."

She actually took a step back. *"What?"*

"Go out with me," he said again. "You were right yesterday," he said. "I *am* interested in you. When I thought you'd gone off with Todd this morning, that became patently obvious. My reaction was not that of a man detached from the situation. I've become attached to you. I'd like to explore the attraction I feel for you a little more closely, beginning with a date."

She crossed her arms in front of her. "A date?"

"Yes. Tonight, if you like. I could have a car pick you up."

"Really?"

"Or my helicopter."

"Even better." But she didn't *look* pleased.

"I realize you might be uncomfortable with dating your superior—"

"My *superior?*" she asked drily.

"Well, your boss," he said, because her eyes had begun to narrow. "But I assure you, my behavior will be most circumspect."

"No."

"I beg your pardon?"

"I'm not dating you despite how 'circumspect'

your behavior might be. You're my boss, and no matter what you tell yourself, our dating would create friction with the team. But even more importantly, I'm not interested in dating *anyone* right now."

"No?' he asked, pulling her to him.

"What are you—"

He kissed her. Kristen tried to push him away, but all at once her arms went weak, and her knees did, too. And she started to tingle. Everywhere. All over. The delicious feel of his lips covering hers took her completely by surprise.

Mathew Knight knew how to kiss.

He changed the angle of his head. She let him, and when his tongue lightly stroked her lower lip, she began to tingle even more.

His tongue slid inside her mouth.

She wanted this, she suddenly realized. Wanted *him.* She let his tongue skate against her own, tasting him for the first time. Sweet mint—the cool flavor completely at odds with how hot he was. Her own tongue probed his mouth. One of his hands skated over her hip, his thumb stroking her abdomen. She leaned into him, wanting him to touch her in other places, to—

"Can't go in there."

They pulled apart.

"Why not?" they heard one of the crew members say.

"Boss is in a meeting."

Kristen panted, her gaze never leaving Mathew's.

"You shouldn't have done that," she said when it was clear they would be left alone.

"Why not?" he said softly. "That kiss proved what I'd begun to suspect. We're mutually attracted to each other."

"I know that," she admitted, because she'd be kidding herself if she didn't admit that kissing Mathew had left her reeling. "But you can't do it again."

"Why not?"

She worked to unscramble her thoughts, to be clear about what she was feeling. He needed to understand.

"Because this is my job," she said with a lift of her chin. "And *you* gave it to me. I worked at designing airframes because it was the only option open to me, but this…" She motioned around her. "*This* is what I want. Not you. Not Todd. Not anything else but this."

"That's no way to live," he said. "Believe me. I know."

"Not when I've dreamed about this my entire life." Her eyes darkened for a second. "Once before I let that dream get away from me, and I'm not giving it up now."

"You let that dream get away from you when your sister died."

Her cheek twitched.

"I know about the wreck, Kristen. I know you had your whole life in front of you before your car hit that tree, your sister at the wheel. You lost feeling in a portion of your foot, the part that would work a gas pedal. There was muscle damage, too, and bone damage. It ruined your driving career, but more importantly, it took your sister's life."

"How do you know this?"

"Rob is thorough in his background checks."

She stared up at him, openmouthed, but then she started to turn away.

"Kristen, don't," he said, stepping in front of her.

"I don't want to talk about this."

"We should," he said. "You should know that I know it all. That you put yourself through college in the hopes of working as an engineer for a race team, only that dream crumbled, too, didn't it?"

"It's none of your business."

"Of course it's my business. You work for me."

Her chin flicked up. "All the more reason we shouldn't date."

"Nothing would have to change if that occurred," he said. "We make an announcement. Tell the team what's going on. That way there's nothing to hide. In time, people will come to accept our relationship."

"Are you that naive?" she asked. "Do you really think that's how it'll go? Don't delude yourself,

Mathew. The minute you make that announcement I'll have zero credibility. My skills as an engineer will be questioned. I'll never be able to propose another idea without people wondering if I came up with it while on my back."

"You're wrong."

"No, I'm not," she said, shaking her head. "I've seen it before. When a woman engineer gets involved with another engineer, suddenly everyone's talking about how she's getting her ideas from her lover."

"Your reputation speaks for itself."

"What reputation? I don't have one in motorsports, and the last thing I want to do is start out here ruining my image by sleeping with the boss."

"We're not sleeping together."

"We would."

He felt a jolt and knew her words were true, especially after their kiss.

"I've worked too hard to get to where I am today," she said. "I've got my dream job now," she said softly. "I'm not going to give it up, not even for the man who gave it to me."

CHAPTER SIXTEEN

KRISTEN WALKED BLINDLY away. She glanced over her shoulder, wondering if Mathew would follow. He didn't. And so she walked away, bumping into Todd on her way out.

"Not now," she warned him, hand held up to silence him.

She left the garage, finding a spot out in the crew member parking area. The back bumper of the team's blue rental van. No one was around, everyone already in the garage. Even the stands were empty, although fans were straggling in to watch the morning practice.

She heard it then. Children's voices. High-pitched screams of delight. The raised voices of adults.

"Terrence, you better not spray that stuff at Cindy again!"

She looked left. Out beyond the gravel parking area sat a white mobile office. The letters MCS were painted on its side, and below that *Motorsports Children's Services.* A waist-high fence made out of gray plastic surrounded a play area. Picnic tables and chairs were spread beneath a wide awning that kept the children and their caretakers out of the sun. They were doing crafts.

A squeal of delight made her turn. A little girl was chasing a younger child, squirt bottle pumping water onto the girl's back.

She'd chased Trina like that when they'd been younger.

No. Don't think about it.

But she couldn't seem to stop herself, Kristen leaned forward and clutched her stomach. She had to leave, to get away from the pain that struck her out of the blue.

I know about the wreck.

The littlest girl ran away, giggling. It was all so raw. Her forgotten dreams. Her sister's death. Leaving home.

Home. She hadn't been back to Oklahoma since right after the accident. She'd left under the pretext of going to college, but she knew better. She hadn't been able to face her parents—their misery, their sorrow, but most of all, their censure.

It'd been her fault Trina had died.

She clutched her hands to her head, then stood up. This whole trip down memory lane was over.

One foot in front of the other, she reminded herself. The way she'd survived the past ten years.

TODD WATCHED HER WALK BETWEEN the parked cars. She still looked upset, which was why he'd tailed her in the first place. Where was she going now?

He'd kept his eye on her for the past few minutes, surprised none of his fans had spotted him. Fortunately, no one had and so he'd been able to study her. She looked sad. And lonely.

She ducked her head as she entered the stream of people entering the garage. So she was headed back to work. Figured. He'd never met anyone who put in as many hours as Kristen.

Was she crying?

Maybe. He tailed her a bit longer, but then someone called out his name. Kristen stopped and turned right as one putz booed—Todd abruptly turned on his heel, heading toward...well, he didn't know where he was headed. Actually, he did, he thought, abruptly spinning on his heel again. He had to round the line of haulers parked opposite the car stalls and use the back entrance. His face was recognized once or twice, but he was moving at such a clip, most people realized who he was too late and so he sailed on by unassaulted—a favorite trick of drivers.

The golf carts were lined up right where he'd spotted them earlier. He didn't know who owned the dark green four-seater he climbed into, all he cared about was that the keys were in it. Always amazed him that people left their carts with the keys in them.

He spun the back wheels when he took off, the guard who manned the back gate shooting him a look. Todd ignored him.

All right, so he could admit that Mathew Knight putting the moves on Kristen irked the hell out of him. But what surprised him the most, what had him driving a stolen golf cart like a madman, was how hurt he felt that there seemed to be something going on between the two of them. One of the guys had told him they were in a meeting. Todd had been on his way in to find out what they were talking about when Kristen had stormed outside. He'd seen something in her eyes just before she'd noticed it was him standing in her way, something that had him concerned: sorrow. And regret. And…longing.

Kristen McKenna *longed* for Mathew Knight, not Todd Peters.

That stung. That stung a lot, so much so that it suddenly hit him how much he wanted Kristen for himself. Amazing. He'd never, *ever* let a woman slip under his skin before. And yet that's exactly what had happened.

One kiss.

That's all they'd ever shared. But that one kiss had been enough. He'd known, just *known* there was something between them.

Damn it, he thought, making a sharp left and heading out toward the infield tunnel. He just about ran over an orange-vested parking attendant who waved him toward a parking area, not even lifting his hand in acknowledgment.

All right. So Kristen liked Mathew as much as he liked her, he thought, shutting off the engine when he found a spot out in an empty RV parking lot, an area that would fill up by nightfall. The question was: what could he do about it? He never gave up on things easily. Crap, that was how he'd got to the top of the motorsports game when other drivers had faded away. When you were running at the back of the pack, you kept digging and digging until you made some headway, because that was the way to get things done.

"You there?"

It took Todd a moment to realize his phone was talking, or more specifically, the speaker on his phone.

"Hello, Todd. You there?" the voice asked again. Jen.

Todd glanced at his watch. Holy shit. Where had the time gone? He'd been parked there for nearly a half hour. Jen was probably freaking out.

"I'm here," he said.

"Dan and I would like to know if you're going to practice?" Jen asked.

"Uh, yeah," Todd said. "I'm on my way."

"Good to know," Jen said.

"Yeah, whatever," Todd said to himself, stuffing

the phone back in his pocket and knowing Jen would give him grief when he saw her next. Reluctantly he fired up the golf cart and took off.

"You ready?" Dan asked, when he finally sauntered into the garage a little while later and suited up in his blue-and-black fire suit.

The dark blue car looked ready to roll beneath a row of fluorescent lights, his crew still making some last-minute adjustments. They'd put the car in rear end first so he could pull right out of the garage without having to worry about backing up. Air ratchets whirred, tools clinked, generators rumbled.

Same as last week.

Same as *every* week.

"I'm ready."

"Good. I thought for a moment there we'd have to send out a search party. It's not like you to disappear like that."

"What are we running?" Todd asked, refusing to discuss the matter.

Dan took the hint. His crew chief went over the setup, Todd listening with half an ear. He kept glancing around. Looking for *her.*

She's in your head.

Yeah, she was.

"You want anything else?" Dan asked.

Todd shook his head, but in disgust at himself,

not in response to Dan's question. He hadn't even been paying attention.

"All right then. Guess you're ready to roll."

"Is it true you guys call me His Holiness?" Todd asked abruptly.

Dan's face went slack. "Who told you that?" he asked.

"Doesn't matter," Todd said. "I can tell by your face that it's true."

Dan held his gaze, obviously trying to gauge how honest he should be. "A few of the guys do, yeah."

"You?" Todd asked.

His crew chief ducked his head for a second, then straightened his shoulders. When next their eyes met, his expression was the same one he wore on race day, usually when they were on the last lap, and they were running on fumes—in other words, serious. "You're not the easiest driver to work with."

"What do you mean?" Todd asked, glancing around. His crew hung back, almost as if they knew he and Dan weren't talking about racing. "I'm about the easiest going driver out on the circuit."

Dan didn't say anything.

"Aren't I?"

"You want the truth?" Dan asked.

"Of course."

"Even if it might hurt?"

"Yeah."

Dan nodded, jerked his eyes away for a second, seemed to take a deep breath and said, "You're one of the biggest assholes I've ever worked with."

Todd felt socked in the gut.

"Seriously?" Todd asked.

"Seriously."

It was like learning he'd been cheated on.

"Good to know," Todd said. He straightened away from the car, setting his helmet on the roof.

"Todd—"

"Hey, no need to discuss this further," Todd said, getting ready to climb into his car. "I get the point."

"No," Dan said, stepping into his line of vision. "Todd, I didn't tell you this just before practice to piss you off. I thought it was important to be honest with you, and to let you know that I still consider you a friend even though you can be a king-size jerk. Sometimes I want to kill you after a race, especially when you're complaining about what a piece of junk the car I gave you is, but the thing is, once you leave the track, you can be an all right guy."

"All right?" Todd asked, not sure whether he should be insulted or appeased. "Just *all right?*"

"Yeah. All right. Some of the other drivers can be total jerks to be around, but they're like that all the time. You have a habit of shrugging things off. Hell, sometimes you even do things that are pretty nice."

"Sometimes?"

Dan began to look uncomfortable. Todd didn't like the direction this conversation was going.

"I don't mean that the way it sounds," Dan said.

"Yeah, you do."

Dan shook his head, "Look. Maybe we should finish this conversation after you're done driving."

"Maybe we should," Todd said, lifting a leg and preparing to climb inside the cockpit. He caught a glimpse of himself in the dark blue paint scheme of his car, the letters of his name scrawled across the top of the door frame intersecting the image of his face.

He looked pissed.

Pissed was good. He always drove better when he was pissed. And at least Kristen was off his mind. That had to be worth something.

But when he turned back to Dan, he couldn't stop himself from saying, "I'm a jerk, huh?"

"Todd—"

"Let's get the show on the road," he said, slipping inside.

"See you after," Dan said.

"Yeah, after," Todd echoed back.

Dan leaned down into the window frame. "Todd, I don't want this to affect your driving."

"Are you kidding?" Todd asked as he taped on his earpieces. "Nothing affects my driving. I'm good no matter what my mood."

"Yeah, you are," Dan said, handing him his helmet.

But Todd was too well versed in bullshit not to recognize when he was witnessing a first class con job.

"Good luck," Dan said when it was time for him to roll.

"Don't need it," Todd said back, starting his car, as up and down the garage, other drivers did the same. Whistles blew outside of the garage, white-clad NASCAR officials clearing pedestrians from the road. A few seconds later he heard Dan say, "Go, go, go."

His Holiness.

Well, okay. So Kristen hadn't been lying about that, he thought, turning right at the end of the garage and then left onto the track. So what? Half of his crew were wannabe drivers. They were just pissed *he* was sitting in the catbird seat and not them.

Yeah, but what about Dan? Dan had never aspired to be a driver. Yeah, there were reasons why Dan could be jealous of him, too.

That's what he told himself. But as he accelerated down pit road, the high-compression cylinders causing his seat to vibrate and his radio to crackle with interference, he found himself growing more and more angry. Who was Dan to call him a jerk? Todd was just trying to do his job. And if sometimes he came off as testy it was because he didn't have the time to be nice. It was critical he got his car right. So what if he conveyed that in a harsh way?

He mashed the pedal, his car lurching right, but a full lap later he wasn't feeling any better. If anything, he felt worse, so much so that he found himself clicking his radio and saying, "Someone better do some adjusting on this car. I've driven golf carts that handled better than this."

CHAPTER SEVENTEEN

"CHARMING," DAN SAID, glancing at Mathew.

"No kidding," Mathew agreed, the two of them perched atop the hauler's viewing platform. Dan, Victor and Floyd were watching Todd's practice with him, all of them listening in on headsets—although Mathew's earpieces looked more like hearing aids. He'd had custom inserts made, but he left one side out so he could talk to his crew chief and team manager. A television screen showed them their driver's progress, a metal visor across the top of it shielding the LCD screen from the sun.

"I mean it, Dan. You better do something about it quick," Todd said.

"Roger that," Dan said, but only after he'd squeezed the call button on the side of his blue headset. He'd slid one side of it above his ear so he could listen to Mathew's questions.

"I think Kristen's change is causing it to run like crap," Todd added.

Mathew stiffened. He knew wherever Kristen

was, she was listening in, too, and no doubt seething at the direct attack.

"We'll change it back," Dan said, the crew chief shooting Mathew a look. But it wasn't a glance of disappointment, it was a look of disgust accompanied by a roll of his eyes. He moved his mic out of the way and said, "He goes from loving the car yesterday to hating it."

"He's in rare form today," Floyd said, echoing Dan's sentiments. The team engineer pressed a different button on the TV screen. The display changed to a spreadsheet, one that listed the cars out on the track and their up-to-date lap times. "You'd think he was running dead last instead of second quickest."

"You want me to talk to him?" Mathew asked.

"Nah," Dan said. "Wouldn't do any good. Whatever bee's up his bonnet, it'll pass."

Was it *Kristen?* Mathew wondered. Had her rejection made him mad? It sure seemed like it, especially when he was making snide comments about her engineering skills when earlier he'd loved them.

Just as Kristen had predicted.

"He's so damn smooth," Floyd muttered. "It's too bad he's such an ass."

"What do you mean by smooth?" Mathew asked, peering between Victor and Dan's shoulders and looking at the TV screen which was back to showing the cars out on the track again. They could hear the front runners approaching their end of the track.

"You see the way he throws his car into the corner? He doesn't slam on the brakes. You can hardly tell where his braking begins. Or later, as he's coming out of the turn, where his acceleration starts. Smooth."

"And this is important?"

"I'm telling you guys," Todd's irritated voice rang out. "This car sucks compared to yesterday."

Dan shook his head. "Yes, it's important. It's not easy to drive that way."

"He's good," Floyd said. "You're lucky to have him."

"Think we'll need to change the tranny, too," Todd grumbled. "This one's geared too high. No bottom end."

"Roger that," Dan said, making a note on his clipboard.

"So what *is* bottom end?" Mathew asked next.

"How a car accelerates." But it was Floyd who answered this time. "If a driver can accelerate quickly from low speeds, he's said to have bottom end. If he puts his foot into it and all that happens is the car bogs down, he'll probably have top end because his car will be fast at top speeds."

"And here I thought the only bottom ends that

race car drivers cared about were the ones on the trophy girls," Mathew said, trying to be more personable.

It worked. Floyd almost smiled. "You might have that right where Todd is concerned."

"Nah," Dan said. "Todd's many things, but he doesn't fool around like some of the guys."

"Really?" Mathew asked in surprise.

"He likes to talk, but the truth is he's pretty standoffish."

Interesting.

"How's the rest of the track feel for you?" Dan asked next.

"Like shit," Todd answered.

Floyd shook his head.

"Ten-four," Dan said. "Bring her on in then so we can make some adjustments."

"You're going to have to do a lot of adjusting on this piece of crap."

Dan leaned back, saying, "You know, I just had a talk with him about what an ass he can be. I was hoping it might have helped."

"I suspect nothing will help *his* attitude," Mathew said.

"Jen told me he missed a PR appearance this morning," Dan said. "Some kid from the Wishing Tree Foundation. She said she thought the caseworker would blow a fuse."

"I'm bringing it in," Todd said.

Dan leaned forward again, replacing his headset before saying, "Roger that." And then he darted off the big rig, leaving Mathew and Floyd behind.

"You want to go down and watch them make changes?" Floyd said.

Mathew was surprised by the offer, and then pleased. Kristen had obviously been right. He needed to loosen up a bit around his team.

"That's all right. I'll watch from here."

Todd came in, the crew making the requested changes, and Mathew noticed they left Kristen's part on. He supposed it would be pretty difficult to remove, anyway. He scanned the garage for her. He had a bird's-eye view from where he stood, leaning against the rail and watching crew members dart back and forth. No Kristen. She must be watching from someplace else. But he could see Rob in his black T-shirt at the end of the garage. His security specialist wasn't supposed to be on duty—NASCAR provided enough for Mathew's peace of mind—but Rob took his job seriously. Too seriously, Mathew thought.

Like him.

And that, he reasoned, was why they got along. They were workaholics, although Mathew had promised his doctor he would slow it down. He hadn't been heeding his promise all that well lately.

“All right,” Dan said a few minutes later, and Mathew could see the crew chief heading back toward the hauler at a sprint again. “We changed the tranny. Put on stiffer springs. Messed with the track bar. Pretty much changed everything we could. We’ll see if it helps.”

Todd didn’t say anything, just started his car, the engine crackling to life. A few seconds later he was backing out of his stall with the help of one of his crew members, the man waving him out. Todd took off with a squeal of tires, disappearing around the end of the garage and prompting Mathew to look back at the television screen.

He loved it.

It surprised him how much he enjoyed watching Todd practice, even if he couldn’t stand the man. Something about the sound of the cars, the tension in the air, the electricity one could feel just standing atop the hauler—it was addictive.

On the flatscreen, Todd brought the car up to speed, but it quickly became obvious that his mood had gone from rotten to rank. “That’s it,” he said, his radio crackling to life. “If you guys can’t get this car working any better, I’m bringing it in and parking it.”

“Roger that,” Dan said with a shake of his head, the man’s arms resting on the rail, a clipboard held in one hand.

"And I thought you were taking away Kristen's change."

"We thought about it," Dan said, "but we're sticking with it for now." He took his hand off the speaker button. "Because we can't remove a rear deck lid," Dan said, "which he damn well knows."

"Asshole," Floyd muttered.

"Do you really think Kristen's part is influencing the car's performance?' Mathew asked Dan.

"Hell no," Dan said. "The wind tunnel doesn't lie. Neither did Todd's lap times yesterday. Kristen's part is working just like it should."

That was good to know. "Then I suppose I don't need to ask you two if you feel Kristen is an asset to the team."

Floyd shook his head. "I never thought I would have said this, but she is, Mr. Knight. She's damn good. She recalculated the fuel mileage in her head yesterday, then confirmed it with the computer. She's good."

"I'm done," Todd said. "Until you get this car working better, I'm done."

Dan covered his mic. "I'm half tempted to tell him he's got the best lap times."

"Why don't you?' Mathew asked.

"Because he'd just brush it off with a snide comment about all the other cars running like crap, too. That's the way it is with Todd."

Mathew felt his grip tighten around the aluminum railing that surrounded the viewing platform. If Kristen hadn't been insistent about not firing the man, Mathew would have tossed him out on his ear. But he couldn't, and so he was forced to listen to him rant and rave. Even after Dan told him to bring the car in, Todd still complained bitterly. The man made it sound like he drove the worst car out there—and all because of Kristen.

Mathew couldn't take it anymore. He started to climb down with his crew chief and Floyd, having every intention of reading Todd the riot act, but when he paused for a second on the aluminum ladder, he glanced out at the garage. Todd was just pulling in.

Kristen was waiting for him.

"WHAT THE *HELL* IS your problem?"

Todd unzipped his fire suit. Kristen watched as he tied the sleeves around his waist, his shoulders pulled back as he turned to confront her.

"Kristen," he said with a slight inclination of his head. "You have something you want to discuss?"

"Don't give me that," she said, just about spitting the words at him. "You know damn well what I want to *discuss*."

Todd glanced around. Kristen became aware then that they were attracting attention. Dan was walking toward them, clipboard in hand, his blue-

and-black work clothes unmistakable in a garage full of bright colors.

She took a step toward him, all but hissing up at him, "There is nothing wrong with the rear deck lid, and you know it."

"Oh yeah?" he asked. "You a driver now?"

"No," she snapped, inwardly seething. "I'm an engineer."

"Oh, yeah? I thought you were the boss's mistress."

Dan walked up right then, but he must have heard the tail end of the conversation because his face registered surprise. "You two need some privacy?" he asked, looking between them.

"No," Todd said just as Kristen said, "As a matter of fact, we do."

Dan's gaze bounced off both of them, but instead of looking put out, he looked amused. "You've got five minutes."

"Don't need it," Todd said, starting to move away.

"Don't you dare leave me standing here," Kristen said.

The other guys kept shooting them glances. A few of them pretended to work, but Kristen knew better.

"I'll do whatever I want," Todd shot over his shoulder.

Kristen caught him just outside the garage, warmth radiating off a nearby toolbox, although that might be rage turning her face hot.

"You truly are the biggest jerk that ever walked the earth," she said, blocking his way.

"Oh, yeah? Why don't you tell your friend to try to fire me? Again." He smirked down at her.

"If he wanted to fire you, Todd, he would." And her voice was dead calm.

"Wrong," he shot. "My contract's ironclad. I only walk when I want to walk."

"Really?" Kristen said, realizing in that moment that she'd never been so mad in her life. "Then why don't you?"

"Excuse me?"

"To hear you talk, we're all a bunch of bumbling fools, anyway. And I'm the biggest fool of them all." She pointed to herself. "If we're so subpar, why don't you leave?"

"I never implied *you* were incompetent, just the deck lid you designed."

"Bull," she said. "You were making digs at me through my work and that is *not* right."

"Don't take anything I say while driving personally."

"Huh?" she said, stepping toward him.

"That's just the adrenaline talking."

"Are you kidding?"

"No."

"Is that what you tell yourself? How you excuse your rotten behavior? It's okay," she said, mimicking a man's voice. "Everyone knows I don't really mean it."

"It's true."

"No, it's not true. Your ego's so huge you don't even see your own faults. You're blinded by your own magnificence."

"That's a little harsh."

"Is it, Todd? Is it really? In my experience every driver thinks they're the greatest."

"Shows what you know."

"Have you forgotten I used to drive?"

"You were an amateur."

She huffed out a breath. "You think you're so smart." She took a step toward him, glad they were pretty much outside the garage stalls. It was still a "hot" time, so not even fans wandered around at least none who dared to intrude upon what was obviously a heated discussion. "I was a professional driver, Todd. And I was good. Really good. So good, in fact, that I'd just signed a development deal to drive for Toyota."

Todd tried but failed to hide his shock.

"People were whispering my name," she said, happy to enlighten him. "There was even mention of Indy in a few years. I was eighteen years old and the only female driver in the nation worth a damn. You want to talk about ego, Todd? I had an ego. It was so huge that I thought I knew all there was to know about driving. But I learned the hard way that I didn't."

"What'd you do?" he asked, crossing his arms. "Get in a bad wreck and lose your nerve?"

"That's exactly what happened," she said. "Only I killed my sister along with my dreams."

TODD THOUGHT HE'D MISHEARD HER. But the mixture of disgust and sorrow on her face told him he'd heard her correctly. Still, he found himself saying, "You killed your sister?"

"I was one of the hottest open-wheel drivers around, and so when my mom and dad told me not to let my sixteen-year-old sister drive my car unless they were in there with us, I thought they were being stupid. I could drive around a corner at over a hundred miles per hour. What did they know? I thought I knew better than my parents. Yeah, I was young, but I was mature beyond my years. Really. And I thought I could keep my sister in check. I was wrong."

She shook her head and turned away for a second. And for the first time in a long time Todd didn't know what to say.

"I should never have let her drive. It was late. We'd been at her softball practice for hours. She was tired. I'd been up the night before helping my dad put a new engine in my car." She shook her head. "But she begged me to let her get behind the wheel and so I let her, and when she started to drive faster, and then faster still, I let her do it because we were young and stupid and I honestly thought I would know well before we got into any trouble. And then that damn dog darted out in front of us. I tried to turn the wheel, to move my leg over and hit the brakes, but there wasn't enough time. Had I been driving, things might have been different. I was used to thinking fast, to avoiding wrecks. But my sister wasn't."

"Kristen—"

She held up a hand. "My sister died that night, and I…I was left with scars and a limp and an overwhelming sense of guilt."

"You couldn't have avoided the wreck, either."

"You think? I'm not so certain. But one thing I do know, Todd. If my parents had been in the car we would never have been going that fast, and if we hadn't been going fast, Trina would have had more time to react. Believe me, Todd, I've analyzed the situation in my head at least a million times, and no matter how often I replay it, it all comes down to one thing—I should have listened to my parents."

Todd moved toward her. The guilt and sorrow in her eyes did things to his gut. "We all think we're invincible at that age, Kristen."

"Feeling invincible is one thing, Todd," she said softly, flicking her head again when the breeze kicked up and blew a lock of hair across her face.

"But I thought I was untouchable," she said, tucking the dark-blond strand behind her ear. "Turns out I was wrong. Now I'm stuck with the consequences of my actions for the rest of my life."

"Don't blame yourself."

"Easier said than done."

"And I'm not blinded by myself," he said, redirecting the subject. "I know I can be difficult to deal with."

"Your idea of difficult and other people's idea are two different things."

"Maybe."

"And either way, life's too short to treat people like crap."

He wanted to argue with her, but his earlier conversation with Dan came up and slapped him in the face.

"Good luck qualifying," she said, sliding past him and disappearing quickly down the narrow aisle. He let her go this time. To be honest, there was really nothing else to say. Actually, maybe there was, he thought, slowly turning so he could watch her disappear around the back of the big rig.

I'm sorry.

That's what he should tell her, but for some reason he couldn't get the words out.

CHAPTER EIGHTEEN

POMPOUS, OFFENSIVE, delusional ass!

"Don't take anything I say personally," she mimicked, so furious she didn't look to the right when she left the garage, a NASCAR official frantically waving her back and tooting on his whistle.

Lance Cooper nearly ran her down.

She jumped back. Air from his car's passing crept under her slacks, warming her ankles.

"Careful," someone called. She didn't know who, she didn't care. Cheeks burning, she darted between the haulers and the garage, down an aisle created by tires and toolboxes and director's chairs. But she didn't go inside the tractor-trailer. Instead she slid between the two big rigs. A chain-link fence covered by black tarps kept people from peering into the garage, but she could still see feet walking along the access road outside. For a moment she wished she was one of those race fans, someone completely oblivious to the inner workings of a race team—and its big-headed, intolerable driver.

Still, she warned herself as she sat down on the warm asphalt, she better watch herself. If she pushed Todd too far, she wouldn't put it past him to demand her resignation.

But if he did, so what? At least she'd go out fighting. There'd be a certain amount of satisfaction in that.

"I thought you might need this."

Kristen's gaze shot up. Mathew appeared in front of her. Terrific. Just what she needed.

"Here," he said, holding a small, rectangular object.

"What is that?" she asked warily.

"Take it," he said, and there was a slight smile on his face as he said the words. *That,* more than anything, got her attention.

She took the thing from him, her brows lifting when she realized what it was. A brick. A *foam* brick, one that looked real with its bumps and pockmarks and beige-orange color.

"I thought you might like to throw it."

"Where did you get this?" she asked, a smile spreading across her face. She stood up, tossing the thing from hand to hand.

"One of the guys picked it up in the souvenir area. It's a promo item. Some house paint company."

She flipped the thing over. "Tough as bricks," she read, the name of the company printed above that.

"One of the guys is looking out for a cardboard

cutout of Todd so we can all take turns throwing the brick at his head."

"You're kidding?"

For the first time since meeting him, she saw laughter on his face. "I'm not."

"Seriously?" she asked, her own smile showing.

"Scout's honor," he said, crossing his heart and holding up his hand. "Dan thought it was a great idea. The team loved the idea, too. I had more than one guy volunteer to find the cardboard cutout."

She laughed. She couldn't stop herself. She just couldn't believe Mathew Knight had come up with the idea all by himself. And that he'd told the team about it. "Thank you," she said, shaking her head.

"You're welcome."

When she glanced up at him something tickled her insides, something warm and soft and momentarily unidentifiable.

Gratitude.

He still smiled at her, and though he didn't laugh, humor lit his eyes. They turned a light shade of green when he was amused. His whole face changed, actually. He looked younger. And more handsome.

Some of her amusement fled.

"But I didn't just come back here to bring you the brick," he said.

"You didn't?" she asked, breath held.

"I came back here to tell you that your team loves you."

Her breath escaped in a rush.

"They see your brilliance, Kristen. They know you're good at your job. They respect you and admire you and don't want you to leave."

And suddenly, unbelievably, she was close to tears.

"You can see it on their faces when you walk by. Hear it in their voices when they talk about your rear deck lid. They think you're pretty amazing. Dan told me so himself."

She stared down at the brick, her hand clenching it so tightly her nails left furrows in the plastic surface. "Thank you," she said softly.

"I thought you should know that," he said gently.

She nodded. Had to take a deep breath. She needed to do something to keep from crying.

"I'll see you at qualifying."

He turned away.

"Mathew, wait," she called.

He turned back to her. His face had gone completely blank, his eyes no longer glowing, they'd turned so serious.

"Thank you," she said.

"You're welcome," he said with a slight smile.

"I want to be first in line."

"I think everyone agrees you've earned that right today."

Her own grin turned wry. "I think you're right."

This time when he walked away, she didn't stop him. Instead she stared at the brick, grateful to him in more ways than one. Not only had he made her laugh at a time when she didn't think it possible, but he hadn't brought up their previous conversation about dating, either. He appeared to have dropped that matter. She appreciated that.

Didn't she?

She tossed the brick in the air.

Yes, she firmly told herself. But there was a tiny corner of her heart that whispered the word *no,* and all because of the stupid plastic brick he'd brought her, and the kind words he'd said.

No one had been kind to her like that in ages because she had no one in her life who cared. *No one.*

"You ready to go?" Dan asked when she emerged from between the haulers a little later.

"Is it that time already?" The hour had flown by.

"It is set," he said with a smile.

"What'd you change?" she asked.

The crew chief stood by the side of the dark-blue-and-black car, a portable generator whirring nearby. "Nothing. The car's good. We all know that, including Todd."

"Not to hear him talk about it," she muttered under her breath.

She looked away, and right at Todd. Her spine

popped, she straightened so quickly. He was fifty yards away, a slew of race fans trailing in his wake like the Pied Piper and a pack of mice. Most people held out hats or scraps of paper. Todd took the items blindly, scribbling his name and then handing it back without really looking at anyone.

"Here he comes," Dan said, following her gaze.

Yeah. Here he came, their driver's cool eyes covered by a pair of dark glasses, fire suit tied around his waist, the white, fire-resistant shirt he wore beneath it making him look as if he'd just gotten back from the Bahamas. For a moment she thought about dashing away, but that would be cowardly. Besides, she had nothing to be ashamed of.

"Hey, Kristen," he said, stopping right in front of her and smiling at her as if nothing had happened.

Maddening, infuriating man.

"Todd," she said with a small nod, but her heart pounded against her chest.

"Dan, can I talk to Kristen for a sec?"

Dan shot her a look, one that clearly asked if she wanted to be left alone. She nodded.

"You're the boss," Dan said, stepping toward the pit wall and the rest of the crew who hung there, waiting to push the car forward as qualifying moved on.

But Kristen wouldn't make it easy. She crossed her arms. In his Ray-Ban glasses and fire suit, a day's growth of beard making his chin look dark, he looked the consummate driver. Proud. Confident. Afraid of nothing.

"Look, Kristen, this isn't easy for me to say." He said, glancing around. "I'm not one to apologize."

"Then don't."

"No," he said quickly. "You were right. I was an ass earlier. After you and I talked, I sat down and thought about it and I could see how you and the crew would get upset at the way I was talking."

Kristen nodded, still refusing to make this easy. She wondered what he'd say if he knew about the brick and the cardboard cutout.

"I heard you," he said. "And I'm sorry about your sister." He lifted his sunglasses, allowing her to see into his eyes. "Really, truly sorry," he said.

And despite her resolve to remain angry, Kristen found herself saying, "It's okay."

He flicked his sunglasses in place.

"Thanks for making my car go fast."

"You're welcome."

And then he did something even more surprising. He gave her a hug.

She was so shocked she couldn't move.

"I'll see you after," he said.

She nodded. He gruffly set her away.

"Todd," she called.

He faced her again.

"Good luck."

He nodded, just once, and then faded away. Maybe she wouldn't be throwing bricks at him after all.

HE GOT THE POLE.

Kristen had never been more relieved in her life. But even more importantly, every person on the team came up to her afterward, each one offering congratulations. That gave her a sense of accomplishment unlike any she'd felt before. She was working with race cars again. And she was good at it, just like she'd always hoped.

She wanted to call her mom. But her mother wouldn't understand. She'd never gotten the whole racing thing. To be honest, she'd probably chastise her for leaving the aerospace industry to go work on race cars.

"You stickin' around for the race tomorrow?" Dan asked when she walked into the catering area, a motorcoach with a canvas awning pulled out on one side, food laid out buffet-style beneath. Their car manufacturer provided food for all the teams, something Kristen was eternally grateful for. Now that qualifying was over, she was starved. "You're allowed to, if you want."

She hadn't really thought about it. All her attention had been focused on making it to race day. But obviously the new material worked. Thus, her job was done. Technically, she could go home with the B team.

She glanced around. The air smelled of hot dogs and barbecues, the familiar odor turning Kristen nostalgic. Some of her best memories were at racetracks. She just wished…but her dad was gone.

"I think I'll stick around," she found herself saying.

Dan nodded and said, "Good," before he helped himself to a giant heap of potato salad.

"Look, Kristen," Dan said while placing a hamburger patty on a naked bun. "I know I wasn't all that friendly when you first came onboard and so I'd like to apologize for that."

"You don't need to," Kristen said, scooping up a patty, too.

"No. I do. You're good. Mr. Knight told us that you were worried we didn't take you seriously because you were a woman—"

"What?"

"He didn't use those exact words," Dan said quickly, grabbing lettuce and some tomato slices off a plate, "but that's the impression I got. I just want you to know that you've more than proved yourself."

Kristen didn't know what to say. She wasn't happy Mathew had voiced her concerns to his crew chief, but there wasn't much she could do about it now. "Thanks, Dan," she said. "I appreciate the vote of confidence."

"And if we ever find a cardboard cutout, you get the first shot."

She laughed. "Thanks."

His face grew serious. "I also want you to know that you don't need to hide your relationship with Mr. Knight, either."

"What relationship?"

"You mean Todd was wrong about your being involved with him?"

"He was."

"Well, I might believe you except that's not how the boss made it sound."

"Excuse me?"

"I told Mr. Knight what Todd said, you know, about you being—" he looked around, and even though the tent was nearly empty, he lowered his voice "—his *you know.* He said that even though you weren't together *like that,* he still hoped to date you at some point in the future, only you were convinced the team would look down on you if that happened."

"I can't believe he said that," Kristen muttered. Why would Mathew air their personal business like that?

"Don't get mad," Dan said, his tanned face showing his concern. "It wasn't like he seemed upset about it. I talked it over with Floyd and we both think—"

"You talked to Floyd, too?"

"Kristen, half the garage probably heard what

Todd said. That's the thing about this industry. Rumors spread fast. Best to nip them in the bud. If you want to date Mr. Knight, date him. Just don't hide it. That always looks bad."

"I'm not dating him."

"Not dating who?"

Mathew. Kristen closed her eyes. It figured.

"She's not dating *you,*" Dan said.

He walked up next to them, empty paper plate in hand. "No, she's not," Mathew said, much to Kristen's relief. "But I'm hoping she'll let me sit with her for lunch."

Kristen opened her mouth to protest. "I don't—"

"You can join us too, Dan, if you like," Mathew quickly added.

"Actually," Dan said. "I think I'm going to take my plate back to the garage."

"No, don't do that."

But with a final scoop of baked beans, Dan spun toward the opening of the tent. "See ya," he said on the way out, lifting his plate in farewell. Kristen was left standing there, her own food held in front of her.

"I should get back to the garage, too."

"No, you shouldn't."

"Mathew—"

"Kristen, we can just sit together. As friends. Like earlier."

Damn it. She was getting tired of men interrupting her.

"I know that," she said, lifting her head. It wasn't like they weren't out in public. Odds were people would think nothing of a team owner eating lunch with one of his engineers. "I just think it's better if I eat with the team."

"And leave me here by myself?"

She tipped her head. "I'm sure you'll be perfectly fine."

"Eat with me," he said, although it wasn't so much an order as it was a question. "Do it out of kindness if nothing else."

She sucked in a breath, reminded of how kind he'd been earlier. But that was probably his point. "All right. Fine," she said, looking in the direction of an empty table near the far corner of the covered eating area. "We can eat over there."

Not that she was hungry anymore.

"Your leg bothering you?" he asked after he'd filled his plate.

She hadn't even noticed she'd started to limp. She immediately lightened her step. "Just a little," she said, pulling a chair out.

Out on the track, some type of smaller stock car began to practice, the whine of the motors fading in and out, a breeze carrying the sound.

"Do you miss it?" he asked next.

She'd just picked up her fork, determined to eat at least a little something. "Racing?" she asked. "Sometimes."

All the time.

She still dreamed about it. Still woke up in the middle of the night, sweating, the roar of cars in her ears, her hand seeming to tingle from the force of holding the wheel.

But it was always just a dream.

"Why'd you give up trying to design race cars?" he asked. "You don't seem like the type of person to let people chase you away."

"Long story," she said.

"And you don't want to talk about it, do you?" he asked, lifting his fork.

"Not really," she said.

He nodded, the two of them watching the cars go around for a moment or two before he said, "Actually, there's something I want to talk to *you* about."

"Oh?"

"I want to know why you refuse to go out with me, Kristen, because after today it should be obvious that there's no reason you should keep telling me no."

CHAPTER NINETEEN

"IS IT THAT YOU'RE NOT interested in me? Because I'll leave you alone if that's the case," he said, his attention darting left when someone walked by. He leaned forward, nearly whispering, "I will."

She didn't say anything, her food forgotten in front of her.

The truth was she *did* like him. She hadn't been lying yesterday when she'd told him that she wouldn't be surprised if they slept together. She was attracted to him. What red-blooded female wouldn't be?

But it was more than that.

She *liked* him, too. Liked how kind he could be. How even though a sense of humor didn't come naturally to him, he tried. Plus, there was the way he made her feel. Every time he was near, her insides seemed to tingle and her face seemed to heat and she wanted, oh how she wanted, to forget about business and engineering and race cars.

That wasn't like her. That wasn't like her at all.

"What if it doesn't work out?"

"What if it does?"

The cars out on the track roared by again. She tried to spot them between the outbuilding and big rigs and various other things.

"Just one date, Kristen."

"One date or two, it'll all turn out the same."

"Why are you afraid of getting close to someone?"

Her head jerked up.

His eyes were serious. And gentle. It was that gentleness more than anything that she liked about him. She'd never met someone who worked so hard, and yet who obviously cared about his employees.

"You are scared, aren't you?"

She thought for a moment, then answered honestly, "I don't know."

Her sister had died. Her dad had died, too, not long after. *Was* she afraid?

"Go out with me," he said. "Please."

She shook her head. "I don't think I can."

"Then let's leave it in fate's hands."

'What do you mean?"

He leaned forward. "If Todd wins the race tomorrow, you go out with me."

"What?"

"If he loses, I'll walk away."

"You're crazy."

"Perhaps. Perhaps not. But it's worth a try."

"Mathew, I'm flattered, really, but I just don't think it's a good idea."

"You racers believe in Lady Luck, don't you? Why don't we let Lady Luck do her thing."

She shook her head again.

"Tomorrow Todd races. If he wins, we go out."

"Mathew—"

He reached across the table and clasped her hand. "Give it a try."

"I can't," she said softly.

"Even if I promise that if Todd wins tomorrow and it doesn't work out, I'll leave you alone?"

"Todd won't win," she said. "Luck never goes my way. And fate is never kind."

"Is that a yes?"

Was it? She didn't know.

"I'll take it as a yes," he said, kissing her hand before getting up from the table.

She melted. Just one kiss and she went all mushy inside.

"I'll see you tomorrow," he said, and walked away.

She didn't call him back—didn't move, didn't do anything—because she suddenly wondered which she would consider lucky: Todd winning? Or Todd losing?

SHE STILL COULDN'T BELIEVE what she'd inadvertently agreed to the next morning. Even worse, it seemed as if the whole team knew about it, too.

"So what we all want to know," said Chuck, their car chief and part of KEM's A team, the moment they'd all climbed into the van for their ride to the track, "do you secretly want Todd to win, or lose?"

Kristen felt her mouth open at the verbal echo of her thoughts, "You guys know about that?"

"One of the guys on the team knows one of the guys on the catering bus. You were overheard."

What? Did everybody spy on everyone else in the garage?

"Great," Kristen muttered.

"So, seriously," Chuck said. "What are you hoping for?"

Kristen shook her head. "He's not going to win so there's no point in talking about it."

"Better not let Todd hear you say that," one of the transmission specialists said.

"Todd would understand," Kristen muttered.

And he would. Heck. Todd might lose the race on purpose just to thwart Mathew.

She thought about that for a second.

Nope. Todd would never do that but she had a feeling he wouldn't be happy.

They left her alone the rest of the way to the track. Kristen almost used her Sprint NEXTEL phone to alert Mathew and call off the whole thing. But she didn't. That more than anything told her a lot.

She wanted to go out with Matt.

And when had he become Matt?

She didn't know, but the new name felt…right. Despite the silly bet, it all felt right.

She could tell immediately that the whole garage knew about it, too. For someone so low on the racing totem pole, she was getting a lot of attention from other teams.

"Tell me everyone on the circuit isn't talking about this, too?" Kristen asked one of the guys on their way in.

"You want the truth? Or you want me to lie?"

That, she supposed, was answer enough.

"Great. Terrific," Kristen said. "Just fabulous."

"Nah," the guy said with a dismissive wave. "Don't worry about it. To be honest, everybody probably thinks it's cute."

"Cute?" she asked.

"Sweet," he offered instead, a duffel bag slung over his shoulder. "You know. Most of the time people try to hide their relationships around here. You two have it all out in the open."

"And my credibility as an engineer is zero."

"Are you kidding? They're talking about how fast Todd's car is going, too, and since you're the only new blood on the team, it didn't take them long to put two and two together. Stop worrying about your reputation. You're a bona fide engineering star."

She didn't feel like a star. She felt like a rock. Actually, she wanted to *hide* under a rock, especially when she bumped into Mathew near the hauler.

"You ready for our date?" he asked softly.

Kristen glanced around to make sure no one was near. Ha. The garage bustled with pre-race activity—tours going on, media setting up, crew members dashing back and forth.

"He's *not* going to win."

The look he gave her made her shiver. "Then I guess we'll just see what happens afterward, won't we?"

How had it happened? How had she managed to become so attracted to him? She was usually so calm and cool and detached from people. And yet here she was, practically melting at the look in her boss's eyes.

"I guess we will," she said, trying to act supremely confident as she turned away.

But her legs felt like bearing lube.

And her hands shook like a car with a broken steering wheel.

And her heart pounded like a bent push rod.

Please, God, let this day end quickly. The suspense was killing her.

CHAPTER TWENTY

SHE'D BET HE'D LOSE the race.

"You're early," Jen said when he showed up to the media center.

Todd tried to hide his agitation behind a wide, confident smile.

"Thought I'd come over and see if you needed me," he said.

Jen looked puzzled, but that was to be expected given that he never showed up on time to anything. In fact, he sometimes *missed* appointments.

"I'll be in the green room."

She nodded. "I still have some interviews to line up."

He'd figured as much. But the media center would be as good a place as any to cool off. None of the other drivers would be there early.

Or so he thought.

When he walked inside the twelve-by-twelve room he was surprised to see Lance Cooper. "Hey," his friend said, setting down his newspaper. "What the heck are you doing here at—" Lance checked his watch "—quarter after seven?"

"I could ask you the same question."

"Have a live feed to do at seven-thirty. FOX."

"Lucky you," Todd said, taking a seat on one of the plush couches in the corner. A TV provided background noise, the smell of coffee filling the air. A fresh pot looked to have been brewed, doughnuts and other breakfast stuff set out on a side table. He always thought these rooms looked like hotel suites. Nothing but the best: microwave, soda machine, and a few live plants to give it that homey feel.

"You look like crap."

Todd shrugged. The blond, blue-eyed driver was one of his oldest friends. Not only had they come up through the ranks together, but they'd been rookies on the NASCAR NEXTEL Cup Series, too. Lance had ended up winning the title, something Todd never forgave him for, but they were as good friends as possible given that they did battle week after week.

"Seriously, Todd. You need to quit burning the candle at both ends."

"Hey, man," Todd said. "Don't tell me I look like crap. You look like crap, too."

"I have a reason. Infants have a way of keeping you up at night."

"How's little Melanie?"

Lance's blue eyes lit up. "Good. Real good. Keeping Jarrod company." He tipped his head in question. "When you going to start a family? Or are you still looking around?"

Todd instantly thought of Kristen. If they had kids they'd be smart, gearheads what with the both of them involved in motorsports. She'd be perfect to have a kid with. Except she'd just bet he'd lose a race.

"I have my eye on someone," he admitted, because no matter how much it bothered him, he understood her reasoning. She didn't *want* to go out with Mathew Knight. That *had* to be why she'd done it.

"Oh, yeah?" Lance asked. "Anyone I know?"

"Nope," Todd said.

"You'll have to introduce us."

"I'll do that," Todd said, just as soon as he won this race, told their boss to take a flying leap, and drove off with Kristen in his own damn car.

He picked up a magazine. His hands shook.

Damn it. What the hell was she thinking laying down a bet like that with the boss? From the way some of the guys were making it sound, it almost seemed she was hoping he'd lose. But that couldn't be the case.

Or was it?

It was a question that plagued him all morning. As he went through his usual routine: interviews, autographing, NASCAR-mandated meetings, he wondered. But in the end Todd decided he had the advantage. If Kristen was really interested in Mathew, she'd have accepted a date with him—without the necessary complications of a stupid bet. Nah. She didn't want to date him. No way.

Todd came out of the driver's meeting feeling confident that he'd be able to win Kristen to his side, especially when he saw her leaning against the back of the hauler, staring off into space. She looked disappointed. Maybe even sad. But definitely not happy.

"Hey there, genius," he said warily. "What has you looking so down?"

She snapped upright. When their eyes met, he could tell she was surprised to see him. "Nothing," she answered softly.

"Nah. Come on. Something's bugging you."

She shook her head.

He sat down in the chair next to her. "Spill," he said.

She took a deep breath, straightened her shoulders, a frown coming to her face. "I just heard Mr. Knight is gone."

"Really?"

"He had to go to New York."

"You mean he left the track?"

"Yeah," she said.

"And that makes you upset?"

"I guess I'm just surprised."

He wasn't. The putz was a jerk. He didn't even

want to hang around to find out if he won a date with Kristen or not.

"No biggie," Todd said. "We don't need him."

"No," she said softly. "I guess we don't."

"Hey, you want to walk me out to my car?"

There she went again, back to looking wary—a common expression on her face where he was concerned. To be honest, it was one of the things he liked about her. She didn't fall at his feet.

"Isn't that what girlfriends do?" she asked.

He rolled his eyes, even glanced heavenward for added effect. "I just thought you might like to keep me company. And it's not just the wives and girlfriends who do that. It's family members, friends and crew members—just about anybody who isn't going to drive a driver nuts with stupid questions and chitchat before a race. You fit in the 'friends' category."

Her gaze flitted back and forth as she studied his eyes. But then she looked behind him. "You have people who want autographs."

He turned. Sure enough, a crowd had gathered nearby, someone snapping a picture the minute he turned. It was a tour by the looks of it, a pretty girl who couldn't have been more than eighteen held up a sign with a major sponsor's name on it. She smiled. He lifted a hand in acknowledgment, but turned away before anyone felt comfortable enough to ask for autographs.

"So, you going with me?"

"I don't know," she muttered slowly.

"Suit yourself," he said, turning back to the crowd. "Just let me go inside and change into my fire suit, guys. I'll sign autographs after."

"Cool," someone said.

"Todd, wait," Kristen said as he opened the tinted-glass doors. He had to work hard to hide the smile that tried to form on his face when he saw the look in her eyes.

"You really want me out there with you?"

"I do," he said, not realizing until that moment just how much.

"Okay."

AND SO THAT WAS HOW Kristen found herself walking Todd to his car, a double row of multicolored vehicles on her right, some of them concealed beneath car covers.

"Keeps the cockpit cooler," Todd explained.

"Oh," she said, her mind still on Mathew's defection. He'd text messaged her. Just four words: *I'll see you after.* Someone said it was urgent business, but Kristen didn't understand what could be so urgent that he'd leave on race day.

Before he found out if he'd won the bet or not.

She shook her head. She should just forget about it. Obviously Mathew had other priorities. And his absence made it easier to forget about their silly wager. That's what she told herself it was—silly. Ridiculous. Dumb.

"Tired?" Todd asked, glancing down at her.

"No, no," she said quickly, trying to pretend an interest in the cars.

It was her first experience with the stares and sneers that went along with accompanying a driver down pit road. Stares from race fans. Sneers from the female groupies who took it as a personal affront that Todd was walking with somebody other than them. It didn't matter that Kristen had on her team polo shirt. It was enough that the two of them were chatting amicably. She was a woman. Todd was single. Women didn't like that she walked by his side.

Jen hovered around them, ready to step in should a television or radio commentator approach, which they did periodically. Kristen stood off to one side as Todd answered questions about his car, how he liked the track, and his chances for the day. A warm breeze blew against her face, carrying with it the smell of hamburgers and French fries, and Kristen realized she hadn't touched her lunch. But suddenly she was ravenous. Todd stopped near Lance Cooper's colorful white-and-orange car, the NASCAR NEXTEL Cup Series driver shooting Todd a funny look when he introduced Kristen.

"She's one of the team engineers," Todd explained, and Kristen realized Lance thought they were a couple. She was grateful for Todd's explanation, because she didn't want to start even more rumors flying. That's just what she needed.

"She's the one I was telling you about earlier," Todd added.

"You were?" she asked, having to raise her voice over the sound of the PA system that blared nonstop. Someone who sounded like a used-car salesman was giving out driver stats.

"Yeah. I was telling him how great an engineer you are."

Another strange look from Lance, and then his face suddenly cleared. "Oh, yeah, right," he said. "I remember now. Nice to meet you, Kristen."

"Same here," she said right back.

"Where's Sarah?" Todd asked.

"With the baby, back at the hotel."

"Lucky her," Todd said.

"Yeah, it's a good thing she's out of this heat."

It *was* warm, Kristen thought. A muggy breeze only made it worse, the humidity so high the sky looked gray.

"Time to go," Dan said, coming up to them with a wide grin.

"Luck," Lance said, holding out a hand to Todd.

Todd slapped it away. "I ain't touching you before a race."

Lance laughed. "I was just trying to fake you out."

"Yeah, right," Todd said.

Todd stopped by his car. Fans filled the grandstands, what seemed like a million eyes trained upon them. Out on pit road, various teams did last-minute housekeeping tasks: moving tires, adjusting the shade of a pop-up tent, fiddling with hoses and air wrenches. In the infield, people stood atop RVs. She could practically feel the electrical charge of the fans' excitement in the air.

"Where you going to watch the race?" Todd asked. He stared at the stage near the start/finish line where he'd just had his driver introduction. Kristen followed his gaze for a second, then looked back at the line of cars behind his own. The vehicles rivaled a gumball machine for color.

"From pit road, I guess."

"Why don't you watch it from up on top of the pit box?"

"Nah," she said. "I don't need to do that."

"No, you should," Dan said, glancing at his watch. "Almost time to line up for the National Anthem," he warned.

"Got it," the driver said before looking back at her. "Go ahead and watch the race from the pit box. That way I can see you cheering me on whenever I come in for a pit stop."

"Todd—"

"Oh, don't worry," Dan said. "We'll keep you busy up there. I'm sure Floyd would love to have your mathematical mind nearby to help him make snap fuel-mileage decisions."

She stared between the driver and his crew chief, knowing she couldn't turn down an opportunity to prove herself to the team. Besides, what else did she have to do? Mathew was gone. And that really hurt, for some strange and inexplicable reason.

"All right," she said.

Todd nodded, and then wrapped an arm around her shoulder. "See you after."

She didn't know what to do, wasn't sure if she should hug him, pat him on the back, or what? "Have a safe race," she said, settling for doing nothing.

She met up with the team halfway between the cars and their pit stalls, the bunch of them holding out their hands so she could high-five them as she passed. The gesture made her smile, mostly because she realized at that moment that she'd truly become "one of the team." It was a good feeling.

She waited until the National Anthem was over before climbing aboard the pit box, and even then she felt highly conspicuous. So many people were in the grandstands behind her that it felt as if thousands of eyes peered down at her as she took her place.

"Okay, we've changed a few things since yesterday," she heard Dan say to Todd after he climbed in the car, Kristen adjusting her earpieces so she could hear better. It was hot on top of the giant toolbox, the metal desktop in front of her reflecting the sun's light. "We gave you a little more gear in the back and changed some springs. Let me know if you have more bottom end out of turns two and four."

"Roger that," Todd said, sounding dead calm. His voice never changed, not even once he'd rolled off, the sound of a pack of cars accelerating off pit road echoing through the hills. The noise of the crowd was even louder.

"Check your gauges," Dan said, climbing up next to her.

"All good," Todd reported.

"Remember, turn off your blowers."

"Already off."

And that was all he said before the start of the race, Kristen and everyone on pit road coming to their feet as they rolled across the start/finish line. It sounded like mayhem. Or madness. Or the roar of a dozen C-130s. Forty-three cars headed toward the first turn. A moment later they were out of sight. But built into the desktop, a monitor with a cover over the top of it allowed everyone on top of the pit box—Dan, Floyd, Kristen and Chuck, their car chief—to see. It showed Todd heading round turn one, his nose barely ahead of the Star Oil car. Lance Cooper tried to hold Todd off, but he couldn't do it.

Todd was too fast for him, especially when they exited turn two.

"That's Kristen's handiwork," Dan radioed to her, using the channel reserved for pit crew only.

She smiled, nodded, not certain she was supposed to say something back, figuring silence was probably golden. On the monitor the cars entered turn three and a split second later seemed to come off the ground as all the weight was transferred to one side. When they showed the cars approaching turn four, Todd was a full car length ahead.

"How's she feel, driver?" she heard Dan ask, his voice over the radio a split second behind the real Dan nearby.

"Not bad," Todd said.

She leaned forward, looking past Floyd, who sat next to her, and smiled at Dan who caught her gaze and smiled back. "Not bad" was code for "awesome."

Around turns one and two they went, forty-three engines sounding like Turboprop jets, not less than four dozen V-8s. On screen she could see that Todd had started to pull away. Lance followed. But fourth and back looked like a bunch of scattered cue balls, rear ends sliding sideways, one car nearly spinning out.

Kristen gasped.

Somehow the driver kept it on track.

Lap one down, one hundred ninety-nine to go.

Todd continued to pull away. Thirty laps later it was time to start thinking about pit stops, but a yellow flag, the first of many, changed their pit strategy, which Kristen had learned was an important part of race day. She took on the task of figuring out fuel mileage, but with so many pit stops, worrying about how much gas they had really wasn't an issue.

"You want any adjustments?" Dan asked.

"Nope," Todd said. "You got her nice and tight in the turns, and she just about lifts the front end off the ground when I nail it. I think we're good to go."

Dan nodded, pressing the button on the side of his radio before saying, "Ten-four. No changes." He switched frequencies. "Got that, guys," he said to the crew. "No changes." He leaned toward the gasman, Joe, who was on the wall behind him. "I'll need the numbers on fuel ASAP."

Kristen watched as Joe nodded and donned his helmet, the fire suit he was forced to wear making him look like an astronaut about to descend from the Lunar Rover. Poor guy must be steaming hot.

She heard the cars coming, looked up. Here they came. And, as it always did, her heart started to pound. So much hinged on a good, clean pit stop. One misstep could cost precious position out on the track. Todd was in the most precarious of situations. He was leading the race and so if the crew messed up, he would then be behind Lance Cooper—and passing on a super speedway was difficult at best.

She tensed even more when Todd turned off the track. A stream of cars followed behind him. That was good. No one was staying out on the track, which meant nobody would be in front of Todd when it came time to restart.

She stood up just as the sign man waved a colorful board up and down for Todd to spot. Dan started calling out numbers, reminding Todd to keep his RPMs down low, and then counting down from five when he was about two pit stalls away. Even before Todd stopped, part of the crew was over the wall, the jackman stopping by the passenger-side door as Todd screeched to a halt. All hell broke loose. Wrenches whirred. Motors revved. The crowd screamed. One, two, three seconds. At six they switched sides, repeated the maneuvers, and then Todd was roaring away, his tires sounding like a broken fan belt when they lost purchase with the ground.

"Go!" Kristen yelled, shooting off her chair.

Lance was right at Todd's rear quarter panel, but the fifty-three car had the jump on Todd. Kristen groaned. She glanced at the TV screen, watching the race to the line. Lance beat him.

"Damn it!" Dan yelled.

Kristen knew just how he felt.

But she needn't have worried, because Todd made passing look easy. His car was that good.

Halfway through the race she started to realize they might have a chance.

Mathew might win his bet.

And that made her feel…she glanced down for a second. That made her feel such a conflicting mass of emotions she didn't know what to think.

Three-quarters through the race, her hands were shaking. Numerous yellow flags made the wait all the more agonizing, but the laps ticked off. Eighty laps to go. Seventy. Eighty. Forty.

Would Todd win?

Would *Mathew* win?

Someone drove into turn four a little too hard. One car collected another, and then another, all of it happening behind Todd. But it didn't matter. They pitted—they had to—but a misstep by the rear tire changer put them behind the eight ball. They went in first, came out sixth.

She didn't know if Todd could pass that many cars in such a short time, and the desperation she felt, her disappointment upon realizing Mathew might not win his date after all, well, she obviously had kidded herself about her feelings for the man. Despite how hurt she felt by his defection, she was still anxiously awaiting the outcome of their bet.

She wanted Todd to win. She wanted *Mathew* to win. She wanted Mathew to win *her.*

But now she didn't know if Todd could pull it off. Not only was the risk greater that he'd get collected in a wreck, but passing at the Michigan race was tricky.

"We need to do better than that, guys," Dan said, his disappointment obvious. "We can't afford to be making mistakes."

Even though Kristen knew getting after the crew was part of Dan's job, she still felt bad for the tire changer. The poor guy's mistake had cost Todd the lead, and was broadcast to seventy-five million fans on national TV.

Funny thing was, Todd didn't say a word. Last week he'd been cussing and cursing. Heck, just a couple of days ago he'd been cussing out his crew. Today all he said was, "What happened?"

"Missed a lug nut," Dan said.

"Did he get it on all right?"

"He did."

"That's all that matters."

Kristen glanced at Floyd and then Dan. They were looking at each other as if Todd had just told them he was headed to the nearest convenience store for a Slurpee.

Maybe her talk with him had helped.

That became even more apparent as the race

wore on. Instead of lashing out at his crew in frustration when he couldn't immediately get around slower cars, Todd calmly asked for his lap times, picking off cars one by one.

Until only Lance was left.

She glanced at the nearby score tower with the giant screen across from them, her foot tap-tap-tapping with sheer nervous energy. Ten laps to go. Todd ducked down low coming out of turn four. Kristen came off her seat, arms raised and hands fisted as she urged Todd on. The car's nose reached Lance's back tire, then his door panel. When he passed them at nearly a hundred and fifty miles per hour, they were neck and neck. Kristen wanted to close her eyes. In fact, she must have done exactly that because, when next she looked, Todd was in front of Lance.

She couldn't believe her eyes, had to check the TV monitor for confirmation. Sure enough, it was Todd's car that came into frame next.

"Yes!" she cried, her palms stinging, she clapped so hard.

Todd aimed his car left and then right. His lead increased. By the time he headed into turn three, she knew he was going to win. Still, she almost bowed her head to pray, especially when he headed toward the last turn.

"Come on," she found herself murmuring, waiting for the cars to reappear in turn four.

There he was. But Lance was right there with him. She squeaked in fear. Todd threw it into the corner. The back wheels broke loose. Lance gained a spot.

"Come on," she said, a little louder.

Todd gunned it. Lance fell back. The flagman waved the checkers.

"Come! On!" she all but screamed, bouncing up on her toes as he shot beneath the flag stand once again.

"Waa-hoo!" Kristen cried, pulling her headset off her head and turning to Floyd. They hugged, but he was the first to pull back, Kristen thinking he looked suddenly embarrassed. "Good job, Todd!" she heard Dan yell.

And then her butt vibrated. She stiffened. Her phone.

She looked at the caller ID.

New York.

It was hard to hear, but she managed to make out Mathew's voice.

"My driver will pick you up at six tomorrow afternoon."

CHAPTER TWENTY-ONE

IT WAS A CELEBRATION Kristen would never forget, but it was overshadowed by Mathew's words.

My driver will pick you up at six tomorrow afternoon.

Todd was jubilant in Victory Lane. He even gave her credit, telling the world he had to thank Kristen in the engineering department for their car's extra speed. Kristen had smiled, but that smiled fade when she remembered what she'd face when she got home.

A date with Mathew.

Or not.

She could say no. She didn't have to do it. Not really.

But she *wanted* to. It surprised her how badly she longed to spend time in his arms.

When the team jet flew into Charlotte International hours later, she was wide-awake. They pulled up in front of the old terminal, Kristen staring at the lights inside the building and wondering who could be up this time of night. She dreaded the half-hour drive home. Thank God she had tomorrow off.

"You need a ride?" one of the guys asked as they waited for the rear door to be lowered. No fancy passenger jetway for them.

"Nah, I've got my car here."

The crewman nodded, his face looking pale beneath the jet's muted lighting.

Suddenly, she was exhausted. All she wanted to do was go home. And cry.

Because there was no escaping facts. She was going to date her boss. No denying it. No more trying to fight it. And when they started seeing each other it would create problems. She knew that like she knew the formula for calculating down force. People would talk. It didn't matter how good an engineer she was, there would always be those who would talk.

Let them, she told herself, spotting her car beneath a pool of light. One of the guys called a good-night. Kristen hardly noticed.

There were roses on top of her car. A big, huge vase of them.

Someone noticed, Mark, their race-day tire guy, said, "Wow. Someone really likes you."

They *were* beautiful, Kristen thought, plucking the card out from amidst the blooms.

Sorry I had to leave. Todd's victory is your victory, Kristen. Wish I could have been there with you. I'm so proud. If I could have, I'd have given these to you on Victory Lane. You deserve them.

See you tomorrow. Dress casual.

Matt.

She had to inhale against the sting in her eyes. Her fellow teammates were still getting into their cars and she didn't want them to see her crying.

Crying.

Because it wasn't until that moment that she realized how much she'd missed him, too. He bolstered her spirits. Made her feel part of the team. His confidence was *her* confidence. His belief in *her* made *her* believe in *herself.*

She wiped at her eyes and took a deep breath. She had to get home. She'd need to get her rest. Big day tomorrow.

Her first date with Matt.

DESPITE HER CONFIDENCE THAT she'd made the right decision, she was still a nervous wreck right up until Mathew knocked on the door. She knew it was him, had watched the limo pull up out in front of her condo. Had seen him emerge a few seconds later, looking supremely confident and handsome in his white polo shirt and jeans.

Oh, God, she didn't think she could do this.

He knocked again.

Kristen, you're being silly. Just open the door.

"Hello," was all he said when she finally faced him, his green eyes so piercingly intent it was like being shot with an arrow.

"Hello," she said back.

And then she was in his arms. She didn't expect it, wasn't sure who'd made the first move, but suddenly he was holding her and she was breathing in his scent and she was instantly *aware* of him, of how just being near him made her feel and think—

"I thought you'd call things off," he murmured. "You could, if you wanted to. I mean, I'd be disappointed, but you can."

"No," she said.

And it amazed her. He was usually such a measured and indifferent man, and yet when he held her he seemed out of control.

"Matt," she whispered softly.

"Ahem."

They drew apart.

Rob stood there, two vases of roses nearly obscuring his face. Kristen's cheeks turned as red as the blooms.

"I would have brought you more," Mathew said, "but Rob refused to carry more than two dozen."

"The damn things prick at your face," Rob grumbled, one of the blooms having gotten caught up in the cord that dangled from his ear.

Kristen laughed. She couldn't help it. He looked so silly. And she was so happy. So damn happy. The happiest she'd been since…well, in a long, long time.

"Just put them over there," Kristen said, motioning behind her. "I'll find a spot for them later." She smiled up at Mathew, who smiled back. "After my date."

"WHERE THE HECK ARE WE going?" she asked when they pulled into the Concord, North Carolina, airport.

"It's a surprise," he said, taking her hand and helping her from the limo.

She felt as giddy as a schoolgirl. This man, this wonderful, amazing man wanted her. She didn't know why, she didn't know how it'd happened, cripes, she didn't know where it would lead, but at that moment she didn't care.

"I had a feeling you'd say that," she said.

And so for the second time in her life she found herself escorted to the door of one of Matt's privately owned helicopters, one that took off practically the moment he sat next to her, her headset fitting snuggly against her head.

"Where's Rob?" she asked when she noticed the security guard hadn't followed.

"I gave him the night off," Matt said, putting on

a pair of sunglasses, the same glasses he'd been wearing the day they met. Very James Bond.

"Really?" she asked.

"I told him if anyone pointed a gun at me, I'd duck behind you first."

A joke, she thought with a surprised smile. He'd actually made a joke.

"He thought the idea was sound."

"Well, thank you very much."

"You're welcome."

But then she immediately sobered. "Are you really a target?"

He looked out. The helicopter had started to rise, the pilot tipping the bird to the left before darting away from the ground and turning south. Kristen held on, waiting.

"I was, a few years back," he finally said. "But the threat passed. Rob insisted I keep him on."

"Really?"

"Yes. And it was the best decision of my life. He does far more than just shadow me."

"Like?" Kristen asked, glancing out the window and seeing the helicopter's own shadow. It seemed to grow and then shrink as they passed over hills.

"He's also the security advisor for our planes."

Kristen's gaze shot back to Matt's. "Really."

"We were locking the doors to the cockpit long before Nine-Eleven."

"I had no idea."

Matt nodded, then glanced out the window. "Look," he said.

Kristen followed his gaze. The sun was starting to set, the sky such a mix of red, yellow and orange it looked like melted sherbet. "It's beautiful," she said.

They flew north east, the occasional town passing beneath them. "Can you give me a hint about where we're going?"

"No," he said. "That would spoil the surprise."

A surprise. When was the last time a man had done something nice for her? She felt a smile come to her face. When was the last time a man had done *anything* for her? And yet here was Matt, flying her off to goodness knew where and she was so excited her stomach tingled. Butterflies, she realized. She had butterflies in her stomach.

"Almost there," Matt said.

"Yeah?"

He nodded, smiling at her. She fought the urge to pinch herself.

"I can't wait for you to see what I have planned." Knowing Matt, it would be spectacular. He never did anything halfway.

But when the helicopter began to descend less than ten minutes later, she felt herself frown.

"That looks like—"

"It's a racetrack."

Her gaze snapped to his. "That's a road course."

"I know," he said with a wide smile. "I rented a car for you to drive."

"You did what?"

She didn't look half as happy as he'd thought she would.

"I rented a car," he said as the helicopter descended. "From the track's driving school. You have about an hour before we lose the light."

She just stared at him, her face unmoving.

"I thought you'd be pleased."

"Pleased?" she echoed.

"Yeah," he said as the helicopter landed. "Aren't you?"

But he could tell by the way she glanced out the window, by the way she sat up ramrod straight, that she wasn't pleased at all.

"I won't do it." She faced him, her face as hard as a headstone. "I won't do it, Matt."

"But you used to drive all the time."

"A long time ago."

"Don't you miss it?"

"No," she said firmly as the helicopter landed with a thud that jerked them both in their seats.

Matt looked outside. Rolling hills covered with trees spread far and wide. Single-story industrial buildings made of galvanized metal sat a few hundred yards away, a gray-haired man coming out of one and waving at them. The words Owen Wilson Driving School were painted on the front door.

"Kristen, please. I went to a lot of trouble—"

"I won't do it."

"Why not?" he asked, frustrated. Surely she wasn't afraid.

She ripped her headset off so the pilot couldn't hear them. He did the same. "Because I haven't set foot in a race car since the day my sister died."

"I realize that. But the gentleman I talked to said your leg won't be a problem with these cars."

"It's not my leg."

That took him aback for a moment.

"Take me home."

"Kristen—"

"Take me home," she said, shoving her headphones back on. Matt stared at her a second or two longer, noting the flush that stained her neck and cheeks and the tips of her ears. She was furious. And upset. And he knew he'd get nowhere with her right now.

Matt leaned forward and tapped the dark-haired pilot on the shoulder, saying, "Let's go," his plans obviously failed for the night.

The man nodded. The rotors changed pitch, and Matt glanced over at the gray-haired man who'd come out of the shop. He was staring at them in puzzlement. Matt knew how he felt.

"Where are we going?"

And now she was leaning forward again, her head looking left and right as they took off.

"My place."

She didn't say anything.

"Is that okay?"

She shrugged. "Suit yourself."

That was all he'd get out of her, he realized, her mood suddenly somber. And he was right, because a half hour later she muttered, "Let's get this over with," when they landed, the words like a punch to Mathew's gut.

CHAPTER TWENTY-TWO

"WHERE ARE YOU GOING?" MATHEW asked when she slipped from the helicopter, not even waiting until the pilot cut the rotors.

"I need a moment alone."

"Kristen," he said softly. But she ignored him, ducking low to clear the blades. She didn't want to go to his house, the light yellow structure with its clapboard windows looking strangely lonely a couple hundred yards away. She ran toward the lake, stopping near the water's edge, arms crossed.

"Kristen!" he called.

She almost kept going, but she couldn't outrun him forever. Behind them, she heard the helicopter lift off. Kristen glanced up and spotted the pilot at the controls just before he tipped the thing almost sideways, heading goodness knows where.

"We should talk about this," Matt said, his eyes suddenly a vivid green as the sun dropped lower. And then, as if a curtain had been drawn, it grew dark, the earth rotating into early dusk.

Kristen shivered.

"I would never have arranged for you to drive if I'd known this would be your reaction."

She crossed her arms in front of her, suddenly cold. "I thought you knew," she said softly, the sound of the helicopter fading into the distance. "I thought you understood."

"Understood what?" he asked.

She shook her head, silent for a moment.

"Kristen, please," he said, "talk to me."

She glanced out at the lake. The sweet scent of honeysuckle filled the air, crickets and frogs singing their song.

"Driving meant *everything* to me," she said. "*Everything.* And for you to take me to some racetrack, and then tell me to just climb in—"

She shook her head, emotions nearly choking her. "It was thoughtless."

"It was supposed to make you happy."

"Happy? How? By giving me a glimpse of something I can never have again? By reminding me of everything that I lost?"

"I had no idea you would think of it that way. I wanted to give you something special. Something no other man had given you."

"And you thought driving a race car would do that for me? That secretly, deep down inside, I wanted to drive open wheels again?"

"Yes."

"Well, I don't," she said, shaking her head, having to inhale sharply when she realized her eyes had begun to burn. "I don't ever want to race again. Not if I can't be the best. Not if I can't do it like I used to. Not if it means climbing out of that car on a foot that's numb, walking away on a leg that aches every single day, that's so misshapen and ravaged by scars half the men I've dated can't stand to look at it."

"Not me, Kristen. Not me."

"I don't want to talk about it. This was a mistake. I should go home."

"You're going to do it, aren't you?" he asked, catching her as she walked by. "You're going to use this as an excuse to walk away."

"No," she said. "I'm ending this before one of us gets hurt."

"Which one of us? You? Or me?"

"Does it matter?"

"Yes, it does matter, because I don't care if I get hurt. I'll take that chance if it means getting to know you."

"That's ridiculous."

"But you won't take that chance, will you?" he asked, his eyes suddenly narrowing. "You're afraid of ever getting close to someone again."

She froze.

"Afraid they'll leave you, like your sister left you."

She shook her head.

"Maybe even afraid that *you'll* have to do the leaving…one more time."

Her gaze snapped to his. "That's a horrible thing to say."

"But I can see in your eyes that it's true."

She turned on her heel. She wouldn't listen to another word.

"Kristen," he called again.

She ignored him, heading back to the house to call a cab. This "date" was officially over.

Maybe even afraid that you'll have to do the leaving.

It wasn't true. He was just saying that because he was mad.

But there was one bit of logic that she couldn't deny. She had left her family. She'd even left her mom. Not once had she been back. She never visited on Christmas. Heck, it was all she could do to pick up the phone and call on Thanksgiving.

"Rob?" she called when she opened the door, even though she knew he had the night off. "Are you there?"

He wasn't. Kristen stepped inside.

And froze.

You'll do the leaving…

She began to tremble.

You'll do the leaving.

"Oh, God," she moaned.

It was the house, so like her mom's—the one she'd left when Trina had died. The one she'd never gone back to, even when her father had passed away.

She'd been too much of a coward to attend her own father's funeral.

She clenched her hands.

Her mother had called her up, furious. Kristen had pleaded work, but she and her mom knew the truth.

She couldn't face the ghosts. Couldn't face a house without Trina and her dad.

"Kristen?"

She jumped.

"You don't have to be afraid," Mathew said behind her, his voice achingly tender. "I'm not going to leave."

"But, see, that's just it," she heard herself say. "This isn't about fear of losing you. This is about losing, period. About trying something and then failing. I failed as a sister and I failed even more as a daughter, and I just don't think I can stand to hurt someone again."

"Shh," he soothed, because suddenly she felt like crying. "Shh."

All he did was hold her, and rub her back, while she broke down for the first time in years. She cried for her sister, her beautiful, carefree little sis who'd been trying too hard to impress her on that fateful night. Who'd been teasing her that one day she might give Kristen a run for her money, but who'd never had the opportunity to grow beyond her sixteen years because Kristen had failed in her duty.

She cried for her father, who'd put so much faith in her and who she'd let down, first with Trina, and then later, when his heart started to fail.

God, she hadn't even visited him in the hospital.

"It's okay," he was saying. "It's going to be okay."

"No, it's not okay," she said, drawing back and wiping at her eyes. "Don't you see? I suck as a person. I hurt everyone around me. There's something wrong with me."

"There's nothing wrong," he said, stroking hair away from her face. "Kristen, there's nothing wrong with you. You were a young girl when everything happened. Too young to know how to handle things. Your parents should have known that. They should have tried harder to bring you back into the fold."

"This isn't my parents' fault.

"No," he said softly, his green eyes never leaving her own. "It's not. It's nobody's fault. That's what you have to remember."

Nobody's fault.

She wished it were true.

"Come on," he said when she started to shiver again. "Let's go. We'll start a fire. I'll make you a cup of hot cocoa. I hear it's good for calming people down. Nobody can cry and drink hot cocoa at the same time—or so Rob tells me."

She tried to smile, but it didn't work. "I don't want to drink hot cocoa."

"Tea?"

"I want you to make love to me."

A songbird broke into an aria outside. Kristen would forever associate that sound with this moment. For the first time in a long, long time she knew what she wanted.

Him.

"Please," she added, feeling so desperately needy all of a sudden she could barely breathe.

He stroked her cheek, his thumb lightly grazing her skin. "I wanted to make this night special. To take you out, not take you to bed."

"You *can* make this special," she said, pulling his head down to hers, his lips startlingly hot against her chilled flesh. "You can make love to me."

In the end he was the one who warmed her up, his hand reaching around her to draw her closer, his palm so hot against her that she gasped. Or maybe it was the feel of his tongue invading her mouth that made her gasp. She pressed against him, the apex of her thighs rubbing against him.

"Let's go upstairs," he said.

But she slipped her hand between them, stroking his chest.

"Let's go upstairs *now.*"

And then her hand was sliding into the waistband of his jeans. She felt elastic, slid a finger beneath that.

"Kristen," he gasped when she made contact.

She broke off the kiss, having lost patience, too. "Let's go," she said.

And they did.

IT WAS A NIGHT SHE'D NEVER forget. A night where Mathew showed her a man's touch could do more than arouse. It could soothe a woman. It could make her feel alive. It could make her feel beautiful. Because never, not once, did he comment on her leg. He touched her as if the scars weren't there. As if each leg was exactly the same. In his mind, maybe they were.

He made love to her all night, both of them dropping into an exhausted sleep near the early hours of the morning. It was exactly what Kristen needed, the emotional toll of the previous night having faded.

Nobody's fault.

Could it be true? Had she blamed herself all these years for nothing? Certainly she wasn't without blame. She *had* abandoned her old life, her family, after Trina's death. But after a night of Mathew holding her, telling her how special she was, how remarkable he thought her, and how nobody should blame themselves over the death of a sibling, she'd started to think, and maybe even believe, that it was time to move on.

Maybe even call her mother.

She glanced at the clock, sitting up suddenly. Noon. Wow. *Where was Mathew?*

She pulled on her clothes from the day before, glancing around the room while she dressed. She loved the old-fashioned pedestal sink and claw-foot tub. If she had any say in it, Matt wouldn't be tearing down *this* house. But that was a mighty big "if," she admitted, her fingers resting on the ancient railing that lined the narrow staircase leading to the floor below.

She heard noises in the kitchen, the hardwood floor squeaking under heavy footfalls. She could smell something cooking. Bacon, she realized, crossing the foyer to the back of the house.

"Hey there, sexy," she said to—Rob?

She drew up short.

"Wow. This must be my lucky day," he said. "I haven't been called sexy in a while."

"What are you doing here?" she asked.

"Mr. Knight asked me to look in on you," he said, his eyes filled with laughter. "I was making some bacon for when you got hungry."

She glanced around the kitchen. But it was just Rob. And for once he was wearing casual clothes.

Beige shorts and a white T-shirt. And then his words registered.

Mr. Knight asked me to look in on you.

"Did he leave?"

"The boss? Yeah. He had to run up to New York this morning."

Gone.

"He said he'd be back tonight," Rob said, turning back to his bacon and flipping it, the grease sizzling in the pan.

Kristin nodded, even though she knew Rob couldn't see her. Gone. "Did he say what time?"

Rob shrugged his shoulders, turned back to her. "Could be early, could be late. You never know with Mr. Knight."

"I'm surprised you didn't go with him."

"Today's my Sunday, even though it's technically Tuesday." And at her look of surprise he added, "I do get days off."

"And you're cooking that breakfast for me?"

"Actually, it's for lunch. And I'm cooking enough for both of us."

"I don't think I'm very hungry." Which was ridiculous. Her mouth watered, even if she did feel a little sick to her stomach. Was this how it would be with Matt? she wondered. Always jetting off?

"You sure you don't want some?" Rob asked, opening up a cabinet and taking down one of the antique plates. “Nothing like a BLT for brunch. I even think there’s some avocado in the fridge if you’re into amino acids.”

“No thanks,” she said. “I think I’ll just head home.”

But she’d only taken a couple steps when Rob called her back.

“Kristen, look,” he said, fork still in hand. “I know it’s really none of my business, but I can tell you’re upset. But you shouldn’t be. Mr. Knight is…” Rob waved the fork around as if he were conducting an orchestra. “Mr. Knight works hard. Really hard. That shouldn’t come as a surprise given all that he’s accomplished. He built his empire from the ground up. It’s his baby. Doesn’t mean he doesn’t care about you. Far from it. He really, really likes you.”

Likes?

Well, of course, Kristen, you’ve only been on one date.

“I’ve never seen him do so much jetting around to be with a girlfriend.”

Girlfriend. Why did the word feel like an insult? They *were* dating.

And he’d just left her high and dry after an evening of passion. She didn’t feel very much like a girlfriend. She felt like a call girl.

“He’ll be back tonight and then you guys can talk about his schedule. He probably would have talked to you about it this morning except he didn't want to wake you."

"Thanks, Rob."

"Now, you sure you don't want some bacon?" he asked, sounding like the Godfather with his Bronx accent. Or maybe one of the Godfather's henchmen.

"I'm sure," she said. "I'll grab something on the way home."

"You don't have to leave."

"Yes, I do," she said. "I, ah, I need to do some housework and stuff. I'll give Matt a call."

Maybe.

"Ten-four," Rob said, turning back to his bacon.

But she ended up having to wait for Rob, anyway. Kristen's irritation mounted when she realized her car wasn't there and Rob would have to drop her off at her condo. She just wanted to get away. And think.

When she finally got home, she did exactly that. Once she took a shower she headed out to the lake, which was practically at her front door. Nothing but the best for KEM employees. She'd have taken the job for the condo alone, not that she spent a lot of time in it.

That was what bothered her, she realized, her leg aching a bit today—another reason she wanted some exercise. Her days off were so few and far between that she was really disappointed Matt hadn't woken her up to tell her he was leaving. She'd have begged him to stay. Or maybe convinced him to let her go with him. Or something. After the emotional toll of the previous evening, she didn't really want to be alone. But after Rob's little speech, she doubted Matt would have stayed, anyway. His business was more important, and that hurt. *That* was the sickness in her stomach. She wanted to spend time with him, but that seemed to be a precious commodity, one he didn't want to share with her.

It was a beautiful day, bright and sunny and sparkly. It must have rained in the early hours because she still could smell moisture in the air. The ash trees that rimmed the lake looked freshly washed, their leaves a dark jade in shadow and a warm, lemony-green where the sun shone through. She found a bench beneath some shade trees and sat, staring out at water that glittered as brightly as water crystals atop snow.

So pretty. Matt would have thought so, too. And then she wondered if she was being too possessive. Maybe she was overreacting to his disappearing act this morning.

She wished she could talk to her mom.

That thought was such an aberration that it made her jerk upright. Then again, it was probably just a holdover from the previous evening. She had some serious issues on her mind, and at the top of her list was how to mend things with her mother.

"Penny for your thoughts."

There he was. And the funny thing was, it didn't even surprise her that it was Todd.

"What are you doing here?" she asked, making room for him on the bench, dapples of sunlight spotting his rust-colored shirt.

"What do you think I'm doing here?"

"Looking for a condo to buy?" she asked.

"No," he said, smiling. He looked different away from the track, Kristen thought. More relaxed. Less stressed. The lines around his brown eyes were softened, his black hair a little less neat. "I came to see you."

"Oh, yeah?" she asked, not ashamed to admit she was glad to see him.

Maybe too glad.

"I missed you."

That made her heart stop, made her look away and her cheeks to flush with embarrassment. "Todd, I—"

"Not that way, you nut," he said, shaking his head. "Jeez. You think I'm jerk enough to come on to you when you're dating Matt?"

"What makes you think I'm dating Matt?" she asked.

"Those roses didn't come from me."

"No," she said, surprised he'd heard about them. Then again, nothing stayed a secret in this industry, she was quickly learning. "But you don't have any reason to send me flowers."

He looked as if he wanted to say something, but in the end he must have changed his mind because he said, "Guess not. But am I right? Did they come from the boss man?"

She nodded, wondering what that look had been.

"So, the two of you dating?"

She thought about waking up alone and said, "I don't know." At this point it was possible she was a one-night stand.

"So what were you thinking about?"

"How'd you know I was here?"

"I took a chance." He leaned forward, turning so that they were practically eye-to-eye. "So?" he prompted.

She shrugged. "Actually, I was thinking about my mom."

"You two close?"

"No," she said. "Not since—"

"The accident," he finished for her.

She nodded, wiped a strand of hair away from her face. "The thing is, I've never really had any close friends."

"Me, neither," he admitted. "I've always been too busy. And nowadays I've got to be careful. I'm hearing about more and more drivers whose stories have been sold by supposed friends. Used to be nobody cared about stock car racers, but those days have passed."

"That's too bad."

"Yeah, it is, and it makes me especially grateful for my family."

"You have siblings?" she asked, flicking a bug off her knee.

"Three sisters."

"Really?" she said, thinking how lucky he was. All she'd had was Trina.

Trina.

There it came again: the ache, the fear, the worry. Her face must have fallen, because he placed a hand on her knee. There was nothing sexual about the gesture, yet Kristen almost flinched away.

"Call your mom."

"I can't," she said, having to force the words past the lump in her throat. He was rubbing her knee, squeezing it, trying to reassure her without words that he understood.

"All you have to do is pick up the phone," he said.

"It's not that easy."

"Of course it is," he said. "I'll even dial the number."

"No, Todd."

"Come on."

She stood up, such a mix of emotions running through her she hardly knew what to do. Suddenly she wanted to leave. She *needed* to leave. "Thanks for coming by," she said. "And congratulations on winning Sunday."

"Kristen—"

"You did a great job."

"Kristen," he said again, walking toward her. "I'm just trying to help."

"Yes, I know." And that was the problem. It should be Matt consoling her. Matt stroking her leg. Matt saying these things to her. Not Todd.

She shook her head. "See you at the shop."

"Kristen, wait."

She kept walking.

He stepped in front of her and placed his hands on her shoulders. "I'm sorry," he said. "I'm just trying to help. To be a friend. I shouldn't have pushed."

"It's okay." Because he was right. She *should* call. She just didn't know what she'd say.

Hi, Mom. It's your long-lost daughter. Long time no see.

"Come here," he said, pulling her into his arms.

Just yesterday it had been Matt doing that. Matt holding her while she'd cried her eyes out.

Now hugging Todd felt like hugging a sibling.

"You do what you want to do," he said, stroking her back. There was nothing sexual about it, but Kristen still felt the need to pull away…for other reasons.

"Thanks, Todd," she said. "You are…a…a good friend. And I've, well, I've got to go."

She hurried away so quickly he'd have been rude to try and stop her. He didn't, and Kristen stepped inside her condo feeling nothing but relief. She couldn't keep meeting up with Todd. He confused her, and he made her think things she shouldn't be thinking.

But she would not betray Matt, despite his defection. She'd give him time to explain, and then she'd ask him to never leave her like that again. She *needed* him.

And that was the most disturbing thought of all.

CHAPTER TWENTY-THREE

MATT CALLED.

She almost didn't pick up the phone, but she knew it'd be childish if she didn't and so she reluctantly answered.

"Rob said you're upset," he said without preamble.

"Who? Me?" she asked, because now that she had him on the phone she realized how silly she'd been.

"Don't lie to me, Kristen. Rob's excellent at reading faces. You were upset that I left this morning without saying goodbye."

She clutched the phone, then felt her grip suddenly loosen. "I was," she said, sitting down on the bulbous edge of her off-white couch. "I don't know why, but I was." She picked up a decorative pillow, hugged it to her stomach.

"You thought we'd had a one-night stand."

"I—" She played with a tassel on one of the pillow's corners. "All right, yeah, I suppose the thought did cross my mind."

"Kristen," he said softly. "After everything we

talked about last night, I would have thought you'd realize you're not the kind of woman a man has a one-night stand with."

No?

"You're not," he said, as if hearing her silent doubt.

"Thank you."

"Can I see you tonight?"

"Hmm," she said, suddenly in better spirits. "Let me check my schedule."

Soft chuckles filled her ear. "*Clear* your schedule."

"Is that an order?"

"It is."

But when his limo pulled up in front of her house later that same day, she was still raw with emotion. Their physical intimacy of the night before mixed with the emotional turmoil of this morning. Her hands shook as she opened the door.

"Still mad at me?" he asked, thrusting a dozen red roses her way—these ones wrapped in plastic.

"The local florist must love you," she said, inhaling their scent.

"Are you?"

"No," she said, realizing the moment she looked into his eyes that everything would be all right. "Of course not."

"Too bad," he said softly, pulling her into his arms, the blooms crushed between them. "Because I was going to try and make it up to you."

Her whole body flushed. She took a deep breath, steeled herself not to fall at his feet in a puddle of goo.

Damn, he was gorgeous.

Eyes as green as grape vines stared down at her. His hair was mussed, his shirt pulled taut over a chest she'd kissed and stroked and—

"I missed you," he said softly.

"I missed y—"

Her words were crushed beneath the onslaught of his lips. He tasted of coffee. Smelled like citrus. Felt hot as molten metal. And he was hers, she thought, running her free hand up his arm, loving how hard it felt, how sculpted, how masculine.

He pulled back. A few petals fell to the floor.

"I'll buy you new ones tomorrow," he aid.

"I don't care about the flowers."

She only cared about *him.*

"No?" he asked softly, still holding her.

"No," she said, placing the flowers on a side table. "Kiss me again."

He did, her body going slack as he warmed her in the same way he'd heated her up the night before. Only now it was better. She knew what it was like to be stroked by him. Knew how it would feel to have him pressed into her, to have his body—

"Take me to your bedroom," he said.

Yes, because if he did that, just for a little bit she could forget…

"Is that another order from the boss?"

"You know it is."

"Hmm," she murmured between kisses. "I never refuse a direct order."

SHE LEARNED OVER THE NEXT week that every time Matt disappeared, he would track her down wherever she might be, greet her with a dozen red roses and offer her dinner…or something else. Since he went up to New York just about every day, Kristen's condo began to resemble a float from the Rose Parade. She appreciated that he tried to make it up to her, but he was away more than he was at home.

She didn't see Todd much, either, although that was good because she still hadn't called her mom. She knew he'd give her grief about that, and she dreaded bumping into him again for fear he'd ask her.

So a few days later, she called from work.

She really wasn't expecting an answer. Truth be told, she'd waited until around lunchtime in the hope that her mom would be out, but she picked up on the second ring—wouldn't you know it. Kristen stared at the phone in shock and then hung up. Her actions were childish, she knew. It was her mother on the other end. Sure, there might be skeletons in the closet, but she was still her flesh and blood.

So when she called back a few minutes later and

her mom answered a second time, she immediately said, "Hi, Mom."

Silence. Kristen waited. But the only thing she could hear was the sound of someone typing the next cubicle over.

"How are you?" she added.

"Fine," her mother said coldly.

And that was it. That was the reason Kristen didn't like to call. Because even though she knew it was her fault her mom was so bitter, the truth of the matter was, it killed Kristen to hear her sounding that way.

"Oh, ah, good," Kristen said, thinking it was obviously far too late to mend broken fences.

"What's the matter?" she asked. "Do you need money or something?"

Her cheeks heated. "No, Mom. I was just calling to see how you are."

"I see."

"So, ah, what have you been up to?"

"Kristen, I've got to go," her mom said. "I have a lunch date that I'm late for."

"Oh? Are you seeing someone?"

"Nobody you'd know," she answered.

She was right. It had been so long since Kristen had been back home—ten years—she doubted anybody in their small Midwestern town would recognize her.

"Well, all right then. I guess I'll just talk to you later."

"Goodbye, Kristen."

And that was it. That was the way their conversations always ended. "Damn it," she muttered after setting down the phone. She should have never called. She should let bygones be bygones. Leave things the way they were.

Except she couldn't.

Her life had changed. She was tired of running, tired of trying to expunge the memories of her past—tired of pretending she didn't care. She would never forget. She knew she had a lot to atone for, but with Matt by her side she really thought she could do it. She wanted her mom to move on with her.

"YOU SHOULD GO VISIT HER."

Kristen looked across the table at Matt. They were in a tiny restaurant that had been built in the corner of one of Charlotte's downtown high-rises. The soothing strains of a Spanish guitar drifted through the air, the smell of flour tortillas and spicy salsa stirring Kristen's taste buds.

"I'm not so sure." she said, savoring the salty tortilla chips.

It had been two days since she'd seen Matt. Two days of missing him and wishing he'd hurry and finish up his business. But it didn't look as if that would happen anytime soon. Tonight's dinner was a going-away dinner of sorts. He'd be gone for a few days next week and she was trying hard not to let her disappointment show. She'd asked to go along, but he'd be working long hours and he didn't think it'd be worth her while. Plus, he'd pointed out that taking time off work to fly away with the boss might not go over very well with her fellow employees. He had a point.

"Do you think she'd want me to visit?"

"Don't tell her," he said, taking a bite, too, the crunchy chip crackling apart. "Just show up on her doorstep."

She didn't think she could do that. What if her mom slammed the door in her face?

"In fact, I'll go with you."

Kristen's chin jerked up. "You will?"

He leaned back in his chair, looking superbly handsome in his denim shirt and tan slacks. More than one feminine eye had followed his progress through the restaurant. Of course, that might have something to do with Rob trailing in their wake, the big security guy sitting at a table a few feet away.

"Of course I will," he said, leaning forward and taking her hands. "I know I haven't been there for you lately, but that's going to change after next week. We'll get all this nastiness with my board of directors over with and I'll be able to spend more time with you." He smiled, and his eyes looked so green by candlelight—as green as sea glass, worn smooth and soft by ocean currents.

"That'd be great," she said.

He collected her hands in his. Kristen felt her face heat at the look in his eyes. "I think I'm falling in love with you."

She nearly choked on her chip.

"When we're together, Kristen, I feel different. More alive. More happy, and lonely whenever you're not with me."

"Oh, Matt."

"To be honest, I've been thinking I need to meet your mother, anyway. Introduce myself to the woman who gave birth to such a remarkable person."

Damn it. He was going to make her cry. "Then we'll go," she said.

THAT NIGHT THEY MADE LOVE with an intensity Kristen would never forget, and when he held her in his arms later, she knew it was already too late for her. She'd fallen in love with Mathew Knight. But that was okay, she reassured herself. Matt was a wonderful man. Yeah, he was busy, but that was to be expected given that he ran a Fortune 500 company.

She threw herself into her work while he was gone, counting the days until they left for Oklahoma, although, to be honest, she wasn't really looking forward to their trip. There was a very strong possibility that her mom wouldn't be happy to see her. But Kristen knew she needed to take the chance. Suddenly it was important to her to mend fences.

"So, I hear you're going home to Oklahoma?" Todd said to her one day.

"How did you hear about that?" Kristen asked, pausing in the hallway. She'd only seen Todd a few times since that day by the lake, but that was because he'd been avoiding her. Probably because she'd acted like a complete freak that day, she figured. So she strove to be extra friendly, giving him a wide smile.

"Word travels fast in this building," he said, looking the consummate driver in his dark blue polo shirt with his sponsor's name over the pocket. He must have had an interview in the building.

"We're leaving tomorrow."

"Good. I think it's a smart move."

"Todd," she said. "About that day by the lake—"

"Nah," he said. "No need to talk about it. Popping in was a mistake. I should have called you first or something."

"You don't need to do that," she said, hoping they could be friends. With things having become so serious between her and Matt, that's all they could ever be.

"Just the same, I'll call before I come over next time."

If there *was* a next time. Matt was talking about Kristen moving in. She doubted he'd welcome his driver over uninvited. He'd already made a few comments about Todd hanging around her more than he should.

"Good luck," he said.

"Yeah. And good luck this weekend."

"You're not going?"

She shook her head. "I'm working on some new stuff right now. Hopefully I'll have everything worked out before Chicago."

"I'm sure whatever you do, it'll help."

"Thanks, Todd."

"See ya, Kristen."

"See ya," she echoed, wondering what would have happened if she'd encouraged Todd—

Whoa! Wrong direction to go with her thoughts. They would never have made it as a couple. He was too…Todd, and she was just plain-Jane Kristen.

"Kristen McKenna to Mr. Knight's office, please."

Kristen looked up at the round speaker above her head, as if she'd see the face of Maddie, who'd paged her. Matt was here? Really? Wow, that was the first time in weeks. Lately the only time he'd been in Charlotte was in the evenings after flying down from New York.

"Hey, Maddie," she said to his receptionist.

"Oh, hey, Kristen. Go right on in."

"In" was a massive suite in a corner of the building. Double doors to the right of Maddie's desk opened into a conference room with burgundy carpet and a dark-oak conference table that would seat twelve. Beyond that was another set of doors. And Matt. It dawned on her that she'd never been to his office before. That was strange. Then again, given how often he traveled—

"Kristen," he said, looking up from the papers he'd been studying.

The office was an homage to all the different race teams the previous owner had fielded over the years. Poster-size photos hung on the wall, some of the cars recognizable even to Kristen. There were no trophy cases—those were downstairs in the main lobby—but she knew there was one trophy in particular that was missing. The championship.

"What's up?" she asked, wondering if she should go over and kiss him. They were in his office and so she felt a little out of place, which was a strange way to feel, she admitted.

"First of all, what did Todd want?"

Her brows jerked upward. He'd seen that? How?

"He was just wishing me luck in Oklahoma." Matt didn't look like he believed her, but what else could he say? It was true.

"Speaking of Oklahoma…"

"What?"

"I have some bad news."

And she knew. She knew just from the look on his face what he was going to say. "You can't make the trip."

He came around the side of his desk. He looked very corporate today in his fitted dress shirt and pants. He must have come straight from New York. "Something's come up."

Yeah. It was always something.

"My board's threatening to sell their shares to one of my competitors. I may have given up controlling interest of FFL when I decided to 'retire,' but it would make my life hell to have to work with a hostile corporation whose ultimate goal would be to drive FFL into the ground."

"What?" she asked, forgetting her disgruntlement momentarily.

"Sometimes companies will take over a competitor."

"That's not right."

"That's big business." He shrugged.

She looked away, knowing there wasn't a whole lot she could say. But her disappointment felt almost physical in its intensity.

"I'm sorry, Kristen," he said, pulling her into his arms.

"I know you are."

"But if I don't fly up to New York, things will get ugly."

"Would that be so bad?" she asked softly.

He drew back. "You don't really mean that."

"No. Of course not." But maybe she did.

"Can you postpone your trip?" he asked.

She could have, easily. But something made her stick to her guns. "I'd rather do it now."

"You can still use the corporate jet."

"No," she said. "I'll fly commercial."

"That's ridiculous."

"No really. I can deadhead on one of your planes. I *am* still an employee of FFL. Sort of."

"But it'd be so much easier to use the jet."

And it'd be so much easier to face her mother with him at her side, but that wasn't going to happen. "I'd really rather fly commercial," she said.

He stared at her a long time, his green eyes never wavering. "You look upset."

She was, but she wouldn't let him know it. "Just a little disappointed," she said, lifting up on her toes to give him a kiss. "But you can meet my mom later."

"Thanks for understanding."

She bit her lip. Nodded.

"You want to go to dinner tonight?"

"No. I have to pack."

He nodded, and she could tell it was his turn to

be disappointed. Well, good. She was tired of being the only one with knots in her stomach.

"I'll see you after, then," he said.

But would she? she wondered. "Yeah, after," she echoed.

CHAPTER TWENTY-FOUR

SHE SLUNG A BAG full of books over her shoulder, took one last longing glance at the lake outside her condo and headed off to the airport. She wished she could stay home instead of flying off to Oklahoma. She wished she could stay in bed, reading beneath the covers, feeling safe and secure when the thunderstorms rolled in later in the afternoon. She wished Matt was with her.

"My, my, genius. You sure look miserable."

Her head flicked up.

"Would you like a razor to slit your wrists?"

"Todd," she said, stopping at the end of the path that led to her front door. "You know, I'm beginning to think you're spying on me."

He smiled enigmatically. "Maybe I am."

She shook her head, her ponytail flicking her on the side of the head. "Do you mind?" she said when he blocked her path. "I have a plane to catch."

"We're taking my jet."

"Excuse me?"

He gave her his patented Todd's-so-cute smile. "I'm taking you to Oklahoma."

"You are not," she said, totally convinced he was joking.

"No, really. I am."

"But...that's impossible. Well, I mean, I suppose it could be done, but why the heck would you want to do that?"

He didn't answer right away, and Kristen grew uncomfortable beneath his scrutiny. And it wasn't because she was thinking he looked handsome in the early-morning light, either. Sure, his black hair was mussed and little-boy charming. And he looked nicely casual in his jeans and dark green, button-down shirt. Good. She liked him better when he wasn't in Mr. Star Race Car driver attire. But that wasn't what made her edgy. There was a look in his brown eyes, one that seemed to pin her to her spot like a butterfly on display.

"I want to take you because I'm your friend," he said, his eyes never wavering. "Because I feel I owe it to you. Because friends do things for friends and I happen to know this is pretty important to you and so I'm thinking you might need someone, especially seein' as how you told me the other day you don't *have* any friends."

Kristen released a breath she'd been completely unaware that she'd been holding. "That's sweet of you, Todd," she said. "But I don't think it's a good idea."

"Too bad."

"Todd—"

"We're going together and that's that. I've got my jet all fueled up and ready, my pilot's at the airport—I even asked him to bring snacks. We're going together, even if all I do is drop you off at your mom's house."

"This is ridiculous."

"No, it's not," he said, stepping forward and taking her hand. She tried tugging it away, but he wouldn't let her, the two of them engaging in a tug-of-war until Todd said, "Come on, get in the car."

"What are you going to do? Kidnap me?"

"If I have to, yes."

She finally wrested her hand away. "I appreciate the offer, Todd, I really do. But Matt wouldn't be happy if you went with me, and I—"

"Why?"

She blinked and shook her head a little, remembering the possession in his eyes the other day. "What do you mean 'why'?"

"Why would he mind?" Todd asked. "If Mr. Knight offered to take me someplace, would you get upset?"

"You're a man. I'm a woman going off with another man. It's not the same thing."

"Then don't tell him."

"I can't do that," she said, stepping around him, book bag just about banging him in the foot.

"Kristen, come on," he said, stepping into place alongside of her. "Let me do this for you."

She unlocked her Ford Fusion with a push of a button. "Todd, I appreciate the offer, but—"

He turned her toward him, his hands lightly grasping her shoulders. "Kristen, do you really want to do this on your own?"

No. She hated the thought of flying all the way to Oklahoma by herself. There and back in one day. But that was beside the point. She needed to do this.

"Well?" he echoed.

"I can't. It's a kind offer," she said quickly. "And I appreciate it a lot, but I can't."

"Then I'll meet up with you at your mom's front door."

She felt her eyes go wide. "What? Don't be ridiculous. You don't even know where she lives."

"Twelve seventy-eight Howe Street."

"Oh...my...gosh. How the heck did you find that out?"

"Doesn't matter. What matters is that you should know I'm prepared to go to any lengths to see you through this, even if it means flying across the country and knocking on the door of a woman I don't know."

He would, too. She could see it in his eyes.

"Matt's not going to like this."

His hands moved from her shoulders to her face. "Then don't tell him," he repeated softly. "Now, come on," he said, taking the black bag off her shoulder. "My pilot's waiting."

SHE CALLED MATT AND LEFT him a message. That, at least, assuaged some of the guilt. But what was she to do? She knew Todd, and she knew he'd do exactly as he threatened and so catching a ride with him to Oklahoma seemed like the prudent thing to do—maybe not the smartest, but prudent.

And she couldn't complain about her accommodations.

She knew drivers made lots of money, but she didn't expect Todd's jet to be every bit as luxurious as Matt's—just on a smaller scale. The Lear seated six, but the inside looked more like somebody's living room than a private plane. A buff-colored leather couch hugged one side of the fuselage. Across from that were two seats that were more like armchairs, a table in the middle of them. She chose to sit in one of those. Todd took the other.

"You gotta admit," Todd said, "this is better than flying commercial."

"Oh, it is…it is," she said, looking out the window, her ponytail catching on the back of the seat. The pilot had started to taxi practically the moment they took their seats.

"Remember, we've got food in the galley, too, in case you're hungry."

"No, thanks. I'm fine."

"Coffee?"

"No thanks," she said.

"Water?"

"Todd, I'm okay."

"You don't look okay. You look worried."

She wasn't. Was she? "I just can't help but think Matt's going to freak out when he hears you and I flew to Oklahoma together."

"Why? We're just friends."

"*You* know that and *I* know that, but I really think I should have stuck to my original plans."

"Kristen," he said. "If you were my girlfriend and I was too busy to take you somewhere, I would feel better if I knew you were making that trip with someone else."

Too busy to take you somewhere.

Was that how Todd saw it? She frowned, the plane pausing at the end of a runway. Kristen leaned back in her seat in preparation for the inevitable thrust of takeoff, remembering the first time she'd done that with Matt.

Waa-hoo.

Yeah, she thought as the jet's engine's revved.

"Matt's dealing with some serious stuff right now. One of his competitors is trying to put him out of business."

"I didn't mean that the way it sounded," Todd said. "I know Matt's a good guy. I just think I'd do things differently."

Maybe he would. But he must understand that Matt had his priorities. She did.

Didn't she?

THEY ARRIVED BEFORE NOON, Todd asking her yet again if she was hungry. She wasn't. The thought of eating made her want to vomit.

So they drove toward the outskirts of Beaumonte, Oklahoma in the rental car Todd had reserved for them. He'd thought of everything, actually. He'd even programmed the directions to her mom's house in the car's GPS. They were quiet the whole way over, Todd seeming to sense that she was in no mood for idle chitchat. As her eyes slid over the familiar countryside—rolling hills, pastures of alfalfa, numerous small towns—a multitude of emotions overcame her. A sense of comfort, the single- and double-story brownstone buildings like old friends from her childhood. Nostalgia when they passed her high school on the outskirts of town. But most of all, an intense jolt of sorrow when they neared the area where her life had fallen apart, a narrow stretch of highway with a tall elm tree alongside the road. The only tall tree for miles.

And they'd hit it.

Todd clutched her hand.

She glanced over at him in surprise. She wondered if he knew where it had happened. It wouldn't surprise her if he did.

The tree still bore the wound, the bark missing from the trunk like a picked-at scar. The shoulder of the road had long since been repaired, but Kristen's life was far from that.

"It's okay," Todd said softly, the GPS system telling them to turn on Howe Street. It wasn't much more than a gravel road. Years ago the county had come out and paved it, but the concrete they'd used had long since broken down, making it look more like a jigsaw puzzle than an actual street. And the closer they got, the higher her pulse climbed, galloping along like a frightened pony. They passed the old maple tree she and her sister used to climb on hot summer nights, the grass field behind it still overgrown and wild. And there was old man Tillman's farm on the right. His cows were long since gone, the barbed wire fence that used to keep them contained tangled and broken as if one day the cows had staged a revolt and run for the hills. They passed the Rienards next on the left and then the mailbox with 1278....

She swallowed.

Her mom's. She felt tears fill her eyes as she stared at the place that held so many happy memories…and so many bad ones. To the right of the two-story clapboard was the old shed they'd used to work on her cars. First go-karts, then open wheels. They'd spent so many nights out there, her dad used to joke that they should just install a kitchen and a couple of beds.

Daddy, I miss you.

Todd paused before turning onto her mom's short gravel driveway. Jeez, she didn't think she could do it.

"Kristen," Todd said. "You can't run forever."

He sounded like Matt. Were the sins of her past so obvious to everyone?

Kristen stared at the off-white house. "Pull in next to the shed."

Todd smiled, gave her an encouraging pat on the leg and Kristen admitted she was glad he'd come.

Her mom's car was nowhere in sight. Of course, she had no idea what her mom even drove these days. For a half second she found herself hoping nobody would be home. She'd leave a note, she thought, shutting the rental car's door. She'd come back later.

It still smelled the same.

The scent of her mom's flowers—roses, daisies, lilies—nearly drove her back into the car.

"Let's go," Todd said, placing a hand on her back.

She hesitated a moment. Later she wouldn't remember climbing the five steps to the front door. She wouldn't remember lifting her hand to knock. All she would remember was the door opening, her mom answering less than ten seconds after she knocked, the look on her face one of astonishment and incredulity.

"Hello, Kristen," she said softly.

It was that same thing she always said on the phone—and it sounded the same, too, the words in a monotone voice. But it was the look in her mother's eyes that made Kristen take a small step back, that made her own eyes fill up with tears, because there was joy in those eyes, something she would never have seen if she hadn't been standing in front of her.

"Hello, Mom," she said.

They stood for a moment, Kristen thinking that was as far as they'd get, that perhaps she'd imagined the softness she'd seen. She took a chance then, though it was one of the hardest things she'd ever had to do. She moved forward, stepped into the house and opened her arms.

Her mom hesitated. Then they were hugging and Kristen was crying, and saying, "I've missed you, Mom. Gosh, I've missed you so damn much."

"Kristen," her mom said, her arms loose at first,

then tighter and tighter. "Kristen," she said again, and this time her voice was soft and seemingly filled with wonder. "Kristen," she said one final time.

TODD LEFT THEM ALONE. But as he turned away, he couldn't help the smile that came to his face. So far, everything had gone according to plan. It had taken a little bit of convincing to get her to use his jet, but he'd done it. Now if he could just get the rest of the day to go as smoothly, Mathew Knight would be nothing but a distant memory by the time they got back to Concord.

He looked around, surprised by what he saw. For some reason he had expected Kristen to have grown up in the suburbs, not out in the sticks like this. But maybe that's what drew him to her. He was the son of an Idaho potato farmer, and he'd grown up in much the same environment. In fact, he would bet his Michigan winnings that in that detached garage he'd find…

He opened up the swinging door, dust motes preceding a gust of heat. Ah. Just as he suspected. Inside was a car, obviously Kristen's mom's, an old Buick that'd seen better days. But along the walls, on shelves built into the garage's sides, were trophies and banners and photos. The banners were from races, a few of them stretching almost the entire length of the wall. The pictures were of

Kristen. He squinted his eyes. There was a window set into the back wall, the dirty glass allowing muted light to shine onto the equally dusty pictures.

Kristen when she was six or seven, standing next to a man who must have been her father, both of them wearing proud smiles and sharing the task of holding a trophy.

Kristen behind the wheel of a go-kart, her face completely shielded by her helmet, her tiny body leaning to the right as she rounded a turn.

Kristen, older now, standing by a sprint car, the name McKenna Construction on the aluminum wing that hung suspended over the car.

The next photo showed a teenage Kristen standing in front of a bigger car—an F3 similar to those driven at the Indy 500. The Kristen in the photo was a younger version of herself, right down to the big blue eyes and mouse-blond hair. And that must be Trina, he thought, something tugging at his insides as he stared at the carefree girl standing next to her. Crap, no wonder Kristen felt so bad. He felt bad just looking at the photo and knowing that she'd never made it past her teenage years.

"What are you doing?"

Todd glanced over his shoulder, seeing Kristen standing in the garage's opening. "Checking out what must have been your shop," he said casually, knowing by the sound of her voice that she was bothered to find him there. "You were a cute little kid."

"That was a long time ago," she said. She looked so wrung out by emotion, Todd was amazed at how hard he had to fight the urge to take her into his arms. The lashes around her blue eyes were rimmed by red, and her cheeks wore the stain of someone who'd recently cried.

"You should be proud of your past," he said. He knew he was. How many other drivers could claim their girlfriends raced open wheels? Not that Kristen was his girlfriend. Yet.

"I am proud of it," she said, tipping up her chin.

"Come on in here and tell me about these photos."

"Actually, I'd rather go back inside."

He thought about insisting, knew the moment wasn't right and said, "Let me just close this up," not wanting to pressure her. He shut the garage with one last look at the photos and trophies, thinking what a shame her driving career had ended so abruptly.

"I can't believe she left that stuff out here," Kristen muttered, the words spoken so softly he wasn't sure he was supposed to hear.

"Maybe she likes looking at it."

"She kept my room intact, too."

"Yeah?"

She nodded, tucking away a lock of hair that had slipped free from her ponytail. "Everything," she said. "From my National Karting Championship trophy to my fire suits."

"Now that stuff I'd like to see."

"Maybe later," she said.

"Whenever you're ready."

She paused just at the bottom of the steps to her mother's porch, her big blue eyes huge. She looked hauntingly beautiful to him then. Not classically so. She wasn't even cute. But she was *gorgeous* to him.

"Thanks for bringing me here, Todd."

"You're welcome," he said softly, his heart pounding.

"I couldn't have done it without you."

"I'm glad I was here for you," he said, his hands tingling from the effort it took not to touch her. "Have you talked to Matt?" he was unable to resist asking because, damn it, she needed to remember that it was her "boyfriend" who had let her down.

"He's in a meeting," she said.

"Isn't he always?" Todd asked.

Kristen shrugged and turned back toward the house.

"Kristen," he said. She paused, then turned back to him. With her standing on the middle step, their two heads were level. "Why do you put up with it?"

"Excuse me?"

"Why don't you stand up for yourself? Tell Matt you need him. Make him come with you."

"Todd, now's not a good time to be making demands on Matt."

"Yeah, but when does it stop? When does he realize that he needs to be there for you, too?"

"He knows I need him."

He clutched her hands, and it was so nice, and yet so bitterly unsatisfying to just hold her hands. "Kristen, I know Matt's business is important to him. I know he's going through some serious shit right now. But I blew off an appearance and a sponsor's dinner tonight to be here with you."

"You *what?*"

He clenched her hands tighter. "And you know what? I didn't care *who* I had to piss off. I'd risk losing my sponsor, my lifeblood, my ride, just to be here with you."

"Todd, you're not saying what I think you're saying, are you?"

Cripes, he didn't know. All he knew was that when he stared at her, something inside him burned. He'd never felt this way toward a woman before. Never.

"I'm saying you deserve better," he said. "You deserve a man who wants to be there for you."

"Like you?"

He almost said yes, almost pulled her to him right then and there, but he held back. "No," he lied. "I'm not saying that. Someone…else. Someone who cares for you." *As much as I do.*

"Matt cares for me."

"Does he?" he asked, wondering if he was fighting a losing battle. But Todd never gave up on battles. He might lose a skirmish, but he never, *ever* lost a war.

"Tell me something, Kristen," he said. "If you were in Matt's shoes, if you had some important things going on in your life, say you were invited by NASA to engineer one of their shuttles, but you couldn't go because Matt needed you—really, truly needed you—would you go to NASA?"

"Of course not."

"Then why is Matt at NASA right now? Why isn't Matt here for *you?*"

CHAPTER TWENTY-FIVE

WHY ISN'T MATT HERE for you?

Todd's words echoed in her ears the whole way home.

He's not here because he's worried about losing his business.

But would it have hurt to spare her a day? Just one day out of his busy life? She understood that he had important matters on his mind, but so did she. Surely he could have spared an afternoon?

"Todd says he's cool with having dinner here, too," she told her mother, stepping into her kitchen and indicating Todd behind her.

Her mom looked up, a smile on her face. Kristen felt her throat tighten all over again. Mom was so much older now. The black hair was liberally sprinkled with gray, but it was pulled into her schoolmarm bun—something Kristen used to tease her about when she was a kid because her mom really was a schoolteacher—up on her head in a tight little knot.

"That's great, honey."

But she was still pretty. Her mom had always been beautiful.

"Todd," she said. "This is my mom. Mom, this is Todd Peters."

"Nice to meet you, Todd," she said, shaking his hand politely.

"Todd's a race car driver," Kristen said.

"Really?" she asked. "Kristen used to drive race cars."

Her mom's eyes dimmed all of a sudden. And there it was again, the past that lay between them. But they couldn't keep pussyfooting around the issue. So Kristen sat down on a rickety chair, saying breezily, "And I was good at it, too, wasn't I, Mom?"

Her mom caught her eyes and seemed to realize what she was doing because she straightened her shoulders, pasted a smile on her face and said, "Yes, she was. Very, *very* good."

And that was that. The dirty laundry had been scattered on the table, and Kristen had taken it out, brushed it off and hung it back up to dry. It was a start.

"Do you drive go-karts, too, Todd?"

Kristen just about spit out a laugh. She couldn't help it. She looked between Todd and her mom, watched as Todd shook his head and said, "No, ma'am," with a straight face.

"What do you drive?" her mom asked. There was a teapot on the table and her mom offered Todd a cup.

"No, thanks," Todd said, though Kristen would have given much to see Todd holding the floral china. "I drive for the NASCAR circuit."

"NASCAR?" her mom asked, but she said the word as if it had two parts. *Nass...car.* "What's that?"

"Stock car racing."

"Never heard of it," she said with a curious look.

"You're kidding," Todd said. "Not even when Kristen was racing?"

Her mom waved her hand. "My husband, God rest his soul, did all that with Kristen. To be honest, I never understood her fascination with going fast."

Kristen tensed, waiting for "that" look from her mom. But this time there was only a twinge.

"Although of course I was always proud of her."

And Kristen relaxed. It was going to be okay.

"Todd's actually a pretty famous race car driver, Mom."

"Really?" she asked, taking a sip of her tea. "That's great. Kristen, you ought to go upstairs and show him your trophies."

"You mean there's more than what's out in the garage?" Todd asked.

"There's a lot more," her mom said, setting her tea cup down and standing. "Come on. I'll show you myself."

THEY SPENT THE NEXT HOUR poking around the house, and as they did, Kristen realized yet again how grateful she was that Todd had come. Although she couldn't help but wish it was Matt by her side.

She called Matt a little later on. This time she reached him, but he sounded tense and didn't have a lot of time to talk and Kristen was left feeling disappointed. It didn't help that Todd was so solicitous. He charmed her mom completely, and when her mother made the mistake of calling him her boyfriend, Kristen felt her cheeks warm at the amused expression on Todd's face.

Time seemed to fly. Suddenly, it was time for dinner, and then time to leave, her mom almost embarrassingly impressed that Todd had his own private jet. She shot Kristen a look that clearly asked, *Why* isn't *he your boyfriend?*

She didn't feel like explaining. Time for that later. And there would be a later, because Kristen promised to come back for a lengthy visit the next time.

"You promise?" her mom asked, drawing back from the hug they'd just exchanged.

"I promise."

Her mom smiled. "I'm so glad you came."

"Me, too."

Todd drove them back to the airport while Kristen replayed the visit in her mind. Her "boyfriend" was strangely quiet. That was good. It gave her time to consider the afternoon.

Why isn't Matt here with you?

"You tired?" Todd asked while they were up in the air, his expression concerned.

"Just thinking," she said, leaning back in her chair.

"You've got a lot to think about."

Yes, she privately agreed. She did.

They landed just as the sun was setting. Kristen was amazed at how quickly and efficiently she'd managed to get to Oklahoma and back in less than a day. It seemed almost surreal, she thought as Todd drove his car into her condo's parking lot. Only a few hours ago she'd been sitting down with her mom.

"You okay?" Todd asked, sounding concerned this time, the car engine idling, the sun casting an orange glow over the two of them.

"I'm fine," she said, her hand on the door.

"You need me to come in with you?"

"No, that's okay."

"Sure?"

"I'm sure."

They were silent, Kristen growing uncomfortable beneath his gaze. There was something there, deep within the depths of his brown eyes, something that made her grow warm.

"Thanks, Todd," she said, pulling the door handle

and darting away before she could analyze what was in his eyes. She didn't want to know, because if she looked too deeply, she might see…

What?

She shook her head and heard him drive off a second later. She didn't know what was wrong with her. Suddenly she was thinking the strangest things about Todd.

There was a message on her answering machine when she let herself inside. It was from Matt, telling her he wouldn't be home until late that night, but that he'd see her in the morning and to give him a call when she woke up.

She stared at the machine in disappointment and, yes, anger. And then she wondered if maybe, just maybe, Matt was mad at her. If he might be angry that she'd jetted off with Todd.

Well, too bad if he was.

She went to bed then, the emotional toll of the day having finally caught up.

MATT LET HIMSELF IN.

She'd given him a key weeks ago, but he'd never used it before. And now, seeing her sleeping there, light from the kitchen ebbing into her bedroom and casting murky shadows, he wanted to scoop her up and hold her next to him.

He'd missed her. Throughout the day, despite

how upset he'd been at her flying off with Todd, he'd still missed her.

"Kristen," he said softly.

She moaned, stirred. He smiled, his fingers catching tendrils of her silky hair. Matt marveled at how soft it felt.

"Kristen," he said again.

She opened her eyes and blinked.

"Hey," she said.

"Hey," he said right back.

"What time is it?" she asked, blinking in the direction of the digital clock, the numbers casting a red glow on her face.

"A little after three."

She nodded and wiped hair off her face. She looked tired, a sleep crease marking one side of her cheek.

"Kristen," he started to say, "I'm sorry I wasn't there for you."

"Did you get your problems worked out?"

"Well." He had to switch gears for a moment. "No. Not yet."

"So going to New York wasn't really necessary?"

"It was necessary," he said. "What I'm dealing with right now is delicate, and I can't afford to mess it up. I might lose everything."

"But aren't *I* supposed to be everything?"

He leaned back, thrown by her comment. He wasn't expecting an instant confrontation, but he noticed that in the yellowish half light she looked hurt. And sad. Maybe even angry.

"You *are* everything to me," he said, realizing at that moment that she really was. He loved her.

Loved?

Yes, loved. He loved her spirit and her intelligence and her generous nature. Even when he'd let her down more often than not, she never held it against him. No wonder she'd gone off with Todd today. He hadn't been there for her lately.

"I'm sorry," he said softly. "I know I was a little short with you on the phone earlier."

"Yes, you were."

"But that was because Todd wants to be much more than a friend. He wants *you.*"

She started to shake her head, but something made her stop.

"Just like *I* want you," he said gently. "I love you. I want to be with you and I'm sorry that lately that hasn't been the case."

She didn't say anything, just sat there, her blue eyes staring into his own with an intensity that seemed to doubt and question everything about him. "Do you?" she asked softly. "Do you really love me?"

"I do."

"Then make the commitment to spend more time with me."

"Of course I'll spend more time with you, just as soon as I have things sorted out with the FFL board."

"But not before."

"Kristen, we've already had this discussion. I can't do that right now."

But Kristen knew better. She knew Matt maybe better than he knew himself, and she knew he'd never give up his workaholic lifestyle. Rob had been after him for years to slow down, and he'd yet to do it. This latest crisis—the issue with his board—was just another excuse to throw himself into work, to hang on to everything he'd built. And while a part of her didn't blame him, another part knew she could never compete. Ever.

"I love you, Matt," she said quietly, and it nearly killed her to watch his eyes light up. "I love you," she said again, "but I can't be with you."

Silence. She heard the creak of a floorboard as he shifted on his feet.

"What do you mean you can't be with me?"

"You're too…" she searched for the right words, "set in your ways." She held up her hands when he opened his mouth to protest. "No, not really that. Just…" Damn it. Why couldn't she think? "Just too in love with your work."

"That's not true."

"Yes, Matt, it is. You choose work over spending time with me every time."

"No, I don't."

"Don't you?" she asked, crossing her arms. "How many times have you sacrificed one of your workdays for me?"

"All the time. When we came back from Michigan—"

"You squeezed me in," she finished for him. "We didn't spend a day together. You penciled me into a convenient time and then you left me behind."

"I had to get back to New York."

"You could have taken me with you."

"Is that what this is about? You're throwing in the towel because you haven't become a pampered mistress?"

She gasped, hardly daring to believe he'd said the words. "Don't even go there with me," she said, her jaw tense with anger. "You *know* how hard I've worked to carry my weight at Knight Enterprises."

"Then what is it?" he asked. "What do you want?"

"*You,*" she said, her anger draining away as suddenly as it'd come. "I want *you,*" she said, more softly this time. "Is that too much to ask?"

He didn't answer, and each second he remained silent, the hope drained out of Kristen like rain from a cloud.

"At this point, yes," he said. "But in another week or two—"

She held up her hand. “Don’t,” she said in a near whisper. “Don’t bother.”

“Kristen.”

“You’d better leave, Matt,” she said, lying down and pulling the covers over her shoulders. “Put your key on the coffee table.”

“Kristen, don’t do this.”

She didn’t answer.

“I’ll sleep on the couch.”

“Then I’ll get up and leave,” she said, suddenly slipping from the bed.

“Don’t be ridiculous.”

“I’m serious, Matt. I want you to leave.”

“Kristen, we shouldn’t let this escalate out of control.”

“Too late,” she said.

“Kristen—”

“Please,” she implored him.

“Kristen—”

“Don’t force me to call the police.”

“You wouldn’t do that.”

“Try me.”

He thought about arguing with her. Thought about maybe sleeping out front, in his car. But obviously she needed time to cool down. Time to think things through. She’d be more reasonable in the morning.

"Very well," he said. "But this conversation isn't over."

"Oh, yes, it is," Kristen muttered as he let himself out.

CHAPTER TWENTY-SIX

SHE THOUGHT HE'D CALL. Sure, she'd been the one to kick him out, but for some illogical reason, she'd thought he'd pick up the phone and call her the next day.

He didn't.

So she told herself she didn't care, but she knew it was a lie. After that, she told herself she'd be the bigger person. If she saw him at work, she'd be cordial and polite. But she didn't see him at work.

A day passed. Then two.

She told herself that he meant to call. He was probably wrapped up in some big work problem. He probably meant to pick up the phone a thousand times.

And that was one more reason she wouldn't accept his call—if he did happen to remember to phone. He never made time for her.

By the following week she was hurt. It didn't matter how ridiculous that sounded. Yes, she'd been the one to break it off, but she'd have thought he'd at least call to see how she was doing.

When she saw Todd talking to one of the team's managers, she approached him without thinking. "Want to have dinner tonight?" she asked casually.

Todd looked surprised, and then pleased, and then concerned, but only after his eyes swept her face, undoubtedly noting the telltale signs of fatigue.

"I'll catch up to you later," Todd said to his manager, putting a hand against Kristen's back and leading her to a corner conference room. "What's going on?"

"Matt and I broke up."

His eyes widened. "When?"

"Monday, after we came back from Oklahoma."

"You're kidding."

"It's for the best," she said, tipping her chin up. "You're right. He was never there for me." She looked away, feeling silly, stupid tears come to her eyes all of a sudden. "He hasn't even called."

"Kristen," Todd said gently, pulling her into his arms. He had a wide chest, she suddenly noticed, and big arms. And it felt good to be hugged.

"I feel like such a prize idiot," she said, wiping at her eyes smearing her makeup all over the place. That was why she should never wear the stuff. In case she needed to cry.

"You're not an idiot," he said gently, rubbing her back. "Far from it."

She wanted to stay in his arms, she really did, but

she couldn't, not when they were at work, in full view of anybody who happened to walk by. She pulled away, swiped her hair over her ears. Todd looked disappointed.

"Anyway," she said, sniffing, glad the tears seemed to have disappeared as quickly as they'd come. "I was thinking it'd be good for me to get out."

"Of course," he said, "but I'm supposed to leave tonight, for the race," he reminded her.

Oh, cripes. She'd lost track of the days. Not surprising with her unusual work schedule. If she wasn't at the track, she got the weekends off. If she was at the track, she had Monday and Tuesday off.

"Are you headed there tomorrow? Because if you are, we could hook up Friday night."

She shook her head. "I'm still working on that new idea. It won't be ready to test for a week or two so I'm at home."

"Then come out with me tonight. I'll have my pilot fly me there after we're done with dinner."

"Todd, I can't ask you to do that."

"Yes, you can," he said, placing a hand on her shoulder, his brown eyes filled with warmth. "What's more, you need to do this, Kristen. You need to get out. I can tell you've been locked up in that condo of yours, sulking."

He was *so* right.

"And it's no big deal for my pilot to take me back to the track. We're racing on the east coast this weekend, so it's just a hop, skip and a jump. Come with me," he said. "We'll go someplace nice for dinner."

And that was the biggest difference between Matt and Todd. Todd found a way to spend time with her. Didn't matter where he was going or whether he was busy, he always worked it out.

"What time do you want to leave?"

His face lit up. "As soon as you get off work."

THEY WERE MEETING AT SIX. Kristen drove home that evening feeling better than she had all week. Going to dinner with Todd would be fun. Something to do to get her mind off her heartache.

Nothing more.

So she dressed in a short-sleeved black Lycra top with a V-neck that clung to her body. She tucked that into blue jeans and added a black belt. It was an outfit she'd bought to wear to dinner with Matt. She'd never had a chance to wear it.

When the doorbell rang a little later she answered the door with a smile on her face. "Hey—"

Matt.

She faltered, glanced at the clock. Ten to six. Oh, crap.

"Expecting someone?" he said, eyeing her outfit.

"No. Well, not for a few more minutes," she corrected, so glad to see him for a split second that she found herself opening the door before thinking better of it.

"You look like you're going to dinner," he said, sliding past her, his familiar scent invading the room. He always smelled like citrus, but tonight it seemed mixed with cedar or perhaps pine.

"I am," she said. "With a friend."

"Oh?"

"Matt, what are you doing here?" she asked before he could probe any further. As ridiculous as it seemed, she didn't want him to know she was going out with Todd.

"You know what I'm doing here," he said softly. "I told you our conversation wasn't through."

"Yeah, but it's been over a week."

"I was caught up at work."

Work. Always work. But she noticed that he did look tired. The skin beneath his eyes appeared bruised. His hair, always a bit uneven, appeared rumpled tonight. And he was pale, the dress shirt he wore wrinkled, his gray suit pants no longer creased down the middle.

"Anyway," he said. "I thought it'd be best if I waited a few days for you to cool off."

"And waiting those few days probably worked perfectly with your schedule."

"Kristen," he said, his voice low, "I didn't come here to argue."

"What did you come here for?"

"This," he said, pulling her to him.

"Matt—"

He kissed her hard, and for a split second Kristen was lost. He tasted sweet, familiar…like home.

And then his cell phone rang.

He let her go.

"Don't get that," she warned.

"Kristen," he said, reaching for it.

"Matt—"

"Hello," Matt said, turning away from her.

Kristen cursed. She clenched her fists. She turned away in disgust. Damn it. Damn *him.* Didn't he see the problem?

But the answer was very obviously, no.

"Yeah," he said in a low voice. "Tomorrow. Seven." She heard him flip the phone closed.

She crossed her arms in front of her.

"Kristen," he said, placing a hand on her shoulder.

She jerked away, her jaw aching with the effort it took to keep from crying. "Leave," she said softly, warningly.

"Leave? Why? We haven't even had time to talk."

"Because in another five minutes it'll be another

call. And ten minutes beyond that it'll be something else. And tomorrow morning you'll be gone by six so you can get to New York by seven."

"Kristen, I told you—"

"No," she said, stepping back. "No," she said quickly. "I won't do this. I won't live my life waiting by the phone. I won't."

"It wouldn't be like that—"

"Yes, Matt, it would," she said, inhaling sharply because she almost, almost let a tear slide free. "It would. And each time you weren't there for me, it would kill me," she said. "You'd be off to this meeting or that, and in time it'd be our children you were standing up. I won't have it. I won't."

"Kristen—"

"Leave, Matt," she said softly, firmly.

Knock, knock.

The both froze.

"Anyone home?" a voice called.

Todd.

Had he heard them? Kristen didn't know. Didn't care.

Matt seared her with a look. "So that's the way it is."

"No, Matt, it's not that way at all. Todd is my friend. He's been there for me more times than you. Don't turn my friendship with him into something it's not."

He didn't look convinced.

"Kristen?" Todd called, obviously hearing their voices.

"I'll be right there," she said, smoothing her hair. She strode past Matt, opened the door.

The two men eyed each other like two dogs forced to share a kennel. "Mr. Knight," Todd said tersely.

"Todd," Matt said back.

"Matt was just leaving," Kristen said.

"Yes, I was," Matt agreed. He looked at the two of them, eyes narrowed, face growing flushed. "Goodbye, Kristen."

"Goodbye, Matt."

And this time she knew it really *was* over.

CHAPTER TWENTY-SEVEN

"YOU OKAY?" TODD ASKED the moment they were alone.

"No," she said, her face suddenly crumpling.

"Kristen—"

"No," she said quickly, inhaling and staying him with a hand. "It's okay. I'll be okay. Just give me a minute."

He'd give her all his life if that's what it took.

"Do you mind if I freshen up?"

"No. Not at all," he said, watching her go. And even though he tried to hold back, he couldn't seem to do it. So he turned away, finally setting free a smile.

Matt was toast.

Finally…finally, Kristen was his. Well, not right away. He'd have to move slowly. But he'd woo her just as he had other women in his life. Only this time he was playing for keeps.

She returned a few minutes later, her eyes red as if she'd allowed herself a good cry. But he'd chase away her sadness. Starting with dinner.

"Come on," he said, taking her hand, a bit disappointed when she pulled it out of his grasp. "Let's go have fun."

"Todd," she said softly, pausing by her front door, orange light pouring over one side of her face and making her blue eyes look almost purple. "I don't want you to think…to maybe be under the impression that I—"

"Want to be more than friends?" he finished for her.

"Well, I—"

"Kristen, relax. I'm not going to make any moves on you," he lied. "Not now or in the future."

"Thanks, Todd."

And he didn't, either. He kept his hands off her, making her laugh so hard at one point (he did a pretty mean Kermit the Frog imitation) that she had tears coming out of her eyes. People stared at them, but that might have been because of who he was, or because Kristen looked so damn beautiful with laughter in her blue gaze, despite the sadness that lingered there. And when it was time for her to go home, he gave her as impersonal a hug as he could manage, surprised she didn't notice that the minute he touched her, his body temperature rose.

The pattern of his courtship never changed, not at first. Over the next few weeks he charmed her. Gradually she relaxed, at least when she was in his company. It was still difficult for her to bump into Matt at the shop, but that rarely happened.

But the time came when Kristen needed to be at the track for a test, and this time Matt would be there with them. Todd took in the news with a vague sense of surprise. It had been weeks since they'd seen him. Not that he had anything to worry about.

Still, when they were together later that night, she didn't seem herself. "You nervous about testing your new part?" he asked

They were driving to one of his media appearances, a ribbon-cutting that he really didn't want to go to. But it was one of the Ford dealerships and he couldn't really get out of it—not if he wanted to keep his car manufacturer happy. But at least afterward they were going to dinner, which was why Kristen was all dressed up. And she looked damn good. With her hair piled atop her head and a pretty floral dress swishing around her ankles, Todd thought *she* looked good enough to eat. Forget dinner.

"No," she said, looking out the car window, her lashes darker when backlit by sunlight. "I'm confident the new air filter design will work."

"Well, if you're confident, I'm confident," he said, admiring her profile when he stopped at a light. She had the tiniest ears, and he was dying to see what they tasted like.

Damn, she made him hot.

Tonight would be the night he'd tell her how he felt. He was tired of waiting.

"Go," she told him.

The light had turned green. He shook his head, amazed at how just staring at her could turn him on.

They were a block away from the dealership, rows of glistening cars reflecting the early-evening sun and when he turned into the parking lot, he could see a huge crowd had already gathered.

"Here we go," he said, pulling in.

The crowd was lined up near a tent where he'd be signing autographs. More than a few broke out in applause, wide smiles of delight on their faces when they saw it was him emerging from his Mustang. They were wearing full fan regalia, dark blue shirts with black piping, hats, Arcadia or his car number on everything—at least until Fly For Less took over.

"Oh, boy," he said, parking. Jen was waiting for him, her ever-present clipboard in hand—the woman never went anywhere without it.

"Don't you like doing these?"

"I'd rather spend time with you," he said, glancing over at her to see how she took the comment.

She looked pensive. "Todd…"

"Come on," he said, shoving his hands into his pockets. "Let's go."

She followed, but at a distance. He wanted to

wait up for her, but he sensed she needed space. His comment had put her on edge, something that didn't bode well for tonight, but he had plenty of time to convince her otherwise. Right now he had autographs to sign and people to make nice to. "Hey there," he said to the dealership manager. When he glanced back, Kristen stood next to Jen, the two of them talking.

"Thanks for coming," the man said, his hair so full of hairspray he looked like a Ken doll, Todd thought.

"My pleasure."

And thus it began. An hour of smiling at the fans, taking pictures with them, signing autographs. He kept his eye on Kristen the whole time and when his hour was up, he smiled at the late arrivals whom he hadn't had time to meet with and said "Sorry" with a wide smile.

"But—" one woman started to say, his picture floppy in her hands.

"Got another engagement after this," he said with his most charming smile. "But send it to the shop. I'll sign it for you there."

"We don't have to leave that quickly," Kristen said.

Todd turned, surprised to find her at his elbow. "Kristen—"

"Sign the autographs, Todd. There's a little boy right behind that lady who looks crushed."

He noticed the kid then.

"All right. The lady says we have more time. I'll keep going, then."

"Thank you," said the woman. "I tried to get off work early, but I couldn't, and then I got caught in traffic, and I really wanted to get this signed for my husband's birthday…"

"Then Todd will sign it 'happy birthday,'" Kristen said.

He would? He glanced back at Kristen. There was a look of steel in her eyes. He would. But he had to smile. He loved her dedication to his fans. Loved how she greeted the little kid with a warm smile, dug around in her purse, fished out a miniature of his car (although where she'd got it from, he had no idea) and offered it to him. She was a natural, perfect wife material.

"There," she said when they drove away afterward. "That wasn't so hard."

"I guess you can tell how much I despise these things," he said, glad they were on their way to his favorite restaurant.

"I can, Todd. But I don't understand why. These people are your bread and butter. And they *adore* you."

"I know. But after a while the adoration wears thin. I'd rather be with you," he said, clasping her hand and shooting her a smile. "Staring into your pretty eyes."

She didn't say anything. Todd focused on driving, but every time he looked over at her, she seemed even more pensive. She hadn't taken her hand away, and so that was good—he loved holding her hand—but she didn't squeeze his hand back, either. By the time they made it to the restaurant, an old farmhouse situated near a creek, her hand had grown cold. Todd squelched his sense of foreboding. It was a stunning place to eat—an old Victorian. Beautiful, lush foliage surrounding the place. Delicious food to eat. He'd sweet-talk her out of her blue funk in no time. He hoped.

But Kristen didn't look excited. "What's wrong?" he finally asked.

"Nothing."

"Kristen," he said, leaning back as the waitress handed them their menus. "Something is definitely wrong."

"Would you like to hear about our specials?" the perky blonde asked.

"Not right now," Todd said quickly, meeting Kristen's eyes and lifting his eyebrows.

"It's nothing, Todd."

"No, Kristen, it's *not* nothing. What is it?"

"I don't want to talk about it here."

Uh-oh. That sounded ominous.

He glanced around, making sure they were private. They'd been seated in the alcove of a bay window, which meant they were pretty secluded. That was good, because one look at her crumpling face had Todd realizing this was serious.

"C'mon," he said, clasping her hand. "You can tell me."

She started to shake her head. He squeezed her hand. She met his gaze. "I can't stop thinking about him."

It felt like his cheeks had been slapped. "What?"

"Matt," she said, looking at her lap and shaking her head. "I can't stop thinking about him. Seeing him at work this week, bumping into him. It's been hell."

Son of a—

"That man's an ass, Kristen. He treated you like shit."

Several people at nearby tables turned to look at them.

"I've treated people like shit, too, Todd," she said. "And thank God my mom loved me enough to give me time to work my way through it."

"Do you still love him?"

She straightened, her hand sliding out of his grasp. "I…don't know. I think so. Maybe. I don't know."

He took a deep breath, knowing it was now or never. "Forget about him, Kristen. Forget about him now."

She glanced up at him sharply.

He reached for her hand again. “Stay with *me*,” Todd said softly.

There. He’d said it, and damned if that hadn’t been as hard as driving blind into a bad wreck.

“What?”

“I’m falling in love with you.” He squeezed her hand.

“Todd, I—”

“No, let me finish. The past few weeks have been some of the best of my life. I look forward to coming home every weekend, look forward to spending time with you. You’re good for me, and I’m not going to let you go.”

“Todd,” she said, her blue eyes huge with shock. “Please tell me you’re not serious.”

“I *am* serious, Kristen. Serious about *you*.”

“Oh, God.”

That wasn’t the response he’d wanted. “You can’t have been that blind to my feelings.”

“I *was* blind, Todd.” she said, her eyes blinking rapidly. “Sure we went out together, but as friends.”

“I don’t want to be your friend, Kristen. I want to be your lover.”

She let go of his hand. “We should go,” she said, setting her napkin on the table. “Really, I think we should—”

“Kristen, stop,” he said when she started to get up. He scooted around the edge of the table, shielding her from everyone's view. "Don't do this. Let's have dinner. Let's talk."

She looked up at him, and he could see that she was close to tears.

Crap.

"Would it change anything?" she asked softly. "Would it change how I feel toward Matt? Or how you feel toward me?"

"It might," he said, grasping at straws.

"No, it won't," she said softly, the redness around her eyes increasing. "You're one of my best friends," she said, reaching up and stroking his chin. He almost closed his eyes. "My only friend. But Matt..." She fumbled over her words for a second. "I think Matt still owns my heart."

"No," he said sharply, quickly.

"I'm sorry, Todd," she said softly, leaning up on tiptoe and kissing him on the cheek. He closed his eyes.

"Goodbye, Todd," she said, drawing back, her cheeks wet from sudden tears. "I'll see you at the race this weekend."

And then she was gone.

Todd stood there for a second, hardly daring to believe the night had turned out like it had. It was like a bad wreck, one he couldn't avoid. Damn it. How could she do this to him?

He picked up a nearby vase, and before he could

think better of it, hurled it at the window. The glass shattered, water sprayed, and the restaurant fell dead silent.

"What are you all looking at?" he shouted before storming out the back door.

CHAPTER TWENTY-EIGHT

KRISTEN DECIDED TO GO HOME.

She had more than enough vacation so when she went to Ralph, the head engineer, and asked for a couple of days off, he gave them to her without question.

It was the first time she'd flown commercial in a while, and to be honest, she'd grown spoiled. She'd forgotten what it was like to have to park and then walk into the terminal with all the other passengers. She'd managed to block from her mind the tedious process of being cleared through security. And the truth of the matter was, she hated waiting to board outside her gate, the seats in most airports as comfortable as plastic lawn chairs. But as she looked around the Fly For Less terminal, Kristen was suddenly struck by it all.

This was Matt's.

Well, not the airport, of course, but the logo above the ticket counter had been designed by Matt. The pretty blonde behind the ticket counter *worked* for him. The passengers sitting around the terminal would not be flying off to visit loved ones, or jetting away to go on vacation, or leaving town for work if not for Matt.

It was a clear day, one of those beautiful late mornings that made Kristen wish for a hammock and a good book to read. She crossed to a window, staring at the jets parked outside, sunlight reflecting off the top of the cockpit.

And she was proud.

Proud of what Matt had accomplished. Proud of what he'd built from nothing. Proud of his determination and dedication to have the best airline, at the best price, so that passengers could fly away and *do*.

And she was ashamed.

Until then she hadn't really thought about all the effort it must have taken to get Fly For Less off the ground. Or how hard Mathew *still* worked to keep it all afloat. She'd never taken the time to congratulate him on what he'd accomplished, first with Fly For Less and then with his race team.

What a remarkable man.

"We're getting ready to board flight number one-eighty-nine with service to Oklahoma…"

She glanced at her ticket, wondered if she should tell someone she worked for Fly For Less, but then thought better of it. She was just a passenger today. That was all. Just a passenger.

THE FLIGHT TO OKLAHOMA took less than three hours. Kristen arrived late in the afternoon, the day as bright and as sunny as it was in Charlotte. Only this time as she drove through the streets of Beaumonte, she felt a sense of peace. She was home and on her way to her mother, who, Lord willing, would help her to sort out her life, because this time she wasn't going to run.

"Kristen," her mom said when she opened the door. "You're back."

Kristen's smile was a bit wobbly as she stared at her mom. "You said I could come back anytime I want."

"Why, of course," her mom said, stepping back from the door.

"It's good to see you, Mom," she said, hugging her for a moment, letting her mother hold her for even longer.

"You look run-down," her mom said, drawing back and studying her face.

"Thanks," she said. "That's good to know."

"You look as exhausted as you used to look after a race."

"Long morning and a crowded flight."

"What? No private jet this time?" she asked, leading her to the kitchen where there was a pot of tea already brewing.

"Not this time," she said softly. Maybe not ever again.

"Did you and Todd break up?"

Kristen plopped down in a chair. "Kind of hard to break up with a man when you were never together."

"Not according to you, but I could tell that young man liked you, Kristen. I could tell he liked you a lot," she said, taking the seat opposite her.

Kristen felt herself straighten. "You could see that?"

"Of course," she said, her upswept hair neatly in place. "But then when you called, you went on and on about this Matt fella. I just assumed I was wrong until you called and told me you and Matt broke up. After that it seemed to be you and Todd and so I just assumed—"

That they'd got together.

"I had no idea he liked me like that."

"Oh, certainly you did."

"Excuse me?"

Her mom clasped her hands. "Kristen, you're a bright young girl. Brilliant, actually. Your dad and I always thought you'd be a surgeon, but that's another story. My point is that you're smart. Certainly you could see the writing on the wall."

Kristen thought back. *Had* she seen it? She thought about all the times Todd had shown up unannounced at her front door. All the times he'd tracked her down at the shop. All the many times he'd invited her out—all under the guise of being her friend. And yet every once in a while she'd catch a hint of something in his eyes, something that had made her step back and think.

"I'm an idiot," she said, covering her face with her hands.

"About men. About relationships. About life... sometimes," her mother answered gently.

"I was too blinded by my feelings for Matt to see what was going on."

"Do you love this Matt person?"

She had to think about it for a moment, really, truly search her heart. "I don't know," she said, shaking her head in self-disgust. "I shouldn't. The man never cared enough to make me his first priority."

Her mom laughed softly. Her face might be lined by age, but nothing had changed about that laugh—it was still soft and husky.

"And you always did need to be number one."

Kristen stiffened.

"What do you mean?"

"You hate to lose, Kristen. You were never the type who could stand being second. I can only imagine how hard it was for you to stand back and let Matt live his life."

"I'm not like that," Kristen said.

"No?"

"No," she quickly emphasized.

Her mom just lifted a brow.

This is about losing, period.

The words came back to haunt her. She'd spoken them by the lake, back when she and Matt had been talking about Trina, and her life...before.

"Oh, God."

"Let me tell you something, Kristen. I spent years and years of my life being second, first when your father was alive and you two were off racing, and then after, when you left, and I was alone. You needed to put yourself first for a while, and I understood that. I waited until the time came when you realized that I loved you and that I'd always be there for you, and you did. Finally you did."

Kristen felt tears fill her eyes.

"I waited. Because I love you." She tipped her head, peering at Kristen intently. "Do you love Matt?"

CHAPTER TWENTY-NINE

DO YOU LOVE MATT?

She didn't know, Kristen admitted as she drove back to the airport the next day. Her whole relationship with Matt seemed like a dream. He'd flown in on his helicopter and swept her off her feet. Handsome, brilliant and kind—what woman could resist a man like that?

But love?

As she returned her rental car and later, flew home, she tried to analyze her emotions. That was the thing about being an engineer. She always tried to see things in black and white, but life was rarely like that, she admitted.

She arrived back at her condo while the sun was still high in the sky. It was another beautiful day, she realized, getting out of her car and staring out at the sparkling lake. Maybe she needed to sit out by the shore and think some more—

"Come with me."

Kristen stiffened, mostly because she thought

she'd imagined the words. They harked back to the very first day she'd met Matt.

"Please," came next, causing Kristen to turn.

Rob stood near the rear of her car.

"Hi," she told him, her gaze immediately sliding past his black-clad form to look for Matt. He was nowhere in sight. "What are you doing here?" She stiffened. "Is everything okay?"

"Everything is fine, Ms. McKenna, but I'd like you to come with me."

"Is it Matt?" she asked, her heart suddenly pinging against her chest.

"No. He's in New York, and as far as I know, he's fine."

In New York. Then why…

"Please, Ms. McKenna," he said, his blue eyes seeming to hold her to the ground for all that they were imploring. "I need to show you something."

Kristen glanced at her car, then back toward her condo. The sun reflecting off the water momentarily blinded her. She clutched her purse.

Don't do it.

"Where are we going?" she asked.

Rob looked relieved, but he wiped the emotion away as quickly as it'd come. "I'll take you there."

He led her to his Mustang, the same one she'd seen parked out in front of Matt's house all those weeks ago. "Nice car," she said.

Rob nodded, but didn't say anything, just opened her door. She slipped inside, palms sweating and pulse elevated, because to be honest, she wasn't at all sure this was a good idea. Whatever Rob wanted to show her, she was certain it had to do with Mathew and she wasn't sure she needed to add to the already confusing mix of emotions swirling through her.

They took off, Rob keeping her confused about where they were going. They hugged the shore of the lake for a little while, then headed east, along tree-lined roads and gently rolling hills, eventually crossing beneath Highway 77.

"Are we going to the airport?"

He shook his head.

That was good. For a moment there she'd thought he was taking her to Matt's jet.

And if he was?

She shook her head. That wouldn't be good. Not now. Maybe not ever.

The road curved north. They traveled along the freeway for a bit, passing the occasional development or drug store or grocery outlet. And then they headed west, back toward the lake, Kristen catching a glimpse of the name of the road.

"You're taking me to Matt's house."

"I am."

"I don't want to see his new place."

"You're not."

"I'm— What?"

They crossed under Highway 77 again, Rob ignoring her. They were definitely headed toward Matt's neighborhood. She might not have been there in a long while—she hadn't been able to stomach the leveling of his historic house—but she still knew the way.

"Why are you taking me to see his new house?"

"You'll see."

And she did. The moment they pulled onto Matt's street, she "saw."

Oh, Lord.

The old house still stood. Kristen felt her breath push itself out of her chest in a big rush. Rob pulled into Matt's driveway. Yes, it was still the same house…just fully restored.

She slipped out of the car without saying a word to Rob, just straightened and stood there, her hands clutching the door.

She stared.

A team of contractors had gone over the home with a fine-tooth comb. Where before the paint had been fading and chipped, now there was a fresh coat—still yellow, but brand new. The railing on the corner porch, the window moldings and the shutters had all been replaced and painted white. The front door, too, looked to be new. Rose and beige stained glass side panels framed either side of a brass and paneled-glass door.

"Beautiful," she whispered softly.

"You should see the inside," Rob said.

"No," she said, her voice suddenly choked with tears.

"Why not?" Rob asked.

"Because I can't."

"He did this for you, Kristen."

"I know," she said over the lump in her throat.

"He loves you."

"Does he?" she asked, closing the door and facing Matt's best friend when he came to her side of the car.

"He does," he said, the words so gently uttered that it seemed impossible for them to have come from such a big man.

She had to look away. The view was spectacular, much more resplendent than hers. Tree-lined shores were visible across a small bay. Boats were out on the water, their white hulls dotting the surface. She wished she were on one of them now.

"He's coming home tonight," Rob said.

But that was just it, she realized. He would always be coming home. She would always be the one waiting for him. She would always play second fiddle.

"I can't," she finally said. "I can't do this."

"Why not?"

She faced him again. "Rob, really, I appreciate

what you're trying to do. But Matt and I—it would never work out."

"Why not?"

For a moment Kristen wondered if Matt realized exactly how good a friend he had in Rob. Probably not. But she did. And she appreciated his devotion. "You know why," she said softly. "Let's go."

Rob didn't protest this time, just went to his car and opened the door.

Kristen felt tears sting her eyes as she climbed into his car. She'd always been the type to cry at the end of sad movies, especially the kind where the hero and heroine ended up living apart. But it was only at that moment that she understood the true magnitude of their sacrifice. It would have been *so* easy to stick around and wait for Matt. To fall into his arms. To take her chances that she could live with just a part of him. But she couldn't do that. For too many years she'd lived half a life.

It was time she started living life to the fullest. And she wanted a man by her side willing to do the same.

That man wasn't Matt.

Maybe it was Todd, a little voice whispered.

Todd. She would see him at the race this coming weekend when they tested her new part.

But despite what her subconscious whispered, she knew that man wasn't Todd. KEM's star driver might still be mad at her, but in time he'd come to realize how completely mismatched they were. It was the same way with Matt. In time she'd come to accept that.

She just wished it didn't hurt so much.

TODD ARRIVED AT THE TRACK the following weekend in a foul mood. Jen asked what was wrong.

"Nothing," he snapped, getting into a golf cart. They'd just finished an autographing session on one of the souvenir haulers, and Todd was glad he didn't have to force his smile anymore. "What's after this?"

"Back to the garage, if you want."

"No," he said quickly. The garage was where Kristen would be, and even though he knew he couldn't avoid her forever, he wanted to put it off a little longer.

"Back to your motorcoach, then?" Jen asked.

Todd nodded.

And that's exactly what he did. He hid out in his Prevost, striding between the living room, whose TV screen flickered with the images of an old race, and the kitchen where Todd snacked. Back and forth he paced, more agitated than he could ever remember being. When it came time for him to leave for practice, he was relieved. Finally, something to do. Something to keep his mind off her.

He zoomed into the garage, walking so fast

hardly anybody recognized him. He went in the back way, too, flashing his hard card at the security guard, then ducking toward the front of the haulers. He used the side entrance to get into the lounge, motioning to one of the crew members sitting there, using a lap top, to leave. He needed to change. He made quick work tugging on his race gear, first the fire-retardant undershirts and pants, then the fire suit. He just about caught his chin in the zipper, though, he pulled the thing up so hard.

His hands shook.

That was to be expected. They always shook before practice. His pupils dilated, too. That was just the way it was. The eye of the tiger, his mom called it.

He ducked out of the lounge, about to shoot out of the side door again when he glanced toward the front of the hauler.

Matt was there, leaning against a gray cabinet, arms crossed, his face partly in profile as he stared out at something. Todd took a small step to the right, following his gaze.

Through the sliding-glass doors, standing in between the big rig and the garage, was Kristen.

His eyes moved back to Matt's. The man stared at her hungrily—Todd could see that all the way down the long aisle.

"Son of a—"

In that moment, Todd let her go.

"You are one colossal jerk," he said, taking a step toward his boss.

Matt jerked, turned. Todd watched him brace himself as if expecting a fight.

"She loves you, you son of a bitch. You know that?"

And now he looked confused. "What?"

"She loves you," he said, pointing outside. "I realized it the other day, and if one of you doesn't come to their senses soon, I'm going to change teams."

"What are you talking about?"

Todd realized suddenly what it meant to love someone. Sometimes it meant giving someone up, because if they weren't happy with you, they should be happy with someone else. And if you loved a person, you wanted them to be happy—no matter what the personal sacrifice.

"The other night Kristen and I had dinner. And while she didn't say the words, it was obvious she's still in love with you."

"It was?"

Todd clenched his hands, tighter and tighter, his nails digging into his palm. This was tough. So damn, frickin' tough. "It is."

Matt glanced back at her. She was still there, taking down notes.

"Go to her, man," Todd said. "Go to her and tell her how you feel."

"Todd—"

"No, no," he said, holding up his hand. "No need to thank me. You can reward me with a raise."

"I don't know what to say."

"Nothing to me," Todd said. "Say it all to her."

"MR. KNIGHT WANTS to see you."

Kristen looked up from the notes she'd been taking to see Jen standing there with a smile on her face.

"He said to bring you on up to the suite."

"The suite?" she asked, the blood draining from her face

"Yup," Jen said, motioning for Kristen to follow. Practice was about to start, drivers darting from their haulers to their cars. Kristen glanced at KEM's own big rig. Todd was coming out, the driver pausing for a moment and catching her eye. He waved.

Kristen was so surprised she found herself waving back.

Mr. Knight wanted to see her.

"Come on," Jen urged as Todd crossed the garage to his car.

"Don't you need to stay here for Todd?" She stalled. What did he want? To fire her? Demote her? Send her back to Florida?

"Todd won't need me for the next hour. Come on."

Kristen followed, her pulse rate rising with each step she took. Part of her wanted to turn back, to tell

Jen she didn't have time for a meeting. To just avoid the coming confrontation, whatever the cost.

Sudden noise exploded in the garage as motors roared to life. The loudspeaker blared. Practice was on.

"Do you have any idea what he wants to see me about?" she asked, climbing the stairs behind Jen. They paused at the landing, the second-floor suites much like a hotel, one with a railing on one side and doors on the other. The suite was the fourth one down, Knight Enterprises Motorsports on a nameplate on the front. Rob stood outside.

"Kristen," he said with a wink. *What* was going on?

"You're not going in?" Kristen asked when Jen stopped at the threshold.

"Nope," she said.

Kristen swallowed again. Yup. She was getting fired. No doubt about it.

It took a moment for her eyes to adjust. The suite was a wide room with an open space near the front and seats lined up near a row of windows. Out on the track a car buzzed by, the engine sounding muffled and echoing oddly inside the room. There was no one around.

Except Matt.

Kristen's whole chest vibrated with the beat of her heart, each thump coming faster and then faster.

Do you love him, Kristen?

She stared into the eyes of the most amazing of men and knew that she did.

"Hey, Matt," she said, taking in the familiar mussed hair, the deep green eyes, the smile on his face. And her heart broke—just shattered—because she knew it would never work out between them.

"Kristen," he said softly.

Her eyes had begun to adjust, the room coming into focus—gray carpet, gray padded chairs—and Matt, Matt who'd started to walk toward her, his hands tucked into tan slacks, black shirt making his eyes look a deeper green…or maybe that was just her imagination.

He touched her face.

She flinched.

And then he was kissing her, and it felt like a dream. This couldn't be happening. She wasn't really in a suite, with Matt, and he wasn't really kissing her as if nothing had happened. But he was, and before she could stop herself, she was kissing him back. No. She threw herself at him, wrapped her arms around his back and held on to him like she'd never let go.

"Matt," she said, tears coming to her eyes at the familiar taste of him. How could she have let him go? *Why* had she let him go? What did it matter if she never saw him?

Except she knew that it *would* matter, sooner or later.

"Todd told me you loved me," he said softly, his hands cupping her head, thumbs stroking her loose hair.

"What?"

He leaned down closer to her. "Is it true?"

She couldn't think for a moment, and then emotions came rushing in. *Was* it true? Did she love him?

"It's true," she finally admitted.

He smiled, and pulled her into his arms again. "This makes things so much easier."

She tried to push away, because this wasn't good. She could feel herself weakening.

"I gave it up," he said softly.

She went slack.

"I walked away."

She leaned back to look him in the eye. "Walked away from what?"

"My company," he said softly. "Three weeks ago, it came down to a final vote, and before they'd tallied the final numbers, it hit me." He stroked her face. "I didn't care," he said softly. "I didn't care who had control. It didn't matter anymore. All that mattered was you."

"What?" she heard herself ask again, convinced this must be a dream.

"But I had to be sure," he said softly. "I had to know that I wouldn't let you down. So I waited. It was the hardest thing I've ever had to do, but I did it. I proved to myself that I wasn't going to go back."

So when Rob showed her the house… "You mean you haven't been working?"

He shook his head. "No. I took some time off. *Real* time off," he quickly added. "And the whole time all I could think about was you."

"Matt?" The word a question, his name whispered in wonder.

"I love you, Kristen. I want to marry you. Now. Tomorrow. Yesterday. And I promise you, if you say yes, I'll never walk away from you again."

Did he mean it? Was it really true?

Yes, a voice whispered, because while she might always cry at sad movies, she also hated it when the heroine was too stupid to grab the happiness right in front of her face. This man had given up his company. For *her.*

Happiness? Oh, yeah.

"Say something," he murmured.

"I think maybe you're going to need a new hobby."

He smiled then and kissed her, Kristen opening her mouth for him the moment their lips touched. And as he did she knew it was true. He *did* love her. It was there in the way he kissed her. The way he held her tight. The way he didn't seem to want to let her go.

"Kristen," he said a long while later, his arms holding her, his heart pounding beneath her ear. "I was afraid I'd never get you back."

Was this real? Was this truly happening?

"Marry me?" he asked gently.

She knew then that it was now or never. She had to trust that this was real. That it wasn't going to fall apart—like her life had in the past. That she could reach for happiness and never look back.

She met his gaze, tears filling her eyes as she said, "Yes, Matt. I will. I'll marry you."

And Matt's world suddenly felt put to rights. Nothing had been the same since she'd left him. Not even working his fingers to the bone. Only now she was here. In his arms.

And he'd never let her go.

"I love you," he heard her say.

"I love you, too," he echoed.

A car streaked by. Matt caught a glimpse of the blue-and-black paint scheme. Todd. Kristen turned, too. They both watched as he threw his car into the corner.

"He's running hard," she said.

"Putting his emotions into driving," Matt said.

"What do you mean?"

"You broke his heart."

She peered up at him, blue eyes wide. "I didn't mean to."

"I know," he said softly. "You have that effect on men."

"There's only one man who matters."

"That better be me," he teased.

"It is."

When they kissed again, they forgot about Todd, and the cars out on the track. They forgot about everything, because suddenly there were only two things that mattered and they were right there in that room. The two of them. Holding each other.

Just as they would for the rest of their lives.

EPILOGUE

THE VEHICLE LURCHED around the turn, the driver clutching the wheel, concentrating.

"Careful there, ace," she heard a man say as her wheels broke loose.

"I'm okay," Katrina Knight said. "Darn it, Dad. I've almost got him."

"Katrina," her mom said, disapproval clearly obvious in her voice. "Take it easy."

"I know, I know," Katrina muttered, but she didn't bother to open the mic. She was too busy racing.

Who the heck did that Jarrod Cooper think he was? She thought, her head starting to ache she concentrated so hard. Just because he'd won a national karting championship already didn't mean he could beat her. No way.

Her kart slid up the asphalt track. It was tight in turn one. But if she changed her line, maybe went into the corner a little more deeply.

She tried it on the next lap.

Better. Much better.

Two laps later and she'd gained on him, but the laps were winding down. Plus, there were other karts on the track. Slower drivers, younger, and she had to be careful when passing them.

"C'mon," she muttered to herself.

But then her kart started to work better. It wasn't as loose out of turn three, not as tight going into turn one. Smoother. Easier to dirve.

Her kart advanced on Jarrod. One lap, two, and suddenly she was there. She saw him glance back, try to block her. Uh-uh. She ducked to his inside.

One foot.

Two feet.

Almost...there.

Jarrod rammed her.

What the—

She turned her wheels into him. Tires screeched, the rubber-on-rubber sound filling her ears. Metal collided with metal, too, but Katrina wasn't about to back off.

And then he was gone.

Katrina glanced back. Jarrod Cooper was in the tires.

Oh, yeah! Score!

"I CAN'T LOOK."

Matt glanced down at his wife, a smile coming to his face. She looked like a frightened little girl with her hands covering her face.

"It's okay," he said, scooting closer to her. They stood on the backstretch, out where all the go-kart trailers sat, a waist-high chain-link fence separating them from the track. "She got him on the inside."

The hands slid away. "She did?"

Out on the track, the engine of their nine-year-old daughter's go-kart whined, Matt filled with a sense of pride as he watched her expertly maneuver her kart between slower lap traffic.

"She did," agreed Sarah Cooper, wife of NASCAR NEXTEL Cup Series legend Lance Cooper. She had to raise her voice to be heard over the sound of the karts—the noise akin to an angry pack of bees. "And she sent *my* son into the wall."

"It's tires," Lance corrected, his blue eyes still on the track, blue headphones on his head. "She sent him into the tires. And it serves him right. That was a dirty move."

"Is he okay?" Kristen asked, looking and then spotting Jarrod Cooper out on the track. He was trying to back up to disentangle himself from the tires.

"Yeah, he's fine," Lance said. "Yelling in my ear, but fine."

Kristen shook her head. "I'll make sure Katrina apologizes."

"Better wait until Jarrod cools off," Sarah said, smiling.

"I wish Lindsey had driven go-karts," Adam

Drake, yet another NASCAR NEXTEL Cup Series driver, said, his arms resting across the top of the fence. He was there with his wife, Becca, his eyes following the progress of their seven-year-old son.

"Are you kidding?" his wife said. "Lindsey was only ever happy when she was watching *you*."

"Yeah, that's true," Adam said, wincing when his son nearly spun out. "And now she has to do it from her dorm room."

College, Matt thought.

It seemed impossible that Katrina would ever be that old one day, and yet she would go off to college eventually. Then again, she might race full-time. She was good, he admitted as she sailed beneath the white flag. Really good.

"Come on," Kristen shouted alongside him. "Come on."

"Kristen," Becca said. "I think she's going to win."

She was, Matt agreed. Now that Jarrod was out of the picture, no one was even close.

The checkered flag came out, their daughter screaming beneath a few seconds later.

"Well, that's that," Lance said, pulling one of his earpieces out. "Guess I better get over to our trailer and try to calm Jarrod down."

"I'll go with you," Sarah said. But she smiled in their direction. "Tell Kristen we'll get her next time."

"I didn't see where Tim finished," Becca said, shielding her eyes with her hand.

"Last," Adam muttered in a derisive manner. "And three laps down."

Becca laughed. "Well, I guess he's not a chip off the old block."

"It's still early days yet," Adam said, waving as they left.

Matt and Kristen headed back to their own trailer, a tiny white thing that they'd bought off a local landscaper. It still smelled like lawn clippings inside, Kristen thought.

A few seconds later Katrina pulled up, the tires on her car screeching as she slammed on the brakes. "Did you see that?" Katrina asked the moment she pulled her helmet from her head. "I put Jarrod right into the tires." She climbed out, her white fire suit with her sponsor's name—KEM Motorsports—speckled with flecks of oil and dirt that she'd picked up on the track.

"*Not* something you should be proud of, kiddo," Kristen said.

"Aw, Mom. Come on." She smiled in Lance and Sarah's direction, but they were already moving off toward their son. "He deserved it," she said, glancing over at the blond-haired, blue-eyed kid who stood glaring.

"Still, you should have made the pass cleanly," Matt said. "If you'd waited a few more laps, you'd have had him. You have to play nice when you're out on the track with other drivers."

"That's not what Todd Peters says. He told me if someone's in my way, I should take him out. Just bump and nudge him right into the wall."

Kristen's mouth dropped open. That sounded like Todd. He was still their star driver, albeit much less of a pain in the butt these days. Most of the time.

"You going to have a talk with him?" Matt grumbled, "Or should I?"

"I'll talk to him on Monday," Kristen said. "And you, missy," she said, pointing at their daughter, "need to load your stuff in the trailer, including your kart."

Their daughter nodded.

"Now, *she's* a chip off the old block," Matt said, pulling Kristen to his side as they watched her begin to clean up.

"Yes, she is smart, isn't she?"

"That wasn't what I meant, and you know it."

"No?" Kristen asked with a teasing grin, smiling up at him.

He pulled her against his chest. "She's a hell of a driver."

"Yeah," she said softly. "She is."

He kissed her. Kristen didn't mind. They might be out in public, but nobody paid them any attention.

Or so she thought.

"Hey, you two," someone called. "That's enough of that."

Blain Sanders, one of the NASCAR NEXTEL Cup Series team owners was walking by, his wife laughing and holding the hand of their five-year-old daughter.

"This from the couple who kisses on national television every time they're in Victory Lane," Kristen called.

"Aw," Cece said. "You're just jealous."

Kristen laughed and shook her head, looking into her husband's eyes. Jealous? Never. Because what she and Matt had was just as precious and rare as what the Sanders had, and what the Newmans had, and the Coopers.

Matt swiped a lock of hair off her face. "*Are* you jealous?" he asked softly.

"Only of the fact that they don't have a newborn to go home to."

Matt smiled. "Speaking of that, we better get going. Your mom's probably ready to pull her hair out."

"Nah," Kristen said. "My mom's in her element."

"So are you," Matt said.

She was. She loved this. Loved racing. Loved the camaraderie and the competitiveness of it all. She might not ever drive again, but this was close enough.

And she had Matt.

Matt who'd officially retired from running Fly For

Less ten years ago. Matt who'd taken KEM Motorsports to the top of the game. They had three championships under their belt—with a little help from her. They were one of the best teams on the circuit now, and Kristen had never been happier in her life.

"I love you," she said softly.

"Good," he answered back.

They kissed again, and this time there was nobody around to interrupt them, because when they touched, the rest of the world faded into oblivion. They forgot about the crowd, about their daughter working in the background, about Kristen's mother and their two children at home. All that existed was the two of them, loving each other, kissing each other—*being* there for each other.

Waiting.

AUTHOR NOTE

Many of you know that I pride myself on the accuracy of my books. Most of the time the "behind the scenes" information is true to form. That said, race schedules change on a yearly basis, as do a particular race's weekly schedule. And so while I try to closely mimic the NASCAR NEXTEL Cup Series current event schedule, by the time you read this, the dates might have changed.

I hope you've enjoyed TO THE LIMIT, and that you get a chance to pick up the next book in my NASCAR series. In the meantime, feel free to visit me on the Internet where you can hook up with other NASCAR fans like yourself:

www.pamelabritton.com

www.myspace.com/pamela_britton

Thanks for reading!